To Catch
a Witch

Also available by Heather Blake

Wishcraft Mysteries

A Witch to Remember

To Catch a Witch

The Witch and the Dead

Gone With the Witch

Some Like it Witchy

The Goodbye Witch

The Good, the Bad and the Witchy

A Witch Before Dying

It Takes a Witch

Magic Potion Mysteries

Ghost of a Potion

One Potion in the Grave

A Potion to Die For

To Catch a Witch

A WISHCRAFT MYSTERY

Heather Blake

CROOKED
LANE

NEW YORK

Published in the United States by Crooked Lane Books, an imprint of The Quick Brown Fox & Company LLC.

Crooked Lane Books and its logo are trademarks of The Quick Brown Fox & Company LLC.

Library of Congress Catalog-in-Publication data available upon request.

ISBN (mass market): 978-1-64385-520-2
ISBN (paperback): 978-1-68331-964-1
ISBN (hardcover): 978-1-68331-708-1
ISBN (ePub): 978-1-68331-709-8
ISBN (ePDF): 978-1-68331-710-4

Cover illustration by Michelle Grant
Book design by Jennifer Canzone

Printed in the United States.

www.crookedlanebooks.com

Crooked Lane Books
34 West 27th St., 10th Floor
New York, NY 10001

Mass Market Edition: April 2020
Paperback Edition: March 2019
Hardcover Edition: August 2018

10 9 8 7 6 5 4 3 2 1

For my family, with much love.

Chapter One

February in the Enchanted Village, a tourist-themed neighborhood of Salem, Massachusetts, was as delightful and charming as it was snowy and cold. A fierce wind sent snowflakes whirling along rustic cobblestone streets and through leafless, twisted branches. Delicate fairy lights strung on the trees created colorful pinpoints in the murky darkness of the breaking dawn.

It all seemed so familiar to me that it was hard to believe it was only my second February in the village. This coming June would mark two years since Aunt Ve had convinced my sister and me to move here from Ohio to embrace a heritage we had known nothing about until that point in time: the Craft, a hereditary form of witchcraft. My sister and I were witches.

Snow pelted my cheeks as I glanced around the village and marveled at how most people had no idea that there were thousands of witches who lived and worked here. We coexisted secretly with mortal villagers who were clueless about residing in such a magical world. Here, Crafters of all varieties were able to practice their magical gifts under the appearance of capitalism—and without the fear of being discovered. Witches were still a bit touchy about the whole burning at the stake part of our history—so much so that we could lose our powers if we told a mortal about the Craft, even accidentally.

The village was thriving with its various witch-themed businesses, such as the Bewitching Boutique, the Magic Wand Salon, the Witch's Brew coffee shop, and the Crone's Cupboard to name a few. Shops with their colorful awnings, charming storefronts, and wrought iron signposts lined the village's main square with dozens more boutiques sprinkled throughout outlying neighborhoods.

The chill wound its way under my hat and beneath my down coat as I perched precariously atop a metal ladder on the edge of the village green. The ends of my long, dark hair blew about my face as I gripped a giant vinyl banner that spanned the main road into the village, desperately trying to keep the sign from flying into the dark gray skies à la Dorothy's house in the *Wizard of Oz*. I'd already hooked the right side of the sign, but the left was not cooperating in any way, shape, or form.

It was a little past six thirty on Saturday morning, and I'd been struggling with my task for nearly fifteen minutes. My fingers were going numb, I couldn't feel my face, and I was pretty sure there were icicles dangling from my eyebrows.

I wished I knew a spell that would finish this job for me, but I couldn't think of a single one that fit. And though I was a Wishcrafter, a witch who could make wishes come true, I could not grant my own wishes so I was out of luck on both counts.

Being unable to grant my own wishes—or those of other Wishcrafters—was just one of the many Craft rules I had to abide by. I couldn't make someone fall in love. I couldn't solicit wishes, either, to help someone out. Or grant a wish that someone would drop dead—mostly because that went against the basic Craft tenet of "do no harm." Above all else, we must not use any Craft ability to harm or hurt anyone, mentally or physically. Each variety of Crafter had their own law book but Wishcrafters, especially, had to be careful. It was easy for others to abuse our powers. Several amendments to our laws had been made to protect us, but every once in a while, someone tried to take advantage.

I'd learned a lot since I moved to this village and my life had changed drastically. Not only because I was a witch, but because I'd discovered long-lost family and made new friends. I'd been appointed an investigator for the Craft—whenever there was a crime in the village involving a Crafter, it was my job to snoop around to ensure that the protection of the Craft and its witches synced with the mortal justice system. I'd also become a business owner, taking over As You Wish, a personal concierge service, which had been run by Aunt Ve.

And I'd fallen in love.

Nick Sawyer, the village police chief, and I were engaged to be married. He and his daughter, thirteen-year-old Mimi, had moved in with me. Along with their Saint Bernard, Higgins, my dog, Missy, and my cat, Annie, we had a full house.

A happy house.

Our *home*.

Thinking of them filled me with a warmth that was more than welcome in this weather. Hanging the massive banner this morning was not supposed to have been a one person job. My twenty-four-year-old sister, Harper, had volunteered to help me, but she was suspiciously a no-show.

She had been volunteering a lot lately, on top of working full-time at her bookshop, Spellbound, and in addition to joining every club and organization—or so it seemed—the village had to offer.

Keeping busy was her way of dealing with a recent breakup, but she'd taken that particular philosophy to the next (obsessive) level, and I was worried about her health, both mental and physical.

I threw a look upward to the apartment where Harper lived above Spellbound. The lights were on but the shades were drawn.

Her absence this morning probably had nothing to do with time-management issues and everything to do with the single-digit wind chill and foot of snow that had already fallen.

She hated the cold.

I wasn't exactly enjoying it, either. The day had barely begun, and I already wanted to go back to bed. That simple yearning was impossible, so I tried not to dwell on the thought. I had a job to do. The village was soon going to be flooded with people arriving to participate in the tenth annual Wicked Mad Dash, which my personal concierge business, As You Wish, had been hired to oversee this year. As much as I'd love to cancel the event altogether, it had been advertised to take place rain, snow, or shine. In fact, Abby Stillwell, the woman who'd hired me, had informed me that the worse the weather, the better for the event.

Which led me to believe that the "mad" part of this dash was associated with the racers' state of mind and not their speed.

I'd known little about the race before I took over managing it, but quickly found out that the Wicked Mad Dash was not only a destination race, drawing competitors from all over the country to the Enchanted Village, but also an adventure race, complete with twenty demanding obstacles along a course that wound through the Enchanted Woods, the forest that surrounded the village.

Apparently, the ultracompetitive racers loved a challenge. The more difficult the course and conditions, the more exciting. They were probably rejoicing with all this wind and snow. I, however, could do with a little sunshine.

Festive heart-shaped wreaths, which were hung in celebration of the upcoming Valentine's holiday, swayed in the wind and knocked a steady beat against faux gaslights that lined the village square. The drums of war, I reflected, bemused as I continued my battle with the banner. It had to be hung as it marked the Wicked Mad Dash starting—and finish—line in front of Spellbound.

I glanced around to see if anyone was nearby to lend a hand, but there was no one. I had commissioned my best friend, photographer extraordinaire, and owner of Hocus-Pocus Photography, Starla Sullivan, to take photos of the event, but with the start of race still hours away she wasn't here yet.

The catering team from the Sorcerer's Stove was inside the large tent set up on the village green behind me. The storm had chased off most of the usual morning dog-walkers and joggers. Nick was at work. As the village's chief of police, he had his own job to do to make sure this race ran as planned, so he was busy overseeing the cordoning off of streets and hanging of "no parking" signs.

Mimi, who often enjoyed helping me with As You Wish projects, had slept at a friend's house last night. She would turn fourteen in a couple of weeks and was at the age where spending time at home with Nick and me on the weekends couldn't hold a candle to a slumber party with her closest friends. While I missed her company, I was grateful she had a somewhat-typical teenage life. Her childhood had been far from normal between her mom, Melina, dying after a battle with cancer, and then finding out her mom had been a Wishcrafter and that she was too . . .

And while I had hired a small crew to work the race today, all were out and about, checking to make sure the course markings were still visible in the snow. The last thing the race needed was for its runners to get lost in the storm, though from what I'd heard of the racers' adventuresome spirits, they might like taking the scenic route through the woods.

Mad, indeed.

With a viselike grip and steely stubbornness, I somehow managed to keep hold of the banner as another gust whipped down the road. If the sign flew off, there was no time to replace it. Not with the race starting in just a couple of hours. Gritting my teeth, I eyed the metal grommets on the sign, willing them to align with the hooks on the coordinating aluminum pole of the portable truss system. But the wind was playing tug of war, and I was losing this battle. My fingers were now numb and my arms ached with the effort of keeping my grip on the banner.

Frustrated, I glanced again at Harper's window, but there had been no change in the status of her window shades since the last time I looked. Then my gaze drifted a little farther down the street, landing on Lotions and Potions, the village's bath and body shop. The lights were on, and I could very clearly see Vince Paxton through the shop's plateglass window, watching me with a smirk on his face.

It suddenly struck me that my current woes could possibly be attributed to him. Tinkering with the banner was just the kind of prank he loved to play with his dark magic. Despite everyone's warnings, he'd been practicing sorcery for months now. While his magical antics tended to be fairly benign and not outwardly malicious, the threat remained that he could cause serious damage on a whim, both to the village and its residents, mortals and witches alike.

In the months since Vince discovered he was a Crafter, he had ignored everyone who implored him to give up sorcery to focus on practicing his inherited Craft. He was a Broomcrafter, a witch who excelled with woodworking, which he considered to be lame. He had no interest in discovering the scope of his magical powers, which were vast and went well beyond working with wood—he had a variety of powerful spells at his command. None interested him, as they were benevolent, not malevolent.

Even the Elder, the governess of the Craft whose true identity was so secret that only a dozen or so witches in all the Craft knew it, hadn't been able to talk sense into him. Most witches around the village had deemed him a lost cause.

I wasn't one of them.

I hated to admit that I had a soft spot for Vince, but I did. I had seen decency in him. Light. I wasn't ready to admit that it had been drowned out by darkness. I desperately wanted him to change his ways and turn toward the goodness of the Craft, but so far he'd ignored everyone who dared to care. Including me. Yet, I kept trying. In that discomfiting vein, I smiled and waved at him.

He waved back, then quickly turned away.

To distract myself, I began to sing under my breath. "'The wind began to switch.'" I tugged and tugged on the banner, wishing my friend Archie, a handsome scarlet macaw familiar (a witch who took on an animal form after death) was here. Archie had once been a London theater actor, and we often enjoyed trying to stump each other with movie quotes. Needless to say, his offerings were usually acted out in overdramatic fashion. Which, if I was being honest, only made them that much more enjoyable.

And though the particular *Wizard of Oz* lyric I sang was fitting of my current situation, it was hardly a challenge. But Archie would have joined me in song, making this task a little more bearable. However, an early bird Archie was not, and he loathed snow almost as much as he despised the TV remake of *Dirty Dancing*.

That was saying something.

"Talking to yourself now, Darcy? Why am I not the least bit surprised? You should get out more. Meet new people. Find new friends. Perhaps you should move back to Ohio. Or . . . anywhere else." Dorothy Hansel Dewitt glared upward at me from beneath the hood of a faux-fur trimmed parka. Redness from the cold colored her plump cheeks and pointed chin.

I hadn't heard her approach, and as I looked down at her, I rather wished a house would come along and land atop her.

Again, unfortunately, I couldn't grant my own wishes. And there was also that pesky Craft rule about doing no harm. Being crushed by a house could definitely be deemed harmful.

To Dorothy.

The rest of the village, however, might be in agreement that the house had done us all a huge favor.

If there was ever a wicked witch, it was Dorothy Hansel Dewitt. She'd despised me from almost the moment I'd arrived in the village, and she'd like nothing better than to get me—and my family—out of town for good.

Like her son, Vince, Dorothy was a Broomcrafter as well, but used her woodworking skills as more of a hobby than anything else. She liked her blonde hair big, her lips bright red, and her clothes extra tight. Dorothy was rude, often crude, mean, and malicious. If she thought you were ugly, you knew it. She'd picked more fights than I cared to count, and had once been arrested for assault, though she'd copped a plea deal and never saw a day behind bars. I knew of two instances where she had set houses on fire, yet there hadn't been enough evidence to prosecute. She'd stalked my aunt Ve, tried to sabotage my aunt's almost-wedding, and then seduced the potential groom—to whom Dorothy is now married. Little had she known, however, that Ve had willingly let Sylar go. I often wondered if Dorothy would have still wanted him if she had caught on to that fact before the wedding.

Probably not.

Dorothy tended to only like taking things that did not belong to her.

And while Dorothy had always been hateful, lately her animosity had become even more pronounced. She was doing little to hide her hostility toward me and my family, even publicly.

When, during the investigation of a cold-case last autumn, it was (shockingly) revealed that she was Vince's biological mother, my first thought was that the apple hadn't fallen far from Dorothy's twisted tree.

But then I reminded myself that Vince did have a soft side. I'd seen it.

I'd never seen Dorothy as anything but hard and bitter, which had nothing to do with her being a witch and everything to do with her simply being a narcissistic, cruel, and heartless person in general.

There was still hope for Vince. And I was clinging to it harder than I was this banner.

Letting out a frosty breath, I decided not to take her verbal bait.

"Nothing to say for yourself?" Dorothy needled, obviously looking for a fight.

I started singing again in my best Judy Garland voice. "'The house to pitch. And suddenly the hinges started to unhitch.'"

She made a face that could have been described as a frown had it not been for the excessive amounts of Botox keeping her skin fairly immobile. "Talk about unhinged," she said with a roll of her eyes. "I've noticed your mental health has gone downhill since you've moved to the village. Your family is rubbing off on you. Crazy is as crazy does." She started to walk off, giving my ladder a good shove as she passed by. Her cackle echoed as she stomped away in heeled boots, heading for the Witch's Brew.

The ladder wobbled, and I would have fallen off except for the fact that I was clinging to the banner for dear life—it was the anchor I needed to keep my balance.

If anyone knew crazy, it was Dorothy. But I wasn't in the mood to point that out to her. I had things to do, and she wasn't one to walk away from a perceived insult without a long, loud, and sometimes violent retaliation.

Instead, I sang more loudly. "'Just then the Witch, to satisfy an itch, went flying on her broomstick . . .'"

Dorothy looked back over her shoulder and shot me the middle finger. At least I thought she had. It was hard to tell with the thick gloves she wore.

I couldn't help laughing. I'd come a long way from being completely terrified of Dorothy. Now I was only moderately terrified. She was downright scary, but I'd learned over the past year and half that I'd lived in this village, it was best to fight Dorothy's fire with fire.

Fortunately, Dorothy's personality type was a rarity around here. Most villagers were kind, generous souls. Take this race, for instance. During its ten-year existence, earnings from the Wicked Mad Dash had been earmarked for local charities. This year veered from the norm in that its proceeds were going to go straight to Joe and Madison Bryant. Along with Joe's mother, Lucinda, they owned Balefire Sports, the village sports shop that had created and sponsored the race, and Joe's younger brother, Ben, worked there as well as a merchandise manager.

Just two months ago, Joe and Madison's six-month-old daughter Aine had undergone hip dysplasia surgery and was now in a spica cast from the chest down for the foreseeable future. When it was revealed the family's insurance had covered only the bare minimum of Aine's medical bills, Abby Stillwell, a professional runner and the assistant manager of Balefire, suggested the race revenue go toward the baby's medical needs. The village rallied behind the idea, and this year's race attendance had broken all previous records. This community was full of heart, and I was proud to be part of it.

I tugged on the banner some more, but it wouldn't budge. I was about to give up when I heard, "Need some help?"

I glanced down.

A man I didn't recognize stood at the foot of the ladder, looking upward. He appeared to be about my age, early thirties, and didn't seem to have dressed for the weather, wearing only a stocking hat, a heavy sweatshirt, jeans, and sneakers. The sneakers were hard to miss. Neon green with orange horizontal laces. Dark brown eyes studied the banner, while a thick beard covered most of his face.

"Yes, please," I practically begged.

He climbed the ladder, edging his way next to my legs until he was high enough up to grab the banner. We both tugged, and with a quick twist of his wrist, he finally hooked a grommet, then another.

"There," he said, jumping down.

I let my aching arm drop and tried not to groan in relief. As I climbed down the ladder, I thought maybe I *did* recognize him. He seemed familiar, but I couldn't place his face. "I can't thank you enough."

"No problem," he said. With a nod of his head, he turned and walked away.

As I folded the ladder, I again looked to my sister's apartment. As much as Harper didn't like being cold, it wasn't like her to stand me up without an explanation. Suddenly concerned, I sent her a quick text and headed to the event tent to organize registration packets.

Portable heaters placed throughout the tent buzzed, doing their best to battle the cold. Dozens of tables were scattered about, and a catering team from the Sorcerer's Stove was busy setting up after-race provisions, which from my spot across the tent looked to consist of bagels, bananas, chocolate milk, and water.

Just as I was wishing for a big cup of coffee, Abby Stillwell stumbled through the tent flaps, two to-go cups from the Witch's Brew in her gloved hands.

It seemed every once in a while the fates threw my wishes a bone.

"Good morning," Abby croaked.

"Are you okay?"

I'd known Abby since I moved to the village, which was also when I had taken up jogging. The running community here in the village was quite small, and it had been easy to get to know those who were part of it, though it was vastly divided in terms of talent.

In one group there were recreational joggers like myself, along with more hardcore fitness buffs. In the other group were the professional runners who ran with Balefire Racing, the exclusive team that participated in elite races including national and world championships and even the Olympics.

I was firmly in the first group.

Abby was in the latter group, along with Joe, Ben, and Madison, as well. Ben Bryant and Abby had been dating for a few months, making the Balefire team seem like one big happy and extremely athletic family.

I'd been working closely with Abby for more than a month now, and never in all that time had I ever known her to stumble or croak. In her late twenties, she tended to glide through life with long graceful strides. And also tended to chirp her words rather than speak them. Starla Sullivan had described Abby as "effervescent." I agreed. Abby bubbled with life. Usually.

Today, a green cast colored her cheeks as she handed me a coffee. "Stomach bug. Lousy timing."

After dragging a chair over to the registration table, she dropped her backpack at her feet and sat down, putting her head between her knees. She was dressed in upscale running apparel. The latest high-tech tights, shirt, jacket, gloves, and trail shoes. Dark brown hair curled out from beneath a red Balefire beanie that I knew was thermal and waterproof, only because I owned the same one in pink.

I noticed her cup had a teabag tag dangling down its side, but I hadn't seen her take a single sip. "Thanks for this," I said of the coffee. "Can I get you anything? Bagel? Banana?"

She moaned softly, and I took that as a no.

My phone whistled, and I glanced at the text message Harper had sent back.

> HARPER: *Dying. Don't know if I can make it today.*
> ME: *Stomach bug?*
> HARPER: *How did u know?*

Harper was well and truly sick if she was using texting slang, which she despised. I glanced at Abby, who still had her head down.

> ME: *Going around.*
> HARPER: *Great.*

"Darcy, can I have a word?" a female voice behind me said.

I glanced over my shoulder and found Stefanie Millet wringing her hands. She was the new catering manager at the Sorcerer's Stove, known locally as the Stove, and I didn't like the look on her face one little bit. With a jerk of her dimpled chin, she motioned for me to step out of Abby's earshot.

"What's wrong?" I asked.

Stef's blue eyes looked pained. In a low whisper, she said, "I was just notified that our answering service is being flooded with complaints about possible food poisoning from the banquet last night."

There had been a prerace get-together at the Stove the night before. Not all the Mad Dash participants had been there, but many of those staying in the village had attended, along with event sponsors and coordinators, including Harper, who had been helping me with last-minute planning. "But I ate there, and I'm fine."

"Did you eat the chocolate cake?"

I hadn't. Simply because it had been gone by the time I had a chance to look for it. "No, I didn't. The cake was bad?"

"*Shh!*" she said, looking around. "We don't know for certain. It's the only menu item consistent with those who've complained this morning."

"How many calls have come in?"

"Two dozen, give or take. I'm so sorry. I don't know what happened. I have the kitchen staff looking into it."

The Stove had a storied history of food poisoning incidents in the past, which had nothing to do with the quality of food and everything to do with abusing magic. It immediately made me wonder which had been at fault this time around.

"Can you get me the names of the people who called?" I asked. "I'll be sure to refund their race fees."

She said she would and walked back to the bananas. Food poisoning. Wonderful. I picked up my phone.

ME: *Good news is it's not a stomach bug. Bad news is it's food poisoning. Chocolate cake gone horribly wrong.*

HARPER: *I'm going to kill somebody.*

ME: *Glad to see you're feeling better already.*

HARPER: *I'd argue, but I have to go throw up now.*

ME: *I'll come check on you as soon as I can get away. Need anything?*

HARPER: *A quick death.*

ME: *I'll see what I can do.*

What Harper really needed was a Curecrafter, a healing witch, but our good friend Cherise Goodwin was out of town with her boyfriend (and former ex-husband), Terry Goodwin, for a winter getaway. Their son, Dr. Dennis Goodwin, was still around, however. While he wasn't my favorite witch in the world, he'd have to do. I made a mental note to get in touch with him to see if he could make a quick house call. He'd have Harper feeling good as new in minutes.

I turned back to Abby. Her head was still down, but she said, "Do I want to know what Stef had to say?"

"Nope."

Abby was a Vitacrafter, so I wasn't the least bit surprised she had picked up on the tension in the air. Vitacrafters could read the energy of those around them.

"Okay then," she said. "In case I forget, thanks for your help with this race. I couldn't have done this without you."

It was true—she couldn't have. I had never met a more disorganized person in all my life. When Abby first hired me, it had taken me a week just to make sense of her paperwork, then another week to get it into order again. Her enthusiasm for the race, however, had more than made up for the headaches. She was quite simply one of the sweetest people I'd ever met.

An amazing feat, considering the life she'd had. Both her parents had been killed in a car crash, leaving her on her own as a young adult. She had no other family than the one she'd created at Balefire. "You're welcome."

Bracing an elbow on her knee, she dropped her head into her palm. "If you have a little bit of time after the race, I'd like to show you something I found in last year's paperwork, get your opinion."

"About?"

She opened her backpack and pulled out a folder. "I think I might have messed up the race's bookkeeping.

Yesterday, I dug up last year's ledger, and mine doesn't come close to matching, even though we used the same vendors. I asked Ben to take a look, but because he's not good with numbers, he suggested I ask Madison or Joe."

Abby handed the folder to me. In it were two ledgers. Accounting books. "What did they have to say?"

"Nothing, because I didn't ask them. I'd rather they not know I messed up. Instead, I came to you. You're so good at fixing my mistakes." She gave me a smile, or tried to. She immediately put her head between her legs again.

The Mad Dash had always been Joe and Madison Bryant's baby . . . but that was before they had an actual baby. And with Aine's birth, her health issues, and Joe's intense training schedule for an upcoming international competition, they had been too overwhelmed to give the event the attention it needed, so they turned it over to Abby. Abby wasn't one for finer details, so she'd come to me. We made a pretty good team, if I did say so myself.

"I'd be happy to take a look," I said, tucking the folder in my tote bag. "I'll do it as soon as the race is over."

"Thanks, Darcy," she said, dropping her head back between her knees.

Racers began to filter into the tent, and I quickly became busy handing out racing bibs, timing chips, and course maps.

Over the next hour, the color slowly returned to Abby's face. In fact, all the stricken racers had made abrupt recoveries and showed up to compete as planned. Abby's best friend and roommate Quinn Donegal had arrived to live-tweet the race for Balefire and smartly planted herself near a portable heater.

Quinn had worked at Balefire for a couple of years, managing the store's and team's websites and social media accounts. She stood out among the others at

Balefire for the simple reason that she wasn't a runner. According to Abby, Quinn preferred yoga.

The Bryants arrived as well, even the baby who looked like an angel in her fluffy custom-made snow suit that had been created to fit around her body cast. Joe, Ben, and their mother Lucinda would be participating in the race, while Madison and Aine cheered them on.

There was still no sign of Harper.

With only fifteen minutes to the start of the Mad Dash, Abby stood and said, "I'm going to head out for my warm-up."

I didn't try to talk her out of participating in such a grueling competition after a night battling a stomach bug. I'd learned runners of her caliber were dedicated and tenacious. I'd be wasting my breath.

"Be careful out there," I said instead, unable to stop the mama hen in me from squawking.

She smiled broadly, and her eyes twinkled. "See you at the starting line."

Snow fell steadily as I left the warmth of the tent to supervise the start of the race. The DJ had set up in a covered booth near the starting line and was playing, of all things, "Let It Snow." The crowd was happily singing along, despite Christmas being two months ago.

Time ticked along, and I busied myself with last minute issues like the race clock malfunctioning, bibs flying off despite safety pins, and the doors to the portable restrooms locking shut. All of which occurred out of the blue, no rhyme or reason.

Or so it would seem to someone not attuned to the magical world around them. I'd bet my Crafting cloak it was Vince and his sorcery behind these troubles. I was going to have to deal with him sooner rather than later.

Despite it all, I was soon caught up in race excitement, setting my worries aside.

Right up until I spotted Stef Millet walking into Lotions and Potions . . . and straight into Vince's arms for a long hug. My stomach churned with the sudden thought that he'd somehow been behind the chocolate cake disaster as well as the other mischief.

Turning away from them, I put it out of my mind for the time being. I needed to focus on the race. There was less than a minute until the starting gun went off, and worry had crept back in, overtaking any remaining excitement.

Because Abby Stillwell had never returned from her warm-up run.

Chapter Two

B y the time the race finished and the trophies, medals, and winners' checks were handed out, my worry
for Abby had turned into full-blown panic.

No one had seen her since she left for her warm-up
run more than two hours ago.

The police were out looking for her, and I, along
with several of Abby's nearest and dearest, were gathered
in the event tent waiting on news. Any news at all.

Nick Sawyer took one look at my face, held my
hand, and said, "We'll find her, Darcy."

Nick and I had been engaged for four months
now and had set a wedding date for this coming June.
Not many knew me better than he did, and he usually
possessed the amazing ability to calm me when I was
frazzled. Not today though. Not with this situation.

Abby Stillwell had vanished.

Both Ben and Quinn, who knew Abby best, insisted
she wouldn't have just gone off without telling anyone.
Especially since her car was still parked in the driveway of
her house, and her wallet and cellphone were in the backpack she had left under the Mad Dash's registration table.

"Abby shouldn't have been running in the first
place, after being ill all night." Ben's square jaw clenched
as he finished the statement.

We were all working on the assumption that Abby had become lightheaded during her warm-up run and had wandered off course. If she was disoriented, she could be anywhere in the expansive woods.

"This is Abby we're talking about," Madison Bryant said, looking upward at her brother-in-law, Ben. About my height, five six, Madison had long, blonde hair that had been braided and pinned in a coil at the nape of her neck. The tips of her ears were pink from the cold, and her breath came out in frosty puffs, but there was fervent heat in her tone. "The woman who competed at the Olympic trials with a stress fracture in her foot. And won." Madison had Aine secured to her chest in a fancy sling. The bright, happy pink of the baby's spica cast peeking out of her snowsuit fairly glowed in the gloomy atmosphere of the tent. The little one was sound asleep, peacefully oblivious to the drama unfolding around her.

"And she paid the price for it, didn't she?" Ben snapped, his blue eyes narrowing. "That decision ultimately ruined her career. She should have known better then, and she should have known better this morning." He shook his head in dismay. "She should have stayed home."

Anxiety seeped out in his voice. It was clear to me he was worried sick. It would do no good, however, to dwell on should-haves. It wouldn't change anything at this point.

Quinn stood back from the group, and looked like she wanted to throw up. She was walking in little circles, her head down and her arms wrapped around herself. According to Abby, she and Quinn were more like sisters than friends, and I immediately felt a rush of sympathy for the woman.

"Hush now," Lucinda Bryant said quietly to her younger son. "Imagine if Abby heard you talking this way."

With a gravelly voice that reminded me of Kathleen Turner, Lucinda was in her late fifties and still had a lithe runner's body. She was slightly shorter than her sons, who were both about six feet tall, and was the most decorated athlete among them, having succeeded as an Olympic marathoner while her sons had never quite reached that athletic mark.

The fact that all three were elite runners wasn't the least bit surprising to me. But that was because I knew they were Vincicrafters, witches who had innate athleticism. They excelled at whatever sport they chose.

While Vincicrafters possessed above-average athletic ability, they still had to take that natural ability to the next level. They trained long, grueling hours and were focused and disciplined.

Lucinda, for example, made it to the Olympics because she worked hard to get there. There were many Vincis—before and after her—who hadn't been able to reach that level. Mortals *could* beat them. And had.

But still . . . among witches, there was no denying that Vincis had an upper hand at athletic events. Which was why there were Craft laws denying Vincicrafters monetary gain from the sports in which they participated. No major league contracts. No Nike sponsorships. No check at the finish line. Most Vincis didn't mind the rule—they weren't in sports for money. They were there for the competition.

Joe Bryant ran a hand down his face, his fingers lingering on his dark, trimmed beard. "Talking isn't getting us anywhere, anyway. We need to *find* her."

Nick said, "Although there is a team out searching, it might be time to recruit some extra help with the search efforts. If Abby is out in this storm, the sooner we find her, the better."

The storm had taken a turn for the worse with whiteout conditions and high winds. Even so, forming additional search parties was not going to be a difficult task. Once word had leaked about Abby's disappearance, most of the Mad Dashers had stuck around, wanting to help in some way. They were not the least bit fazed by the snow and rough terrain.

Out of the corner of my eye, I saw Vince Paxton slip into the tent and make his way over to Stef, who was standing off to the side watching us. She whispered something to him.

So help me if Vince decided to pull one of his *pranks* right now. I was too upset to deal with his shenanigans. Feeling fury rising, I had to look away before I marched over there and had it out with him.

Madison said, "Count me in on the search team. I'm in the woods all the time, so I have a good feel for the spots Abby could have taken shelter."

Madison was a Terracrafter—a witch with the ultimate green thumb. Her affinity for the woods was in her blood. I was certain she had explored every inch of the Enchanted Woods and knew each and every hollowed tree trunk and hidden cave.

Turning to her mother-in-law, she said, "Lucinda, can you watch Aine for a while?"

I loved the way Madison said her baby's name. *Awn-yah*. It wasn't a name I'd been familiar with until I met the little girl.

Lucinda's eyes softened as she glanced at her granddaughter. "Of course."

I pulled Nick aside. "I'll see what help I can round up, too." There were many Crafters in this village who'd be more than willing to risk their own lives to help find a fellow witch.

First and foremost, the Elder. I needed to get in touch with her as soon as possible about this situation. She was the most powerful witch in the village and had endless resources to help in the search for Abby.

A flood of emotions filled me just thinking about the Elder.

The Elder . . . my mother.

My mother, who'd died in a tragic car accident when I was seven years old.

It had been nearly a year since I learned that after my mother's death twenty-four years ago, she had taken on a familiar form—she'd chosen a mourning dove—and then soon after had become the Craft's Elder.

Like all the Elders before her, her identity was a secret from most in the witch world, to protect her and those she loved. Only the Coven of Seven, her advisory council, and a handful of others knew who she was. It was against Craft law to reveal the Elder's identity. If a witch knew who the Elder was, it was because she wanted that witch to know. Otherwise, a memory cleanse would be involved. I didn't know how the Elder chose *who* was allowed to know the truth, but I trusted her decisions.

Harper and I hadn't been told at first because we'd grown up knowing nothing about the witch world since our father had wanted to raise us as mortals. It was only after his death that we even learned we were witches. Above and beyond that was an additional measure in place to protect the Elder: No one, including close relatives, was allowed to know the Elder's identity unless they had lived in the village for a full year. It had taken nearly that long for me to figure out the truth on my own, and mine and Harper's reunion with our mother was something I would never, ever forget.

With all this snow, reaching my mother's home deep in the Enchanted Woods would be nearly impossible for me, but fortunately, I knew just the bird who could help out.

Archie.

Even though he did not live with my mother, he was her assistant, her right-hand bird so to speak, and while he couldn't travel in this weather, either, he would know another way to reach her, as they had many ways to communicate with each other.

As Nick gave instructions to those who'd gathered, I called my aunt Ve. Since she was birdsitting Archie for the next week, she was the easiest way to reach him quickly. While familiars like Archie were not beholden to any witch, they often had caretakers. Archie's usual custodian was Ve's neighbor (and ex-husband), Terry Goodwin, who was currently on vacation with his girlfriend (and former ex-wife), Cherise Goodwin. That love triangle was as complicated as it sounded, but amazingly they were all close friends.

I also wanted to tell Ve about what was going on with Abby and ask her help to locate her. As village chairwoman, Ve could send out an alert to witches and mortal villagers alike in no time flat.

It took three tries to get the call to go through to Ve. My cell was dying from the cold weather, freezing up. Ve's phone clicked over to voicemail. I left a message then tried her landline, but I couldn't get the call to go through and my screen turned black. I tucked my phone into the inside pocket of my coat, hoping body heat would warm it up enough to use.

I walked over to one of the tent windows and peered across the village green to my aunt's beautiful Victorian. The blowing snow obscured the finer details of the house's design, but I could see twin pinpoints of light—the front porch lights—glowing through the storm. Ve was an early bird by nature, so I was surprised she wasn't already out here nosing around among the police cars. I immediately started to worry, being that worrying was the primary marker of my DNA.

As far as I knew, Ve had intended to be home all day. She'd been experiencing empty-nest syndrome since I moved out and was loving every minute of having Archie's company. In fact, I knew she and Archie had plans today to watch as many Doris Day movies as they could.

Since I couldn't reach her by phone, I'd stop over there as soon as I had the chance.

". . . out for her warm-up," Nick was saying. "By all accounts, she would have jogged about a half a mile, gone through a series of prerace exercises then returned to the starting line. As we all know, she did not make it back. I can confirm the last sighting of her was in fact at the trailhead. The half-mile marker is just beyond the turnoff for the Aural Gorge Trail."

Nick finished his speech and the searchers broke into teams of six and started gearing up for a trek into the woods. Pulling on a warm hat and slipping on a pair of gloves, he walked over to me. His brown eyes softened and again he said, "We'll find her. She'll be okay."

I wanted to believe him, so I said, "Okay."

Only minutes after he and the search teams left the tent, it hit me that Harper might be of help in finding Abby as well. In fact, she could hold the key to pinpointing Abby's *exact* location.

Not long ago, Harper had unearthed a centuries-old spell able to locate lost things. A bubble of excitement rushed through me. I pulled out my phone to call her, but it was still dark.

Instead of wasting my time fighting with my phone, I decided to simply go see her. But as I walked toward the tent flaps I was stopped by the sight of Lucinda pacing with little Aine. Anxiety was splashed across Lucinda's face in her furrowed brow and downturned lips, but she held the sleeping baby's hand so very gently. I veered toward them.

When Lucinda glanced up at me, her blue-gray eyes widened, and I realized she thought I might have news. I gave a soft shake of my head and searched for the right words of comfort. I couldn't find any. All I could manage was an echo of Nick's promise. "They'll find her."

She nodded but said nothing. Just kept holding the baby's hand—making me want to hold it too. Aine was just so sweet and innocent, and I craved that, even if only for a moment.

I gave a weak smile and turned to go. I'd made it about two steps out of the tent when Vince stepped in front of me.

"Not now, Vince," I said, trying to sidestep. Snow had been stomped down outside the tent but had drifted into banks two feet tall in some places. The searchers had their work cut out for them.

"Darcy, wait."

"Why?" I asked, marching away. Snowflakes stung my face, tiny icy knives.

Vince dogged my heels. "I want to help."

I spun to face him. "Help? Like with the banner this morning? The race clock? The portable bathrooms? Oh, and let's not forget the chocolate cake."

Snow blanketed his wavy brown hair as a grin lifted one corner of his mouth. "Oh come on. No self-respecting athlete would eat cake the night before a race. Serves them right. Besides, no harm, no foul. The hex expired at seven this morning. Everyone who ate the cake is fine now."

I fisted my hands and shoved them in my pockets. "There is so much wrong with what you've said, like how it wasn't only athletes who ate the cake, but I don't have time to get into it with you."

I spun around, my eye on the bookshop. It had opened at eight, and at the door I could see Angela Curtis, the shop's manager, looking out into the snow. No sign of Harper.

"I have a drone," Vince called after me. "It can traverse the woods much faster than anyone on foot."

I stopped then turned slowly around.

His glasses were fogging, so he pulled them off. I saw earnestness in his blue puppy-dog eyes as he said, "I want to help find Abby. She's a friend. Not a close one, but one nonetheless."

It was times like this that confirmed there *was* good inside him. Deep inside, maybe, but it was there. "A drone? You can use one in this weather?"

"I have my ways."

Ah yes. I knew of his chosen ways. "Your ways don't help. They *cause* harm."

It was the nature of dark magic. To hurt, to harm, to damage. There was nothing remotely benevolent within it. Nothing at all.

"Right. Like *your* magic is doing so much good right now. Maybe you could wish Abby back. Oh, that's right. You can't. Your magic is useless."

I clenched my jaw—he knew how to push every single one of my buttons.

"Besides, I didn't say I'd use sorcery, Darcy." He *tsk*ed. "Don't jump to conclusions."

I wanted to turn him down flat just for the principle of it all, but this wasn't about me. It was about Abby. "Fine. Get your drone and meet me back here in five minutes."

"As you wish," he said with a mock bow, jogging off toward his apartment above Lotions and Potions.

I couldn't help letting out a small growl of frustration as I pressed on toward the bookshop, scooting around a line of village police cars. Each was a MINI Cooper, painted nonthreatening colors like green and pink. I saw Nick's car—I called it the Bumblebeemobile because of its black and yellow coloring—parked across the square in front of our house, and wished more than anything that this morning had never happened. That the two of us were still in bed, enjoying a lazy Saturday.

But I couldn't grant my own wishes. And I couldn't change the fact that Abby was missing. I could, however, help find her.

To reach Harper's apartment, cutting through the bookshop was much faster than walking around to the entrance in the back alley.

Angela Curtis saw me coming and held open the door. "Quite a morning!"

"An understatement," I said, stomping my boots on the winter mat.

"Any word about Abby Stillwell?" Angela tugged down the sleeves of her *Goodnight Moon* sweatshirt to cover her fingers.

I blew into my hands, trying to warm them. "Not yet. Has Harper ventured down here this morning?"

Her thick brown eyebrows dipped low. "She left me a message that she was sick and would be late today. Is she okay? It must be bad if she's not out there, snooping around in police business."

Truly, there was nothing Harper enjoyed more. "Food poisoning. I thought she'd be feeling better by now though." After all, Vince said the hex wore off at seven.

Hours ago. It was disconcerting that Harper wasn't down here, peppering me with a zillion questions.

Angela grimaced. "I had food poisoning once, and I was down and out for nearly a week. Anything I can do?"

"I'll let you know," I said. "For now, just hold down the fort here."

"Will do."

I zipped through the bookshop, barely noticing the fantastical décor. The store was done up in a *Starry Night* theme, with bright yellows and bold blues. There were bookshelves created with logs and twigs, iron shelving made to look like trees, and the most impressive children's forest I'd ever seen. And I wasn't just saying that because I'd painted the murals for the area. I hadn't had a lot of time for my art lately, and I made a mental note to get back to it soon.

I hurried down the back hallway toward the private staircase that led up to Harper's apartment. Light shone beneath her door at the top of the steps, but when I knocked there was no answer. I tried the knob. The door was locked. "Harper?"

When I didn't get a response, I pulled out my keys, found the one for Harper's door, and let myself in. The apartment was small. One bed, one bath, with an open layout. The scent of illness permeated the air, and I automatically winced at the smell. I heard bath water running.

"Harper," I called out more loudly, so she could hear me over the running water.

She didn't answer.

Pie, Harper's orange tabby, stared woefully at me from his spot by the bathroom door. Which was ajar.

Panic snaked its way up my spine as I stuck my head into the steamy bathroom. The bathtub faucet was on, the water running down the open drain.

And Harper was unconscious on the floor.

Chapter Three

Letting out a horrified cry, I dropped to my knees next to my baby sister. I patted her face, and winced at the clamminess of her skin. "Harper!"

Clad in a fluffy terry cloth robe, she let out a soft moan and blinked. "Darcy? What happened?"

Tears sprang. I'd never been so relieved in all my life. I thought she was . . . I shook my head. I wouldn't go there. Couldn't.

I fumbled in my coat for my phone to call for help but realized quickly the screen was still black. Fighting the urge to hurl it against the wall, I shoved it back into my pocket. Harper didn't have a landline, but her cell had to be around here somewhere. "Harper, I need to find your phone to call for help." I pushed off the cold, gray tile floor. "I'll be right back."

Pie, who'd been watching from the doorway, let out a loud *reow* and bolted away, a fuzzy orange blur.

"No, no. No need to call anyone." She weakly grabbed my arm and sat up, leaning against the wall with a small groan. "I'm fine."

Stepping over her stretched out legs, I shut off the bath faucet and thanked the heavens the tub hadn't been plugged. I didn't even want to think of what kind of damage a flood would have caused to the bookshop downstairs. Sweat beaded on my forehead from the sauna-like temperatures, and I wiggled out of my coat and threw it out the doorway, into the living room. It landed on the arm of the couch then slid to the floor. Pie didn't look impressed with my aim from his perch on top of the sofa.

"Fine?" I sat next to Harper. "Oh yes, I can see that."

She had been aiming for serenity when she'd chosen the color palette for the bathroom. Pale periwinkle walls, white trim, and light gray accents. But at the moment, there wasn't a speck of serenity to be found within these four walls.

It had been obliterated by the lingering scent of sickness and a feeling of foreboding.

Cinching her bathrobe, she rolled her bloodshot eyes. "I was going to take a bath and got dizzy. That's all. No big deal."

While she wasn't a girly girl by any means, she loved taking baths as a way to relax—usually at the end of her long workday. One of the first renovations she'd commissioned on the apartment after she moved in had been to replace the old, shallow tub with a deeper one. Candles of varying heights dotted the tub's ledge, along with a jar of lavender-scented Epsom salt, and a stack of books. One of which appeared to have taken a bath with Harper at some point, if its wrinkled pages were any indication.

I didn't argue her "no big deal" comment, though I wanted to. Fighting with her right now wasn't going to help anything. But I couldn't stop a tear from sliding down my cheek now that the rush of adrenaline was wearing off. "You're probably dehydrated."

Harper saw the tear and moisture instantly filled her eyes. She sniffled. "I'm sorry I scared you."

Seeing her tear up broke my heart. "I'm sorry you're not feeling well."

Her lower lip trembled, and I pulled her in for a tight hug. "I'm going to have it out with Vince for hexing that chocolate cake. No harm, no foul he told me. Just wait until I get my hands—"

Harper cut me off. "Vince?"

I pulled back. "Yeah, he thought the runners deserved to be hexed if they chose to eat cake before a race."

She struggled to stand up. "Let me at him." She went ghostly white and sat back down. Weakly, she added, "Later. I'm going to wring his scrawny neck later."

Now that my heart rate had calmed down a bit, I studied her, my emotions warring. Relief versus worry. Sadness versus irritation. Because I knew, deep down, there was more to Harper's illness than a hexed cake. "The thing is," I said, trying to keep my voice neutral, "Vince's hex wore off earlier this morning, so you *should* be doing better by now. The runners who ate the cake were still able to participate in the Mad Dash."

"Don't start, Darcy," she warned, not falling for my detached tone in the least.

I took a deep breath and started. "The racers are fit, healthy. They could bounce back easily."

"*Darcy.*"

"For months, you've been working yourself to the bone, and you are always on the go, go, go. You've joined every group and club in the village. Hula-Hooping. Yoga. Dominoes. Weather chasers. Needlepoint."

Wriggling out of my grasp, she stood. Wobbled. Reaching out, she grabbed the towel bar to keep her balance. She'd always been small and thin, but in the past four months, she'd lost weight. At least five pounds, maybe ten. It was weight she didn't have to spare. She was starting to look skeletal, and it was terrifying.

At the sink, she splashed water on her gaunt face. She used a hand towel to pat her face dry, then sop up wayward droplets on the granite countertop. Tossing the towel into the wicker hamper next to the sink, she glanced at her reflection in the mirror then looked quickly away as if unable to stand the sight of herself. "I like staying busy."

Wind rattled the eaves, shaking them angrily as I said, "There's busy, and then there's worn out. You're not sleeping. You're not eating."

We'd had this conversation before. About a hundred times. After her breakup with village lawyer, Marcus Debrowski, last October, Harper had done everything in her power to take her mind off the pain.

Everything but deal with it.

During those months, I had pushed her as much as I dared, but now I questioned whether I should have been more adamant. More forceful. Made her seek help.

I loathed hindsight.

Her short pixie haircut stuck out in tawny unruly tufts. Darkness circled her big golden brown eyes and exhaustion hollowed her cheeks. Her tiny body bowed as if bearing a weight too heavy to carry. My heart ached for her, and I wished more than anything that I could take this pain away from her.

But I couldn't.

"I eat. I even had cake last night. Look where that landed me." She gestured to the floor in front of the toilet.

Although she had a good point about the cake, I didn't let it deter me. "Since Cherise is out of town, I'm going to call Dennis Goodwin." I had wanted to call him this morning when I thought she simply suffered from food poisoning so he could give her a quick fix with his Curecrafting ways. But now . . . It was crystal clear something other than a stomach bug ailed Harper. Something I wasn't convinced could be cured with a spell. "I want him to look you over, just to make sure everything's okay."

"No."

Fighting back angry tears, I said, "No? Okay. Then brace yourself, because I am not going to stop nagging you about your health and wellness until you do agree. I will move in here, to keep an eye on you. In case you pass out again, which I know you think is *no big deal*, but guess what? It is a big deal. Colossal." There was nothing Harper prized more than her independence, so I was fighting dirty, hitting her where it hurt most. "I will ask you at least thirty times a day if you're hungry or thirsty or want to take a nap. I will follow you to work. Offer to turn the pages of the books you read. Turn down your bed at night. Tuck you in." Winded, I sucked in a deep breath. "I'm dead serious, Harper. It's either one visit from Dennis . . . or dealing with me constantly for the foreseeable future. Your choice."

Her hands clenched into fists. Saying nothing, she carefully walked out of the bathroom, keeping one hand on the wall for balance. Slowly she made her way to the windows overlooking the village green and opened the shades. Snow had drifted onto the windowsills. Wind rattled the panes. At just over five feet tall, she looked puny against the huge windows. Fragile. Ordinarily, she was anything but. However these last few months had thrown her for a loop, mentally and physically. She loved Marcus, and he'd chosen his family over her.

I followed her into the living area, the wood floor squeaking underneath my booted feet. Pie eyed me from his spot on the larger of the two sofas that faced each other in the center of the room. He sat on a crocheted blanket Harper had brought home recently from her crochet club, the Crafty Hookers.

She reveled in telling people the name of that particular club. She had a bit of a mischievous streak, which fortunately hadn't gone missing these last few months along with her appetite and sense of self-preservation.

Waiting her out, I found a lighter and lit a scented vanilla candle, hoping it would help cut through the horrid scent in the air. The living room had a library-like feel to it, decorated mostly with shelves of books. Old books, new books, and numerous in-between. Hardback, paperback, and leather-bound. Many of them were about witchcraft. When we had first moved to the village, she hadn't been too keen on being a witch, but she was slowly coming around to her natural gift. And had become hyper-focused on learning as much as she could about it.

She wasn't one to do anything half way.

After a long moment of staring outside, she turned to face me. "I'll see Dennis on one condition."

I'd been hoping she was too ill to negotiate. No such luck. "What condition?"

"Once he gives me the all clear, and he will, you will not say another word about my schedule or my health." She crossed her arms. "I am almost twenty-five years old. I can do what I wish, when I wish, how often I wish to do so. If I don't want to eat, I won't. If I want to pull an all-nighter, I will. If I want to sleep all day, I will. If I want to become a groupie and follow the Roving Stones around the country, I will."

She wasn't a big fan of the Roving Stones, a rock and mineral traveling show, so I breathed easy she wouldn't follow through on that particular threat. "I wish you would sleep all day. You can use the rest."

Her jaw jutted. "Deal?"

"Forever and ever?" My stomach turned. I wasn't sure it was a promise I could make.

As if sensing my reservation, she said, "At least until my birthday, then we can renegotiate. And I mean it. Not a single peep."

Her birthday was in June, four months from now. It was honestly going to be torture for the mama hen in me.

But I'd do it. I was worried about Harper enough to agree to her terms. "I promise. You have my word."

With a firm nod, she said, "Now tell me what's going on outside? What's with all the police cars? And why is Vince out on the sidewalk in a blizzard, staring up here?"

I went to the window. Sure enough Vince stood in front of the bookstore, his arms wrapped around a back-pack that undoubtedly held his drone.

"He's waiting for me. We're going to use his drone to search the woods because Abby Stillwell is missing. But maybe we don't have to, which is actually why I came up here to see you in the first place. Could you do the lost and found spell on her? The one you used to find the four-leaf clover in my yard last fall?"

Using the spell had been a breakthrough for Harper. It had been the first time she'd practiced any part of the Craft.

"Whoa, whoa. You lost Abby? How did that happen? I thought there were course guides and markers . . ."

"*I* didn't lose her." I quickly explained what had happened.

Harper glared at Vince. I imagined she was pictur-ing her long fingers circling his neck. Fortunately for him, I didn't think she had enough strength in her body to do any serious harm.

"Can you do the spell?" I asked again. "Are you up to it?"

"I keep telling you, I'm fine. So yes, I'm up for it. But I'm not sure I can find a *person* with that spell. Was Abby wearing any jewelry? Carrying her phone?"

I conjured the memory of Abby a few hours ago, sitting with her head between her knees. I hadn't seen any jewelry, and I knew she didn't have her phone on her. "What about clothes?"

"If you can remember a specific item, it's possible."

"She's wearing a red Balefire beanie. I have the same one in pink."

"I can picture it. That should work, but I'll need a strand of Abby's hair."

"I'll get one." There had to be one on her backpack, which was in the registration tent. If that failed, I'd go to her house. Since her roommate Quinn was a mortal, I'd have to come up with some viable reason to borrow Abby's hairbrush, but I'd cross that bridge later.

I went into the kitchen and filled a large tumbler with water and grabbed a sleeve of crackers from the cupboard. "I'll be back as soon as I can. Until then . . ." I handed her the cup and crackers.

She immediately set them on her coffee table and jutted her jaw again.

I let the defiance go. I'd chosen my battle earlier and won. I'd call Dennis as soon as I could.

I gave Pie a quick head scratch, picked up my coat from the floor, and then walked toward the door.

"Hey, Darcy?"

I turned. "Yeah?"

"Should we be worried that Vince has a drone?"

I took a deep breath. "Probably."

It was something else to worry about later. Right now, I had a strand of hair to track down, a woman to find, and a man's neck to save.

Then I scratched that last one off my to-do list.

Vince and his neck were on their own.

Chapter Four

"Everything okay with Harper?" Vince asked as I pushed through the bookshop's front doors and went out into the cold. "You were gone awhile."

Snow blew sideways, and I lifted my hood for extra protection. "She had a piece of that chocolate cake last night."

He fell in step beside me as we practically jogged toward the event tent. "So she wants to kill me."

"Pretty much. She's in the frame of mind to do it, too, so be careful."

Snowflakes froze on his glasses. "'The grief that does not speak whispers the o'erfraught heart and bids it break.'"

It took me a second to realize Vince was quoting Shakespeare, which was a favorite pastime of many in the village. Quite frankly, I was surprised Harper hadn't joined the local Shakespeare society, run by the Chadwick family. It was probably only a matter of time at this rate.

As Vince's actual words sunk in, it was obvious he recognized Harper's current frame of mind stemmed from her sorrow. Which made sense. He'd experienced that grief and sorrow himself. I long suspected his ignoble nature was born from his not feeling loved—by anyone. I'd known him for almost two years now, and I still wasn't sure if that theory was true. Or if *he* simply did not know how to truly love or accept love. It was easy to speculate his confusion on the matter had driven his egregious behavior as he searched outwardly for something that could only be found within himself.

I wasn't sure I'd ever know the truth. He wasn't exactly an open book.

His breakup with my best friend Starla had been an extremely painful experience for both. Months later, the two had made great strides to overcome their suffering to try to salvage a friendship. It wasn't easy, and the progress they'd made was tenuous at best. For example, Starla could now say Vince's name without visibly wincing— most of the time. Vince still winced—every time.

The inside of the tent was chilly, and I realized the portable heaters had already been packed up by the rental company. "The broken heart club is probably the only club Harper would like to quit right about now."

He said quietly, "Has she considered therapy?"

He seemed genuinely concerned for her, which reminded me of the good within him. "No. Have you?"

Too quickly, he said, "I'm not the one falling apart at the seams because of a broken heart."

I lifted an eyebrow and stared at him.

Swiftly, he looked away and opened his backpack. "If we can get a lull in the storm, that's our best opportunity to send out the drone."

I let his lie go. It wouldn't do me any good to argue the truth. I crouched under the table. "I'm not sure we need the drone after all. Harper might be able to pinpoint Abby's location."

"How?"

I glanced around. The staff from the Stove was gone but a few Mad Dashers remained behind.

Dropping my voice, I said, "A lost and found spell."

He rolled his eyes.

I pretended I didn't see as I carefully looked over Abby's backpack. Sure enough, several strands of her long, dark hair were stuck to the shoulder straps.

I looped Abby's backpack over my shoulder. "Come on, we have to get this hair back to Harper."

"Is she going to let me into her apartment?"

It was a good question. "Probably, since you're helping find Abby." Maybe. There was a good chance she might push him down the stairs, too. But I didn't mention that to him. The snow was still falling, but it felt as though the wind had lessened. "By the way, did Stef know you hexed the cake?"

"Stef? Nah. I don't go around telling mortals about my magic, and so far she hasn't really noticed that I'm not exactly normal."

"Not normal? Get out," I teased. His dark magic had no rules about anything, so I was surprised he hadn't tried to show it off to impress her.

He made a face at me. "I know, right? She's a sweet girl, though a bit dim."

"Yet, you're obviously a couple."

"Maybe I like dim."

"Then maybe you're the dim one."

The corner of his mouth twitched. "She's easy on the eyes, doesn't want a commitment, and Dorothy hates her. All positives in my book."

Snow crunched beneath my boots. "Is it wrong that Dorothy hating her makes me like Stef?"

"A little."

I could accept that. "I thought you and Dorothy were getting along."

"We are, but I don't need or want her input on my love life."

"Why doesn't Dorothy like her?"

"Who knows? She doesn't like many people."

That was the truth.

I wanted to ask more about his integration into his new family, but couldn't bring myself to pry. Maybe I'd ask Glinda Hansel, Vince's biological half sister. My relationship with her had started off rocky, had become even rockier, but was now on solid ground. We had slowly become good friends over the past six months. We walked our dogs together a couple of times a week and often went for coffee afterward, chatting about anything and everything.

As if reading my mind, Vince said, "Have you talked to Glinda lately?"

"Not in the past couple of days. Why?"

"No reason."

I skirted along the back of a police car parked at the curb. "Said just like there was a reason."

His lips were sealed as we stopped in front of the bookshop. With a wary gaze, he looked upward at Harper's apartment.

I said, "Well, you can stay out here and wait for me again or take your chances with Harper."

He adjusted his glasses then blew into his hands. "I think I'll take my chances. I want to see this lame spell with my own eyes."

"Maybe you'll finally see our magic isn't as useless as you think."

"Don't hold your breath."

I was glad he was coming along. There was an old idiom about being able to lead a horse to water but not being able to make it drink. So help me, I saw Vince as a wild horse, and I was bound and determined to make him drink up our magic. One way or another.

A quick minute later, we were in Harper's living room.

Vince said, "You look terrible, Harper."

I thought, perhaps, that wasn't the best opener.

"No thanks to you," she snapped.

He looked at me. "Have you called a doctor? Her illness is not just from the cake . . ."

"It's on my to-do list," I said.

"It was the cake, and I'll be fine," Harper said sharply. "The worst is over. A couple of aspirin, and I'll be good to go."

She was still ghostly pale, but I was happy to see she wasn't as shaky as the last time I saw her. The vanilla candle had worked wonders replacing the smell of sickness in the air, but I could still detect it if I breathed deeply.

Harper's big eyes narrowed on Vince. "I should curse you. Give you a bad case of warts, or eternal halitosis and body odor. Boils, maybe. Oozing boils."

I shuddered.

He didn't look fazed by her threats. "But you can't use magic for harm. Such a pity."

"I can't use the *Craft* for harm," she said, "but I think Andreus might have a black magic charm or amulet I can use. Seeing as how he's practically family now, I think he'd indulge me."

Andreus Woodshall was the director of the Roving Stones, and the quality of his character was constantly in question, despite him being my aunt Ve's current boyfriend. Their relationship had lasted a lot longer than anyone predicted. Maybe because they spent a lot of time apart.

Andreus would have absolutely indulged Harper, family or not. Charms didn't fall under Craft law, so

Harper could buy a malevolent charm or amulet from him to suit her needs, and he'd undoubtedly know exactly which one would be to Vince's utmost detriment.

"You wouldn't dare," Vince said. "Unlike me, you're too nice a person."

Still in her fluffy bathrobe, she crossed her arms over her chest and glared. "Am I?"

Although she looked about as threatening as a newborn goose, I saw caution flash in Vince's gaze.

"Now, now," I said, stepping between the two. "Let's focus on the task at hand. The lost and found spell."

It had been less than half an hour since the search teams had headed out, but it felt as though we were running out of time. The sooner we found Abby, the better. I handed Harper the backpack. "Several of Abby's hairs are caught in the straps."

Taking the pack, Harper went to the kitchen and grabbed a small colorful ceramic bowl that I recognized came from the Trimmed Wick. It was undoubtedly charmed. As she went about gathering supplies, Vince and I sat down on opposite couches. I noticed the crackers on the coffee table had been left uneaten but was glad to see the water level in the tumbler had decreased.

Harper came back with a teapot and set it on a trivet on the tabletop. Steam rose from the spout along with a pungent, unappetizing aroma.

"Tea?" Vince said. "You're using tea?"

"Shush," Harper told him as she added the tea mixture to the ceramic pot along with some herbs and a strand of Abby's hair.

Pie stretched his way, one paw at a time, over to where Vince sat and climbed onto his lap. Vince awkwardly reached out to pat Pie's head. The orange tabby purred loudly.

Harper murmured the lost and found spell under her breath and waved her hands above the pot.

A vivid white plume rose up like a cloud. In it was an image of an empty living room.

"I don't see Abby," Vince said, sliding his glasses farther up his nose.

Harper glowered at him and moved her hands together, almost like she was practicing some strange form of tai chi. The image in the cloud narrowed, focusing on a wig laying on a table.

"The hair I used wasn't human," Harper said. "Is that Abby's living room?"

I squinted. "Yeah, I think so. I've only been there twice, but I think that's her sofa."

"Does she wear a wig?" Vince asked.

"Not that I know of," I said. But there was no arguing the wig looked just like Abby's hair, long and dark.

Harper drummed her fingertips on the coffee table. "The spell found the wig, because I used a strand of the wig hair. That's an interesting twist to this spell."

I could practically see her taking notes in her head.

"We need *Abby's* hair to find her hat," she said.

I searched the straps of the backpack and found another hair. "Here, try this one."

Harper repeated the steps of the spell, and Vince and I watched in awe as the white cloud plumed once again.

"Lame, huh?" I said to him.

He shrugged indifferently, but I saw the interest in his eyes.

This time inside the cloud a red dot appeared in the distance. I leaned in but still couldn't see much.

Harper continued to move her hands, back and forth, up and down. The cloud grew with her manipulations, revealing more and more landscape.

"That's the Aural Gorge footbridge," Vince said. He'd relocated Pie and knelt down next to Harper, intently studying the scene in the cloud. He pointed. "It's hard to tell because of the snow, but that's the bridge's double arch."

Harper nodded. "It looks like the hat is partly buried in the snow below the bridge."

"Can you zoom in on the hat?" I asked, trying to ignore the growing pit in my stomach.

She brought her hands close together. The cloud narrowed in on the hat. We all leaned forward, looking for the one thing that was clearly still missing.

Abby.

"She's not wearing the hat any longer," Harper said, unnecessarily. The red hat was lying in such a way that the top half was buried, but the brim was exposed.

She panned around but the flying snow made it difficult to decipher what was what.

"How far is the gorge from here?" Vince asked.

"A little more than half a mile." I knew the distance only because of my work with the Mad Dash. Although the racers hadn't taken that route during the race, early on it had been lobbied as an alternate trail. It had been ultimately ruled out as too dangerous, because if anyone slipped and fell along the footbridge or gorge, it was a long way down into a rocky creek bed. I swallowed hard. "Why?"

Vince had already stood up. "I can fly the drone from here. It can go down into the gorge and search the area more thoroughly."

"It can fly that far?" Harper asked as she cupped a hand over the bowl. The cloud vanished.

"It's a long-range model," he said. "Can I open this window?"

She took the bowl to the kitchen. "You can try. It sticks."

I still had my concerns about flying a drone in a storm, but I didn't want to ask questions I didn't want the answers to.

Vince strong-armed the window crank and shoved on the frame at the same time.

"Yow!" He yanked his hand back, looked at it.

Blood pooled along a deep cut on his palm, and I immediately saw stars. I closed my eyes and sat on the sofa. Blood and I didn't get along.

Harper said, "What happened? Oh geez!"

I peeked through the fingers covering my eyes. Harper went back into the kitchen and came back with a dry rag. She tossed it to Vince.

"It's fine," he said. "Just a nick."

I'd seen the cut. It hadn't been a nick. It had been a veritable crater. "Tell me when I can look."

"You can look," Harper said, "just not at Vince's hand. Let me see what I have for bandages. You should wash that before wrapping it up."

"It's fine," Vince said, giving the window another shove.

It creaked open.

"Here," Harper said, returning with a roll of gauze. "There's one of those urgent care places just outside the village. You might need stitches."

"*It's fine*," he repeated as though we were both deaf. He perched on the snowy windowsill as the winter chill creeped into the room. "The drone obviously works better in wide open areas, but we'll see what we can do."

Within moments, the drone was off. Vince guided it using a handheld monitor, and I had to admit it was rather extraordinary to see the village from above.

However, it was slightly alarming to see how adept Vince was at flying the drone. It was as if it were second nature, especially since he was controlling it with one hand only.

I said, "What do you use the drone for usually?"

"This and that."

For such a banal answer, it sounded ominous.

"Are you spying on the village?" Harper asked in her usual direct manner as she leaned over his shoulder to watch the footage on the monitor.

"Why would I do that? Nothing ever happens around this sleepy little town," he said in a way that told us that was exactly what he had been doing. Spying.

Sad to say it wasn't the first time.

"Why?" Harper glared at him. "You already know about the Craft. What else is there to learn?"

"Isn't there always more to learn?" he asked, dodging the question.

Her fists clenched and for a second I thought she was going to push him straight out the window.

Instead, she took a deep breath. I imagined she was debating on what kind of pox to curse him with, and I wasn't sure whether I was grateful or dismayed Andreus Woodshall and the Roving Stones were currently in Delaware and weren't slated to return to the village for a few more weeks.

Sometimes Vince brought out the worst in me.

The drone passed over some of the Mad Dashers who looked to be returning to the village. All glanced upward in confusion, following the drone's trajectory.

It wasn't long before the drone dropped below the footbridge. The red hat was barely visible in the drifting snow.

Vince flew the drone in concentric circles, widening the search zone with each pass. It went without saying what we were searching for . . . and hoping not to find.

Abby's body.

No one could survive a fall from the bridge.

"Wait, wait!" Harper said. "Go back."

"What did you see?" I asked.

"I'm not sure," she said.

Vince reversed the drone.

Harper's gaze intensified. "Near those rocks."

"I don't see—" Vince said but then abruptly cut himself off.

Because what Harper had seen became quite visible as the drone zeroed in on a lumpy spot near an outcropping of rocks.

Where bone-white fingers stuck out of a snowy grave.

Chapter Five

I pushed open Ve's side gate, giving it a good hard shove through a foot of snow, and the arch above the gate rattled its displeasure. In the spring, summer, and fall the arch was covered in climbing roses. But in the winter it stood bare, looking lonely and forlorn as though in mourning for what it had lost.

The stone walkway leading to Ve's porch and side door lay hidden beneath the snow, but I knew the way by heart. Archie's cage, located just beyond the fence that separated Ve's and Terry's yards was covered with heavy tarp. Archie wouldn't be back in his outdoor home again, entertaining tourists, until the weather cleared. Even though he was a familiar, he had some limitations due to his chosen form. Scarlet macaws couldn't tolerate blizzard conditions, therefore, neither could he.

As I high-stepped through the yard, I reflected how a visit to Ve's usually brought forth an immediate burst of peace and contentment—I'd loved the time I spent living here, in this house.

Today, however, there was no peace to be found.

There was too much going on inside my head, from concern for Ve and why she hadn't been out and about today, worry for Harper's well-being, and grief for Abby.

Abby.

My breath hitched, caught on a wave of emotion. It had been an hour since recovery teams had arrived in the village to retrieve Abby's body from the bottom of the gorge. Looking back at the green, all physical traces of the Wicked Mad Dash had been erased; the tent was gone, along with the starting line trusses. Mad Dashers had dispersed, most leaving the village and going back to their everyday lives. But the emotional toll of the morning weighed heavily in the air and on the faces of the emergency personnel who remained behind, looking for any and all clues of what had happened to Abigail Stillwell.

Word raced through the village about the horrible accident, and I knew Quinn Donegal, who was the closest thing Abby had to family, was already in contact with the medical examiner's office. There was going to be an autopsy to determine Abby's official cause of death.

A shiver ran through me at the thought of falling off that bridge. My stomach ached, and all I could do was hope she hadn't suffered.

As I climbed the porch steps, I glanced around Ve's yard and spotted small footprints in the snow. I knew immediately to whom they belonged: Missy.

My dog, Miss Demeanor, aka Missy, was a miniature Schnoodle, part schnauzer, part poodle, that Harper and I had adopted shortly before we moved to the village. Well, we'd been awarded custody of her in a court case, after Harper had been arrested trying to break up a puppy mill ring. Hence, Missy's formal name. Harper had avoided jail time, the puppy mill had been shut down, and we had Missy, so all's well that ended well with that situation.

Gray and white, Missy was a tiny fluff of a dog who loved cuddles and escaping any enclosure in which she was penned. There was a reason we called her the Houdini of the dog world and had equipped her collar with a GPS tracker.

Mine and Nick's new backyard had quickly proven to be useless in preventing her from escaping, despite our attempt to make it Missy-proof. She never ran far, however. Over and over again, we found her back at Ve's. There had been a time, months ago, when Ve had asked me if Missy could stay with her when I moved. I hadn't been able to imagine leaving Missy behind and had said no. But now it seemed to me that Missy had weighed in with *her* opinion.

After much debate and consideration, instead of fighting Missy's penchant to run away to Ve's, we decided to embrace it. With permission from Terry, whose house was sandwiched between Ve's and mine, we had a contractor build a decorative elevated runway of sorts through Terry's backyard, complete with scroll railings and paint that blended in with the landscape. There were two ramps—one in my backyard and one in Ve's. Nick had also installed electric dog doors at both our houses that were controlled by a tag on Missy's collar, allowing her to come and go between her two homes as she pleased. In the months since these changes were made her behavior had been quite telling: she was more Ve's dog than mine now.

Stomping my feet on the floor mat outside the back-door, I peered through the door's glass panes. Past the kitchen, I could see the flicker of the TV set coming from the family room, but there was no sign of Ve . . . or Archie. I gave a swift knock, and Missy immediately started barking as I turned the knob to let myself in.

The little dog raced to greet me, circling my feet while her stubby gray tail wiggled. "Hi you," I said as I bent to rub her head. "Have you been here long?"

The last time I'd seen her, she'd been eating breakfast at my house.

She barked and I smiled. "I imagine hanging out with Ve and Archie is much better than being slobbered on by Higgins at home."

Higgins, an enormous Saint Bernard, seemed to have an endless supply of saliva. Even though he'd been living with me—and Missy—full-time for months now, we were still adjusting to the copious amounts of drool.

Missy barked again, and I could have sworn she nodded.

"I can't blame you for that. Is anyone else here?"

She barked, then went running into the family room.

"Hello?" I called out.

Tilda, my aunt's cranky Himalayan, eyed me with disdain from her perch at the top of the back staircase. It was nice to know some things never changed. Tilda and I had a love hate relationship that hadn't changed one bit after I moved out.

"Ve?"

I heard a moan from the family room and kicked into a jog. I found Ve curled into a ball on the sofa, and Archie laid out on the love seat. Each had an ice pack balanced on their forehead.

Magic Mike was showing on the TV.

So much for Doris Day.

Then I realized the TV was muted. And that it was deathly quiet in the room and all the shades had been pulled low. Other than the light from the TV, it was dark as midnight even though it was a little past eleven in the morning.

"What happened?" I asked, crouching down next to Ve.

"*Shh*." She lifted a finger to her lips. Redness infused her normally creamy complexion. Coppery hair sprung out about her face, looking like inflamed tentacles.

"What happened?" I said again, more gently this time.

Archie was on his back, his feet and all eight toes in the air. He halfheartedly flapped a colorful wing. "Piña coladas," he said in a hoarse whisper.

"So many piña coladas," Ve murmured, wincing her way through the words. "We partook in a *Magnum* marathon last evening."

I sat on the edge of the coffee table. Now that they mentioned it, I smelled coconut in the air. "Piña coladas?"

"It seemed a delightful idea at the time." Archie's normally grandiose baritone voice with its English accent had lost its peppy edge. "What with *Magnum, P.I.* being set in Hawaii."

"*Alo-ha*," Ve added as she adjusted her ice pack.

I couldn't stop a grin. "Aloha indeed. So, you're both . . . hungover?"

Archie nudged his ice pack with the tip of a wing and cleared his throat. "'I almost regret it.'"

He wasn't feeling too badly if he could still play our movie quote game, and the clearing of the throat was a dead giveaway that a quote was on its way.

I shrugged, lifting my hands up, palms out. "I don't know that one."

"*Raiders of the Lost Ark*," he said gleefully, giving himself the macaw version of a high five.

He loved one-upping me.

Shifting on the coffee table, I turned my back on him. "I'm guessing your phone is turned off?"

"The ringer. Dreadful noise."

"Shrill," Archie added with a full-body shudder. A loose feather floated to the floor.

Ve cracked open an eyelid. "Why? Did you call?"

Her bluish-gold eyes, so like mine, were shot with redness. "Several times."

Missy hopped up on the couch next to Ve and burrowed into the fleece blanket, looking perfectly at home. Ve absently patted the dog's head. "Is something wrong? Are you okay?"

Her gaze skimmed over me, as though checking to make sure I wasn't bleeding and still had complete possession of all ten fingers and toes.

"I'm fine."

"Nick? Mimi?" With a moan, she struggled to sit up and the ice pack slipped off, nearly hitting Missy on her head. Halfway up, Ve's cheeks went from red to green, and I pushed her back down and reset the ice pack.

"They're fine, too. There was an incident this morning at the race. Abby Stillwell went missing while out on her warm-up run."

"Abby? Oh dear."

"Was she located?" Archie asked, studying me with his tiny black eyes. The white ring around them seemed even brighter than usual.

I wrung my hands. "Eventually."

"Oh dear," Ve said again. "She's not . . . ?"

Her voice trailed, leaving the question unsaid.

I tried to block the sudden image of Abby's fingers poking up through the snow. "Her body was found beneath the Aural Gorge bridge."

"She *fell* off the bridge?" Ve gasped.

I explained about the hexed cake and how Abby was likely dehydrated and possibly became disoriented. "Plus, the weather might have been a factor. At times, there were whiteout conditions. One misstep . . ."

"Were there no witnesses?" Archie asked.

"No," I stood and turned on a light. It was much too dark in there. "Not who have come forward anyway."

Both Archie and Ve groaned at the sudden brightness.

I turned the light off again.

"Tragic," Ve said.

I wasn't sure if she meant the light or Abby, until Ve added, "She was so young."

A clinking noise came from above our heads, and we all looked upward.

"Sounds as though we have company." Archie rolled and flapped until he was in an upright position, his tail hanging over the side of the loveseat.

Missy's head came up, and her ears perked a second before she started barking.

"Missy," Ve said sharply, "dear God, stop that yapping!"

Archie covered his ears. "Talk about shrill."

Missy glanced at Archie, gave one last defiant yip, and then began whimpering as the return air vent near one of the windows popped forward an inch. Just enough for two small mice to wiggle through, one white, one brown.

Both dear, dear friends.

"Hello down there! Oh my stars," Mrs. P, the white mouse in the pink velour dress, said. "Have you heard the news?"

In the past year, Vaporcrafter Eugenia Pennywhistle, a witch who had the power to become invisible, had adapted to her familiar form without skipping a beat. Her animated personality almost seemed better suited to this lifestyle than her previous human one. Although so much about her had changed physically, her raucous laugh, her enormous heart, and zest for life had remained the same.

In his endearing French accent, Pepe, the chubbier of the two mice, added, "The news pertaining to Abigail Stillwell?"

Pepe had been a familiar just shy of forever. Hundreds of years. Originally from France, he was a Cloakcrafter, a witch who worked magic with needle and thread, who lived in the walls of the Bewitching Boutique. He was quick to temper, quicker to love.

Both slid down the curtain and leapt onto the back of the love seat. "I didn't know Darcy was here. Then of course you know about poor, poor Abby. Hello, doll," Mrs. P said, using her pet nickname for me. "Do I smell pineapple?"

Ve once again struggled to sit up. She kept a hand on the ice pack this time, and her face merely paled instead of turning a full-on shade of green. "Don't talk about food, please, I beg of you."

"Are you sick?" Mrs. P asked her. A small tuft of white fur stuck up between her ears. "Should we call on Cherise? Oh, wait, she's out of town with Terry. Dennis, then?"

I'd called him myself an hour ago, using Spellbound's phone since mine still wasn't working. It had taken some arm-twisting, reminders of my help to his family in the past, and a threat to call his mother to get him to agree to see Harper this afternoon, but he'd finally conceded. I was going to meet him at her apartment at noon.

"No, no, I'm fine," Ve insisted, suddenly reminding me of Vince.

I hoped he had seen a doctor about his hand.

"Is it a cold? The flu?" Pepe twirled his whisker mustache and took a step back, away from any potentially offending germs.

"Piña coladas," Archie said by way of explanation.

Pepe smiled. "Ah, but of course. *Magnum, P.I.* reruns, I assume?"

"You know what they say about people who assume," Archie intoned righteously as he fluffed his feathers. "For all you know, we could have been watching *Blue Hawaii*, a favorite of Ve's."

Mrs. P sat and adjusted the hem of her dress. "It's not been a favorite since she and Terry broke up again. What's it been, a year now?"

Terry, after all, possessed an uncanny resemblance to a 1970s-era Elvis. So much so that he often wore disguises in public.

"Close enough," Ve said.

Pepe chuckled, an infectious *ho-ho-ho*. "So Magnum it was."

Ve said, "A shirtless, young Tom Selleck tops Elvis any day. Those legs. Have *mercy*." She fanned herself with her hand.

"No doubt about that." Mrs. P barked out her trademark Phyllis Diller laugh.

Ve recoiled at the sound and rubbed her temples. "My head might fall clear off my body by the end of this day."

"Sorry, Ve dear," Mrs. P said. "I'll pipe down. Have you taken some aspirin? Or had some hair of the dog at least?"

Missy, who'd settled back into the fleece, lifted her head and wagged her tail.

"Not you," Mrs. P pointed at her. "A little nip of rum . . ."

Ve went green again.

"Or perhaps not." Pepe sat next to Mrs. P—on the far side of Ve.

I figured it was just in case she tossed her cookies.

Or *hoiked*, as Archie preferred to call the action.

Either way, Pepe was out of the line of fire. Being a tad bit persnickety, he didn't like getting dirty.

Archie flapped a wing. "I wouldn't mind partaking in a driblet or two if someone is offering."

"I think we've had enough to last the whole weekend long." Ve's eyebrows dipped low, and her lips puckered as she tapped her chin with a fingertip. "Or at least for now. The weekend *is* still quite young."

"Excellent point, Velma. There are many more *Magnum* episodes remaining," Archie said.

"Exactly," she agreed.

Mrs. P laughed again, then abruptly stopped when Ve sent a withering glance her way.

"Doll," Mrs. P said, "what's the word from Nick?"

Everyone turned my way. "No word yet. He's still at the accident site."

"*Accident*?" Pepe said, his wrinkly forehead lifting in confusion as one of his big ears twitched.

"Abby's accident?" Surely they hadn't forgotten about Abby so soon, though the thought of a shirtless, long-legged Magnum was more than a little distracting.

"Her death was an accident?" Mrs. P questioned, her tiny dark eyes narrowing on me.

"It wasn't?" I asked.

"It is not what we have heard, *ma chère*." Pepe pressed his hands to his chest, covering one of the gold buttons on his red vest. "We heard it was—"

"Murder!" Mrs. P cut him off, looking quite puffed up to break the news.

Shock dropped my jaw. "Murder? Says *who*?"

"We heard it at the Witch's Brew," Mrs. P explained. "And that the police were questioning a suspect."

I was at a loss. "This is all news to me. Who are they questioning?"

"Alas, it is Ben Bryant." Pepe folded his hands on top of his rounded stomach.

"They were dating, were they not?" Archie asked.

"*Oui*," Pepe said. "Reportedly, they'd had a loud row last night and the animosity carried over to this morning. They were seen arguing shortly before the start of the race. Abby disappeared not long thereafter. Has the Elder not been by?"

Although everyone in this room knew the Elder's true identity—my mother, Deryn Merriweather—most witches did not, so we tended to still refer to her as the Elder out of habit.

"I'm sure she'll be by soon," Ve said. "I know she has a meeting this morning with a member of the Coven and that might be keeping her."

As a familiar, my mother's form was a mourning dove, though I knew she could choose any form at will, including her human form, which would allow her to travel in this weather. Having unlimited access to varied forms was one of the perks of being the Elder—no other familiars could change at will.

The coven Ve mentioned was the Coven of Seven. My mother's special advisors. Their identities were not known to me, and I doubted they ever would be, though I had some suspicions on a few of their identities. Ve for one. Godfrey Baleaux, a family friend, another. I was on the fence about Pepe.

"Well, doll, you don't need the Elder's permission to start investigating, do you?"

"No," I said. "I don't need permission."

As Craft investigator, I was more than familiar with murder cases, having worked many of them in tandem with Nick—a partnership set up by the Elder not long after I arrived in the village. It was never easy to investigate homicides, especially when the victims were my friends. But it was important that I was involved, because more often than not, crimes against—and committed by—Crafters had motivation rooted in our magical world. Whether it be greed where magical diamonds were concerned or someone who wanted complete control over a unique spell . . . I worked the magical side of the case while Nick worked the mortal side. And together, we put the pieces together to bring killers to justice, while being particularly careful to hide some aspects of the truth from the mortal world.

My job as investigator started once I knew there was a crime committed.

Thanks to Pepe and Mrs. P, I knew.

Murder.

Chapter Six

I headed straight home from Ve's, not quite knowing where to start my investigation until I spoke with Nick. If he was interviewing Ben, and Ben confessed then I had very little work to do.

I tried to picture Ben shoving Abby off that bridge, and I couldn't. My brain wouldn't go there.

If he'd done it, what could precipitate such an act? I didn't know Ben to have a temper. I'd seen agitation in him a time or two, instances when he lost his patience. But certainly not the type of rage that would lead to murder. And Abby wasn't the contentious sort. She was a peacemaker, which made her an excellent employee at Balefire. No one did customer service like Abby.

So if not anger, then evil? Or desperation? Revenge?

I tried to think of any motive for murder that fit this scenario, but there was nothing. Most likely because I couldn't come up with a single reason why Abby had been killed.

I gave my head a good shake, and my hood slid off. I pulled it back on and told myself to get a grip.

I was jumping to conclusions. Hurdling, really.

I'd wait to see what Nick had to say about the pre-liminary investigation before I started picturing Ben in prison stripes. While Mrs. P and Pepe were reliable sources of village gossip, I had to remind myself that's all it was. Gossip.

Snow was still falling steadily as I stuck close to the fence line and tromped through the snow piled high on my driveway, then veered off toward the front door.

A thunderous woof greeted me with enthusiasm from inside the house. Higgins had his face pressed into one of the sidelights flanking the front door. Drool smeared the pane, making it appear opaque.

"Hi, Higgs. I'll be right in."

He gave another woof, and I could hear the faint sound of his tail drumming the hardwood floor in the entryway.

I took a moment to brush snow off the dark purple "As You Wish" sign hanging from a porch column and also the smaller sign dangling below it: "By Appointment Only." I couldn't imagine there was anyone out and about today that planned to drop in to secure my concierge services, but one never knew around here.

I backtracked to the driveway and walked along the side of the house toward the mud room entrance. The alarm system didn't beep when I opened the door, setting me immediately on edge. Mimi wasn't due home for another couple of hours, and Nick was at the police station. Higgins came tearing through the kitchen, a brownish red-and-white blur, his feet sliding on the floor. Mere months ago, he'd have hurled his muscular body at me, but he'd been learning manners recently through a dog training class, so he simply knocked into me like I was a human bowling pin, sending me backward into the door.

Baby steps.

"Okay, okay, Higgs. I know. I love you too," I said as he kissed my hands. His tail sliced the air and banged against the washing machine. It sounded a bit like an out of tune snare drum announcing my presence.

If anyone was in the house, it would be enough to alert them that they were no longer alone.

And although Higgins wasn't acting as though anything was amiss, I was still worried about the silent alarm. I knew I'd set it when I left this morning . . . It was possible there had been a power surge during the storm, or something equally quirky that would have messed with the system, but I wasn't taking any chances.

I quickly grabbed Higgins' leash, which was hanging from the hook by the door, and was about clip it on him and slowly back out the door I'd just come in when I heard a voice.

"Darcy?"

Higgins wagged his tail again, resuming the metallic beat, as relief loosened the knots in my shoulders and eased the pit in my stomach. "Mom?"

"Do you want some coffee?"

"More than life itself." The morning had taken its toll on me. My body ached, my head hurt, and I just wanted a cup of piping hot coffee to drink while sorting through the events of the day.

Her laughter filled me with happiness, flooding out the anxiety I'd been carrying around since Abby had run off and never came back.

I shed my outerwear and noted Higgins' woeful expression when I replaced his leash on the hook. "Later," I told him.

His tail banged the washer even harder, making the mountain of clothes atop it wobble. Before an avalanche occurred, I motioned Higgins into the kitchen. "C'mon, now."

My mother stood in front of a built-in hutch that served as a coffee bar, and I took a moment just to watch her. And to appreciate the magic in the world that allowed her to be standing in my kitchen, dressed in shades of white from her long cashmere wrap sweater to her cream-colored leggings.

She glanced my way as she set out two mugs. "Long morning?"

Annie, a beautiful black ragdoll cat who'd joined our family not that long ago, lounged on top of the fridge. I reached up and rubbed her ears, and could feel her purrs rumbling against my palm. "The longest. I'm guessing that's why you're here?"

Thick auburn hair streaked with silver was clipped back off her face. Her bluish-brown eyes sparkled. "Can't a mother simply drop by to see her daughter?"

"Anytime you want." We'd been apart for nearly twenty-four years, so I was happy to be making up for lost time. "But I know travel during this weather is difficult, even in your human form."

She lived deep in the Enchanted Woods, in a weeping tree that stood in a luminescent, warm meadow filled with wildflowers. As Elder, she possessed all Craft abilities, not just Wishing. She could shape-shift at will, evaporate, and glow. But she often traveled about the village as a mourning dove. While we lived in an amazing, enchanted world, our magic did have certain limitations. We couldn't teletransport quite yet. Mom would have had to fight her way through this storm just like the rest of us and a Mad Dasher she wasn't.

The coffeepot gave a final burble. While filling the mugs, she said, "I adore the snow, and the storm isn't blowing as fiercely in the woods."

As I followed her into the living room, I noted her feet. They were bare, as always. When asked about it, she usually brushed off the idiosyncrasy as a quirk, but I'd long ago decided it had something to do with the Eldership. What, I had no idea, but if she wasn't willing to share details, then it had to be something important.

Her feet also did not touch the floor—ever. She floated about an inch off the ground.

I veered off to the back door, to let Higgins out.

"Is Missy at Ve's?" Mom asked.

I watched Higgins play in the snow for a bit before heading for the couch where my mother was already curled up, her feet tucked beneath her.

"She is. I was just thinking about how she's becoming more Ve's dog than my own."

"And how do you feel about that?"

I blew across my mug before taking a sip of coffee. Heaven. I relaxed against the pillows, simply trying to find some peace in this crazy day. "It was strange at first. Now it almost seems normal to share her."

"Ve is quite happy to have the company."

I studied her. It was clear she and Ve had been discussing the matter. "I know."

She laughed. "What I was trying to subtly say—and not doing a good job of it—is that the day might come when Missy stays with Ve. For good. Ve won't mind. But will you?"

"It's hard to say. I guess I'll know when that day comes, won't I?" A soft, melodic sound filtered through the tension in the air, and I said, "It's alive!"

"What's alive?"

I set my mug on the coffee table and jumped up. "My cell phone. It froze up earlier. Literally."

Annie *reow*ed at me as I dashed past the fridge. My cell was in my coat pocket. I found it just as the ringing stopped and the screen started to fade. I didn't recognize the number.

On my way back to the couch, I let Higgins inside and quickly wiped him down with a towel that we kept in a basket near the back door. As soon as I finished, the phone chirped, alerting me to a voice mail. I listened, then frowned.

"What's wrong?" my mother asked as I hung up.

"That was a message from Quinn Donegal. She's Abby's roommate," I added in case she didn't know, which was probably silly of me. My mother seemed to know everyone in the village, witches and mortals alike.

"What did she have to say?"

"She said the Bryants are looking for business ledgers pertaining to the Mad Dash race. Abby had the ledgers last, but now they're missing. Quinn was wondering if I'd seen them."

"Intriguing."

"For a few reasons. The first being that Abby died this morning. Shouldn't they be more focused on her death than business matters? Second, if Ben Bryant is truly a suspect in Abby's death, then the family has bigger worries than missing ledgers, right? So why are they so worried about them *today*? It's odd."

My mother didn't seem fazed by the revelation that Ben was a suspect, so I had to presume Pepe and Mrs. P's gossip had merit.

She said, "The timing is alarming to say the least, but you have to remember people grieve in different ways. There's a chance they're focusing on work to take their minds off the pain."

I turned to look at her. "Are you saying that because, as the Elder, you know Ben is innocent? Or are you simply speculating?"

"Speculating."

"Good to know. And also the ledgers aren't missing."

"They aren't?"

"I have them." I grabbed my tote bag. "Abby gave them to me this morning, asking me to look at them."

"Why?"

I shooed Higgins from my spot on the couch and sat down, explaining how Abby thought she'd made a mistake in the race accounting. I flipped through the pages of the ledgers, but nothing immediately jumped out at me. I needed time to study the columns of numbers.

What I really needed was for Terry Goodwin to be home and not on vacation. He was a Numbercrafter and a certified accountant. A few minutes with these ledgers, he'd have them analyzed down to the last zero.

"Unfortunately for the Bryants it will probably be a while before they get these back. I'm going to have to give them to Nick. They're evidence now."

She raised her mug to her lips. "But there's probably no harm in photocopying them before you hand them over. Just in case the information is pertinent to *your* investigation."

I pointed a finger at her. "Aha! I knew you didn't just happen to drop by today."

Lifting her eyebrows, she smiled. "You clearly get your astuteness from me. Not that I don't adore dropping in for coffee, but I do need your help as Craft investigator since Abby's death might not have been an accident."

"I'm already on the case, and am still hoping it was an accident."

"As am I."

There was something in her voice, a hesitation. "But?"

"I suppose it is possible Abby was dehydrated and became disoriented enough to fall from the bridge . . ."

"But?" I pressed.

"Vince was correct in saying his hex wore off at seven AM, restoring his victims to full health, precake. Abby would only be dehydrated this morning if she had been so before she ate the hexed cake, and I doubt an athlete such as herself would have allowed that to occur the night before a big race."

I had no idea how she knew what Vince had told me. The Elder worked in mysterious ways.

I said, "Abby always carried a water bottle, filling it throughout the day. She constantly touted the benefits of hydration—to everyone, not just runners. It's unlikely she was dehydrated before she ate the cake."

"So we must then consider how she fell off a bridge—a bridge with a railing—by accident."

Put that way, it seemed *highly* unlikely.

But murder? I couldn't fathom someone hurting Abby on purpose.

My mother glanced at the clock, stood, and floated into the kitchen. Her outfit blended right in with the ivory cabinets. After rinsing the mug, she set it in the dishwasher. "I should go. You have an appointment soon, correct?"

It shouldn't have surprised me that she knew I was meeting Dennis Goodwin at Harper's apartment, but it did. "At noon."

"You'll keep me informed about Abby's case?" She pulled open the backdoor. Snow fluttered inside.

"I will. But wait, before you go . . ."

She waited, watching with patient eyes.

"If Vince's hex wore off . . ." I struggled to find the words. I met her gaze. "Harper. How worried should I be? Should *we* be?"

In an instant, her face and her eyes clouded with concern. She tried to mask the emotions with a sudden, bright smile, but it was too late. I'd seen it.

She cupped my face and kissed my cheek. "Darcy, I'm sure Harper will be just fine."

With that, she stepped outside, and in a blink she turned into a beautiful gray bird soaring upward, disappearing into the falling snow.

I stood in the doorway a moment, wishing I hadn't asked about Harper in the first place.

Because after her reaction, I was more worried now than ever.

Chapter Seven

Not ten minutes later, I was back outside. Hat, boots, and gloves on. Higgins' leash in hand. I'd promised him a walk, but it would have to be a quick one. I was due at Harper's apartment in fifteen minutes.

The snow had let up for the time being, and the village looked like it belonged in a snow globe. Everything the eye could see was dusted in white. Village maintenance crews were out and about clearing streets, walkways, and parking spaces.

Higgins was sniffing to his heart's content as we meandered on the village green. I'd left a voice mail for Nick about the ledgers, and sent a text to Mimi to let her know I'd be at Harper's for a while, and she texted back that she would be home soon.

As Higgins and I walked, I was trying to ignore the knot in my stomach. I was kicking myself for not nagging Harper to go to the doctor earlier, but I'd believed she was heartbroken, not truly physically ill. I just hoped it wasn't something serious, and that Dennis could work his magic to cure her completely.

"Darcy, hey! Hello!"

I stopped short and found Glinda Hansel waving a gloved hand in front of my face. Higgins and her golden retriever, Clarence, were giving each other undignified once-overs. Dogs. Sheesh.

"Are you okay?" Glinda asked. "You were in another world. And not a pleasant one by the look on your face."

Glinda, a Broomcrafter like her mother Dorothy, often had an angelic look about her because of her pale blonde hair, light blue eyes, ivory skin tone, and the slightly rounded features of her oval face, like her button nose and full cheeks. But there were many times in the past that I'd believed she was the devil in disguise. But those days were past. Much to her mother's dismay, Glinda had decided she didn't like herself very much. Over the past year, she'd made big changes in her life to eliminate the malicious aspects of her personality. She wasn't quite at an angelic level yet, but it had been a long while since I pictured horns on her head.

I didn't know how much falling in love had influenced her behavioral changes, but it was obvious she was over the moon in love with Liam Chadwick, a local artisan. If they could survive the hell we all went through last winter and come out of it better people . . . then I had no doubt they were meant for each other.

"Sorry," I said. "I have a lot on my mind."

"Abby? It's terrible. I'd just talked with her yesterday at Godfrey's. She was bubbling with excitement. If I'm being honest, it was a little nauseating. I feel bad about thinking that way now."

"I hate hindsight," I said, echoing a thought from earlier today.

"It's a bit like a slap in the face, isn't it?"

It was.

Godfrey Baleaux, a Cloakcrafter who owned the Bewitching Boutique, was Pepe and Mrs. P's guardian, and was practically family to me since he'd once been married to Aunt Ve. He was the third of her four husbands.

A city plow exhaled black exhaust as it rumbled down the street, lining the green with a snowy mountain range. "Did you know Abby well?"

"Not especially. Just in passing. I saw her running a lot while I was out walking Clarence. She was always friendly." She leaned in. "Is it true Ben Bryant is a suspect?"

Clarence heard his name and started enthusiastically wagging his tail. Glinda rubbed his head, and he pressed his nose into her thigh and looked up at her with adoration shining in his big brown eyes.

"I haven't talked with Nick since earlier this morning, so I don't know for sure. That's the rumor I hear. I'm still hoping it was a tragic accident."

"I have a hard time believing anyone could accidentally fall off the Aural Gorge bridge. Even in a whiteout. I'm also having trouble with Ben being considered a suspect. I once saw him stop running to move a caterpillar off the path. Hardly the homicidal sort."

Glinda had once been a police officer on the village force, but had left under less-than-stellar circumstances. Since turning her life around, she'd opened a private investigation agency that was keeping her more than busy. Which was to say, she had good instincts. If she thought Ben was a gentle sort, then I took her opinion to heart. But that didn't mean I'd blindly accept it as fact. "That's good to know about him, but we both also know anger can transform even the most docile person."

"True enough." Keeping hold of Clarence's leash, she tucked her hands into the pockets of her down coat. "And I did hear that Ben and Abby had been arguing."

"I heard that too. Did you hear what they'd been fighting about?"

"No. You?"

"No." I reeled Higgins in so he wouldn't chase after a squirrel climbing a tree nearby. "Have you ever heard anyone say anything negative about Abby? I can't think of a single person who didn't like her."

"You mean other than me thinking her perkiness was nauseating?"

I smiled. "Other than."

Snow crystals glistened in her blonde hair as she shook her head. "Not that I've heard. No, wait. There was an incident at Balefire." She squinted as though trying to remember the exact day and time down to the nanosecond. "It was months ago. Springtime, maybe? Do you remember?"

Now that she said it . . . "The police were called, weren't they?"

"Yeah. There had been a fight at the store. One of the runners went off the rails. But I think there was something about the Craft involved as well. There were whispers about a memory cleanse being used."

"I don't remember that part. I'll have to ask the Elder."

She glanced away quickly and called for Clarence to stop eating so much snow. "Yes, she'd know."

I wondered at her odd reaction, but didn't dwell. "Do you remember the runner's name?"

"I'm blanking. I do remember he and Abby had been dating. Pretty serious, too."

"Duncan Cole?"

She nodded. "Yes. Duncan Cole."

It was slowly coming back to me. Duncan had been kicked off the Balefire Racing team and while no official reason had been given, there were murmurs in the running community he'd been caught doping. He and Abby broke up not long after.

"I assume you're also working the case?" she asked.

Although Glinda had no idea that the Elder was my mother, she did know about my job as the Craft snoop. "I am—since Abby's death is suspicious."

"If you need any help, let me know."

At one point in our relationship, I would have been suspicious of such an offer. But we'd come a long way. "I will."

"What's that smile about?" she asked, her forehead crinkling in puzzlement.

Higgins had his face to the sky, his mouth open, trying to eat snowflakes. I brushed the snow from the top of his head and said, "Sometimes life amazes me."

"How so?"

"I can't help thinking about last year around this time. What happened."

"Please do not remind me. I was horrible."

There was no arguing her words. She *had* been horrible. I put an arm around her in a half-hug. "I didn't mean to make you feel bad. The opposite, actually. I was just thinking about how far we've come. You and me. If you'd asked me last year if we'd willingly work together, never mind be friends . . ."

She laughed and some of the tension eased out of her shoulders. "You know," she said, shifting the leash from hand to hand, "I've worked hard at the changes in my life, but I give a lot of credit to you, Darcy."

Another plow rumbled past. "Me? No. You're the one in therapy."

"That's true, and I have the bills to prove it, but seriously. I don't know how to say it exactly. There's a way about you, how you seem to have faith in people who don't have faith in themselves . . . and are willing to help them see it." She shook her head. "It's hard to explain, but I saw it firsthand all the time in the past year, and now I see it happening with Vince. There's not many people in this village who are willing to associate with him, because of his type of magic. But you . . . You haven't given up on him."

I felt an unexpected rush of emotion at her words. "I don't give up on people easily. I'm stubborn that way."

"Oh, I know."

I shrugged. "I see the good in him. Just like I saw the good in you. I mean, I saw it eventually."

She grinned. "I didn't make it easy for you. But that's what I mean. How is it *you* can see the good when no one else does? That's . . . a gift."

"I don't know about that. The gift will be when Vince starts to see the good in himself. He doesn't yet, but I'm hopeful."

Her gaze met mine, held steady. "Thanks for helping give me that particular gift."

Believing in someone—and helping them to believe in themselves—wasn't always easy. I thought about how many times I'd wanted to cut Glinda out of my life. The times I had, even if it hadn't lasted long. I thought about the pain she'd caused. Not only to me, but to people I loved. Seeing the changes in her, however, made me glad I hadn't given up on her. "You're welcome."

"Well," she fanned the tears in her eyes, "if this isn't the perfect time to ask you a favor, I don't know what is."

I laughed. "What kind of favor?"

She glanced around. "I don't want to talk about it out here, in the open. Are you free tomorrow?"

I tipped my head, studied her. Saw flashes of anxiety in her eyes, but also something else. Joy? An odd combination that left me even more curious. "Eleven okay with you?"

"Perfect. Can you meet me in Godfrey's workshop?"

"Godfrey's workshop?"

"That's right. You can't tell anyone, okay? About meeting with me."

"But Godfrey will be there . . ." Especially since the meeting was before the boutique opened at noon.

"Oh," she brightened, "he knows, so the boutique is safe." She glanced around again. "I should go."

I looked around too. She was acting so oddly. "Everything okay?"

She flashed a big smile. A genuine one. Her blue eyes sparkled. "Everything is great. See you tomorrow."

As she and Clarence walked away. I stared after them, wondering what in the world that had been all about. Then I suddenly remembered Vince's words this morning, asking if I'd seen Glinda lately. Surely he knew what was going on as well.

I supposed I'd find out soon enough.

As Higgins and I walked home, I realized I was grateful I'd run into Glinda.

Because for a few moments, she'd taken my mind off what was going on with Harper. But now I had just enough time to drop off Higgins, run to the Gingerbread Shack to pick up some treats for Harper, and then hotfoot it to her apartment to find out what was wrong with my little sister.

And find out if Dennis Goodwin could fix it.

* * *

The Gingerbread Shack, a bakery specializing in miniature treats, held a corner location on the main square. It was a prime spot along the same sweep of connected shops as Spellbound, which anchored the other end of the buildings. The weathered brick building had brightly colored mint green trim, giving it a splash of whimsy to break up its typical New England architecture.

It was one of my favorite places in the village. Not just because of its delectable desserts, but because one of my favorite people owned the bakery. Evan Sullivan had become an instant friend the moment I met him, just after I'd moved to the village.

The enticing scent of chocolate and cinnamon washed over me as I pushed open the bakery door and promptly came face to face with Quinn Donegal, who was on her way out.

"Darcy, hi. Did you get my message?" Quinn's ash blonde hair was swept back in a low ponytail. She wore little makeup, but truly needed none. Hers was a natural beauty, born from good genetics.

Her hands were full. One hand gripped a to-go coffee cup. The other had hold of a Gingerbread Shack snack box, which was appropriately shaped as a gingerbread house that had a witch waving from a doorway.

The snack boxes—used only for small take-out orders—were new, the brainchild of Evan's boyfriend, FBI agent Scott Abramson. I'd drawn the design, and it was no one's imagination that the witch looked just like Evan's twin sister, and my best friend, Starla.

Quinn and I stepped out of the entryway, off to the side near a pair of high-topped bistro tables. Evan stood at the counter on the far end of the store, adjusting shelves of miniature delights in the display case while clearly trying to eavesdrop.

"I did get the message," I said. "So sorry I haven't gotten back to you yet. I've been waiting to hear from Nick, but he's been understandably busy."

The store was bright and airy with its white bead-board trim and large, bold close-up photos of cake slices that Starla had taken. Only two of the tables were taken, but the shop still felt full of life under the chatter and laughter of those eating Evan's treats. It was part of the magic of his Bakecrafting. His desserts brought contentment to those who ate them.

It was clear Quinn hadn't eaten any recently since her eyes misted and her voice cracked as she said, "Yes, understandable."

There was a fragility about her, the air of a woman just barely keeping herself together. One crack and she'd break in two. The mama hen in me wanted to pull her into a hug, but I didn't know her well enough to know if she'd welcome it. "How are you holding up?"

She held up the box. "With chocolate. Lots of chocolate."

"The mini devil's food cupcakes are my comfort food of choice." Though I sampled all of Evan's creations, I always came back to these.

"Mine are the chocolate cream puffs with hazelnut cream and dark chocolate drizzle." Confusion suddenly wrinkled her brow and she tipped her head. "Why do you need to wait for Nick to call me back?"

"*I* have the ledgers the Bryants are looking for."

"You do?"

"Abby gave them to me this morning. She wanted me to look them over." *This morning*. It seemed a lifetime ago yet it had only been a few hours.

"She did? Why?"

"She thought she made a mistake with the accounting and asked me to take a look. I'm surprised the Bryants even noticed the books were missing, considering all that's going on."

"It is strange," she agreed, her lips pulling downward in a deep frown. "I don't know why they'd want them back so badly today of all days, but Joe was . . . He wasn't happy Abby had taken them out of the store."

Hmm. It seemed to me that wasn't a normal response, either, especially when Abby had been in charge of the race. Was there something in those ledgers he didn't want anyone to see? Had he fudged the numbers, perhaps? It would certainly explain wanting the books back so desperately.

"Who usually takes care of the accounting at Balefire?" I asked as casually as I could.

"Joe, mostly. Sometimes Madison."

Madison and Joe. The proceeds from this year's race had been earmarked to offset the medical expenses from Aine's surgery. With their financial troubles, I could easily see them tinkering with the numbers.

"Does Ben help, too?"

"No," she said with a wan smile. "He's not very good at math, except when it comes to calculating mileage and PRs. He's a whiz at that."

PRs. Personal records. Many of the runners I knew were continually trying to top their best running times. And what she said about Ben jibed with what Abby had told me this morning. "Do you remember if there has ever been any accounting issues with the store?"

Quinn, who was picking at the sleeve on the coffee cup, suddenly looked me in the eye. "Not that I know of, but honestly, it wouldn't surprise me."

"No?"

"The Bryants, Joe and Madison especially . . ." Her eyes welled, and she swallowed hard. "Let's just say they're very different people behind closed doors."

"How so?"

She glanced outside. "They're just not nice is all."

A couple passed by us on their way out, letting in a burst of snow as they left. I put my hand on Quinn's arm. "Do you think they could have had something to do with what happened to Abby?"

In a whisper, she said, "I don't know. Maybe? I don't know. I can't imagine anyone hurting her."

My head spun. I didn't know Madison and Joe well, but what I knew of them didn't warrant this reaction. They had always been friendly toward me, and charitable within the community. But I quickly realized what I knew of them was their public image. What if Quinn was right and they were different behind closed doors?

It was troubling to say the least.

Quinn went on. "I can't believe Abby's gone. This whole day has been nothing but a nightmare."

"Do you know if Abby had any enemies?" I asked.

"No. No enemies. Everyone loved Abby."

"You just said Joe wasn't happy she'd taken those ledgers."

"He's furious. But that doesn't mean he didn't love Abby."

Furious. Anger often caused people to act rashly. Even toward people they cared for. It was something to share with Nick as soon as I could.

"What about her ex? What do you know about Duncan Cole?"

She startled, stiffening up. Weakly, she said, "Duncan Cole?"

"He was on the Balefire Racing team. Dated Abby? Surely you remember him."

Her green eyes widened. "Oh yes. Of course I know Duncan. He and Abby broke up a long time ago." She went back to picking at the cardboard sleeve. "Why are you asking about him?"

I wanted to ask why she'd freaked out at hearing his name, but since she was a mortal, I couldn't out-and-out tell her I was investigating Abby's death. I thought fast. "I remembered there was a big blowout at Balefire with Duncan, and he and Abby broke up afterward. Maybe there's bad blood between them?" I sucked in a breath, since I'd rambled all those words in one big rush. "You know, so I can pass it on to Nick to investigate." I smiled, hoping I didn't come across as a nosy lunatic.

"There's no bad blood," she said firmly.

I moved farther out of the doorway when someone came into the shop, bringing in more snow. Evan's welcome mats were downright soggy at this point. Shifting my weight from foot to foot, I battled inwardly about how much to ask. Especially since Quinn was grieving, and I didn't want to say anything that would split her fragile façade in two.

I chose my words carefully. "Is there any truth to the rumor that Ben and Abby had been fighting recently?"

I noticed she had started to tremble, and I felt instantly guilty I'd pressed too hard.

She said, "They argued this morning before the race because Ben thought she shouldn't run today. That she should rest. But she laughed it off. She seemed fine. Energetic, even."

"You saw her?"

"I did. I was standing in line for the portable restrooms. The trailhead's right there."

"Did Ben follow her onto the trail?"

"No. He went back to the tent to change for the race."

"And you?"

"I went to find a bathroom, since the line for the portable restrooms was a mile long. Angela at the bookshop took pity on me."

The doors of the portable restrooms had been frozen shut, thanks to Vince's magical mischief. And though I had no reason to doubt her, I wondered if there was a way to verify if she was telling the truth about Ben going back to the tent. I immediately thought of Starla. She'd been taking photos of the race. It was possible she'd caught the comings and goings around the trailhead this morning. I made a mental note to check with her.

Looking off in the distance, Quinn said, "The last I saw of Abby, she seemed happy and healthy. No sign she'd even been sick. But I do think something went terribly wrong, Darcy." She faced me, determination overtaking the grief in her eyes. "Because she wouldn't have willingly been on that bridge otherwise."

"Why not?"

"Abby was terrified of heights. She lived in a one-story house for a reason. She went out of her way to avoid all bridges when running. In all the years I've known her, she's never run the Aural Gorge Trail. Not once. She didn't go there willingly this morning. I'm sure of it."

She did sound sure—there was steel in her tone. I said, "It's possible she took a wrong turn in the storm. There were whiteout conditions."

"No. She knew those trails like the back of her hand. She could run them blindfolded." A sheen of tears glistened in her eyes. Blinking rapidly, she opened her mouth to say something more, then closed it and shook her head. Trembling even more now, she said, "I should go. I need to plan Abby's services."

I decided I'd pushed enough, but would let Nick know he needed to interview her sooner rather than later. "Will you let me know about the services?"

She nodded, tucked the snack box under her arm, and pulled open the door.

As I watched her walk away, I had the undeniable feeling she was hiding something.

Something big.

Chapter Eight

Evan was finishing up with the couple who'd come in moments before as I stepped up to the display case. His baked goods were works of art, and I never ceased to marvel at their intricacies.

"I cannot believe the news about Abby," he said. "She was just in here yesterday, so full of life."

Evan wore his usual uniform of jeans, a dress shirt with its sleeves rolled up, and a white apron. His ginger-colored hair was neatly combed in a mini-pompadour style that was new, and his blue eyes blazed with good health and happiness.

I glanced around the shop. It had cleared out, a rare lull. "I can't believe it either."

"Tell all," he said, dropping his voice as he leaned across the countertop, propping himself up with forearms strengthened from years of hand-mixing his batters. "What did Quinn have to say about Abby's death?"

"Seems to me you heard it all. Didn't anyone teach you eavesdropping is bad manners?"

"Only if you get caught." He grinned, flashing pearly white teeth. "But I couldn't catch it *all* because Quinn's back was to me, and then I had a customer. So, spill."

I spilled as I ordered, and he whistled low at the news that Joe and Madison perhaps weren't the people we thought them to be.

"I can see that," he said. "Now that I'm looking for it. Even when they're sociable they're aloof. Kind of cold."

I thought about this morning in the event tent, how they'd kept Quinn outside the group, instead of inviting her into their tight circle. Madison had spent most of the time talking with Lucinda, and I was pretty sure she hadn't even said hi to me this morning, even though I had helped plan the race. I hadn't really thought much of it at the time, but maybe being aloof was the norm for them—and not the exception.

"Do you remember Duncan Cole?" I asked, thinking about Quinn's strange reaction to hearing his name.

"Oh yeah, I remember Duncan." He fanned his face. "Tall, dark, and delightfully buff. He didn't come in here much, but I'd see him running from time to time in those tiny shorts and tank top."

Evan was one of my jogging buddies, and I was starting to suspect he wasn't running as a form of exercise but rather a form of ogling. I couldn't judge him too much. Back when I first started, my jogging workouts had increased once I knew I could bump into Nick from time to time. "Don't go getting yourself all worked up. What would Scott think?"

Evan and Scott had been dating since last spring, and Evan had recently shared that Scott was thinking of moving to the village.

"He'd think it was a damn shame he'd never caught a glimpse of Duncan in those shorts. How long has it been since Duncan moved away?"

I laughed as I ordered a dozen of Harper's favorite bakes and added another half dozen to take home with me later on. "Last spring."

Evan perked up. "Has he moved back to the village? And why are you interested in him? Do you think he had something to do with what happened to Abby?"

"They'd broken up right before he left the village. And I'm not sure he has anything to do with anything, but he's a puzzle piece. I need to find him, see if he has an alibi."

Or, Nick did. I couldn't exactly explain to Duncan why I wanted to know.

"Well, you won't find him in here. Balefire people are usually granola people. Not chocolate ganache people."

"You say that, but you just said Abby was in here yesterday. She's a Balefire person."

Or had been.

My stomach suddenly hurt so much that even the devil's food cupcakes didn't seem appetizing.

"Abby wasn't a regular. I can count on one hand how many times she'd been in here, and that was mostly picking up orders for Quinn and for special occasions, those kinds of things."

"Was yesterday a special occasion?"

He gently set cupcakes, opera cakes, truffles, and chocolate mousse cups into one of his fancy boxes and wrapped string around it. "It's so sad to think about it, really. She was ordering a wedding cake."

"A wedding cake?"

His eyes bright with a secret he was ready to tell, he said, "She and Ben were eloping. On Tuesday."

"*What*!"

"Yeah. She was ordering a cake to be picked up that day."

"What!" I said again.

"I know," he said. "I didn't think they were that serious."

Me, either. I'd spent a lot of time with Abby over the past month, and she hadn't said a word. Hadn't even hinted there was a wedding on her mind.

I cupped my face with my hands. "I can't . . . I can't believe it."

"It's true," he said. "She paid in full. In cash."

"Does Quinn know? Does anybody know?"

"I'm not sure," he said. "Abby came in alone. I've been hearing all morning about how Abby and Ben had been fighting last night and this morning, and I'd been wondering if it was about the wedding. Weddings truly bring out the worst in people. Consider yourself warned."

My wedding was months away, but for some reason I'd been dragging my feet on the planning. "Good to know. Quinn mentioned the fight this morning had been about Ben not wanting Abby to run the race."

"And last night?" he asked. "I heard there was a big blowup between them behind the Sorcerer's Stove."

It never ceased to amaze me how fast gossip spread in this village.

"Quinn didn't say." I made a mental note to ask her about it the next time I spoke with her. "What do you know about her? You said she's a regular?"

"For years she's come in at least twice a week. Chocoholic. Mortal. Late twenties. Grew up near the Berkshires." He tapped his chin as he rattled off the bullet points of Quinn's life. "Moved here and started working for Balefire two, three years ago. Abby was her best friend. They were close. Like sisters."

"Does she date?" I took the cups over to the coffee station. I filled mine with dark roast and wondered if

Harper would prefer tea. I settled on a green tea for her, hoping the antioxidants would prove miraculous.

"Not that I know of. Quinn's a bit of a workaholic."

"Money?"

"I get the feeling she scrapes by. Sometimes she digs for change to pay for her cream puffs. You think she had something to do with Abby's death?"

"I don't know," I said. "I can't imagine it, but you never know. I need to check out her alibi."

I happened to glance out the window as a couple on the sidewalk strode past. I did a double take. It was Marcus Debrowski—Harper's Marcus—and local real estate agent Noelle Quinlan, who looked as though she was in the midst of an animated conversation. Her hands flew this way and that as she talked, emitting a continuous stream of steam from her mouth.

As if sensing someone was watching him, Marcus's head turned my way. Our gazes met through the snow-flecked glass. My heart fell just looking at him. With a hangdog expression, long unruly hair, dark eye circles, and pasty complexion, he looked as miserable as Harper.

He broke the eye contact, and with a few more steps, the two crossed the street and were gone.

"How's Harper doing?" Evan asked, clearly having seen what had distracted me.

"That first box of pastries is for her."

"Damn."

"Yeah."

I hooked a thumb over my shoulder, my hand shaking a bit. "Do you know if Marcus and Noelle . . ."

Vigorously, he shook his head. "No, they're not."

I blew out a breath. Thank goodness. I wasn't sure how Harper would've handled that news.

"Penelope Debrowski sold her house. She's moving south to warmer climes."

Penelope—Marcus's mother. His family dynamics had imploded months ago after a cold case murder had become suddenly very hot. Marcus's mom had gone into hiding the day his father was arrested—I hadn't seen her in the village since. Not even a glimpse. His dad, facing murder charges, had died of a heart attack in early January while awaiting trial. Some thought it was a blessing the family hadn't had to go through the stress and shame of a public trial. But I wasn't one of those people. I knew the pain of losing a parent. There were no *blessings* whatsoever.

At the time, I had believed, incorrectly, that the death of Marcus's father would have sparked a reunion between Marcus and Harper. It was the murder case, after all, which had split them up to begin with. Marcus had decided he didn't have the time or energy to devote to Harper while trying to defend his father and keep his mother from falling apart.

While I could understand his reasoning, I wished he had leaned on Harper instead of abandoning her.

"It might be the best for Penelope," I finally said, wondering if she'd find the peace she longed for somewhere else. Somewhere that didn't remind her of the murder case—and her role in it—day in and day out. Then I wondered if such a place existed. I doubted it. "And it might be the best for Marcus and Harper too. With his mother gone, maybe they can pick up the pieces of their relationship? Hopefully. Maybe?"

Empathy flooded Evan's eyes. Somberly, he said, "I heard Marcus has a contract on his house, too. He's leaving with Penelope."

My chest ached suddenly as if someone was sitting on it, pressing out every last bit of air. "You're sure?"

"Noelle told me herself this morning. She was on her way to meet with Marcus and his mom. You know how she talks."

I did. "I'm going to need to double my order."

Nodding, he quickly added more pastries to my box.

Was it was possible Harper knew the news about Marcus moving already? Was it why she had taken a drastic turn for the worse in the last couple of days?

Wouldn't she have told me, though?

Maybe. Maybe not. She'd been keeping a lot to herself lately. Internalizing her pain and her feelings. It could be one more thing she'd stuffed down instead of dealing with.

"Is there anything I can do for Harper?" he asked.

I shrugged. "I don't know what's going to help her at this point. If she doesn't know Marcus is moving, it's going to . . . I can't even think about it."

"I can start a baking club."

Tears filled my eyes. "She'd actually like that."

"Consider it done."

A mournful silence fell over us as Evan finished the orders. The weight on my chest had lessened, but it was still there. Squeezing. My heart felt like it was literally breaking for my sister.

Evan pushed the pastry boxes toward me and said, "On the house."

"Thank you. You can write it off as a charitable expense."

"Too much paperwork. What the IRS doesn't know won't hurt them."

His words reminded me of the ledgers Abby wanted me to look over. And of Joe's desperation to get them back. I told him about them.

"What're you thinking?" he asked, his eyes lighting up. "Is he embezzling?"

"Whoa there, Sherlock. I'm not sure about anything right now."

"If he was embezzling and Abby figured it out . . . I think Joe could be your lead suspect."

"There's nothing to *suspect* until we get official word from Nick or the medical examiner's office."

He leaned in. "But, come on. What do *you* think, Darcy? Was Abby's death an accident or something more sinister?"

"I'm not sure," I said as I gathered up the boxes. "All I know is that the more questions I ask, the more I'm realizing there's more to this case than meets the eye."

Chapter Nine

"He's late because this house call is a waste of time," Harper said. "I know it and he knows it."

"*Mm-hmm*." I sat on the sofa, sipping my coffee, taking the brunt of her frustration and trying not to panic.

She'd refused to even take a bite of any of the goodies I'd brought, which was a sure sign to me that she was dying. Imminently.

Dennis Goodwin couldn't arrive fast enough to suit my needs. The fact that he was ten minutes late only added to my anxiety. So help him if he canceled at the last minute. I'd bundle up Harper and track him down if I had to.

Pie slept through Harper's ranting, stretched languidly along my thigh. He snored in soft little snuffles that ordinarily I would have found charming. But not now, with my nerves on edge. I gave my leg a jiggle, hoping to stir him enough to change his breathing patterns without waking him up. He kept on sleeping. And snuffling.

Gripping my cup so tightly that the paper dented beneath my thumb, I said, "He'll be here soon, I'm sure. The streets are still a mess." He was driving in from the Salem coastline where he lived with his wife and young daughter.

I watched Harper pace, and wondered for the millionth time since I stepped into her apartment whether she knew Marcus was leaving the village.

Unfortunately, she looked so pitiful it was hard to tell. Hunched shoulders, pale skin, bloodshot eyes, and gaunt cheeks. She was still dressed in her robe but had added thick, fuzzy socks to the outfit.

"Have some tea," I said.

"You promised you wouldn't nag anymore."

I wagged a finger. "Not until you get the all clear from Dennis."

Her chin jutted as she realized she hadn't caught that loophole. "I'm not thirsty."

"It's not for thirst. It's for health."

"No thanks."

It was hard to tell if she truly didn't want the drink or if she was simply being stubborn. I suspected it was both.

She hadn't asked me a single question about Abby Stillwell since I'd come in. I figured that was because she knew I'd barter for the answer, making her eat or drink before filling her in.

She was right. I would.

It was probably driving her as crazy as her pacing was driving me.

I had texted Starla on my way from the bakery to here, and she'd been more than happy to show me her photos of the race later this afternoon. She loved being involved in my investigations. If I ever hired any investigative sidekicks, there would be plenty of applications.

"Has Mom been by?" I asked as innocently as I could.

"We had lunch yesterday. You didn't tell her about this appointment, did you?"

"Nope," I answered truthfully. She'd already known. "Any reason you wouldn't want her to know about it?"

"She spent most of the time yesterday nagging me to go to the doctor, but there's no need to worry her when there's nothing to worry about."

"Well, I'm pretty worried."

She huffed and rolled her eyes. Plopping down on the couch across from me, she crossed her legs and began bobbing the leg on top. Up, down. Up, down. "You're being ridiculous."

"Okay." It seemed to me that she doth protest too much, but I was wise enough not to say so aloud.

We sat in tense silence, save for Pie's snuffles, until we heard heavy footsteps on the stairs.

I jumped up and quickstepped to the door, pulling it open before Dennis even made it to the landing. I met him out there.

"Darcy," he said with a nod.

"Dennis," I said, nodding back. "Thanks for stopping by."

Dennis Goodwin, Cherise and Terry's son, and I had butted heads in the past, but eventually put those days behind us. I hoped. Cantankerous with little tact, he came off as a total blowhard. Yet, I knew that beneath his crusty exterior, he had a big heart. He just didn't like anyone to know it.

"You didn't leave me much choice, did you?" he said with his usual lack of grace.

"Desperate times." I smiled wide, ushered him inside, and closed the door.

Harper was still seething from her spot on the couch.

Dennis took one look at her and said, "I see why you called."

If he had been able to cure a broken heart, I would have called him to check on her months ago, but I knew he couldn't. Only medical ailments.

"Oh, come on," Harper said. "I don't look that bad. I had a stomach bug. For the love!"

Dennis turned to me. "Has she had an eye exam recently?"

"Doubtful since Sylar Dewitt is the only optician in town, and we tend to avoid him since, well, Dorothy." She worked as his assistant.

He took off his coat. "I'll give you a name of a friend in downtown Salem."

"My eyes are fine," Harper said in a staccato burst. "Can we just get this over with? I'd like to put in at least half a day at work."

Dennis tugged off a stocking cap, making his brown hair stand on end. He patted it down, and said, "You'll be taking the whole day off. If you need to make a call to set up the arrangements, I'll wait."

Harper opened her mouth, clearly ready to argue, but she must have seen something in his features that made her snap her lips together. After a moment, she said, "It can wait."

"Good." He handed me his coat. "You're going to lie down the rest of the day, drink plenty of fluids, eat some soup, and get what appears to be some much-needed sleep."

I wanted to give her a smug "I told you so," but Dennis was making my anxiety have anxiety. He hadn't even laid a hand on her yet—a Curecrafter's method to diagnose—and he could already tell there was something terribly wrong.

"Sit here," he said to Harper, motioning to a wing chair that had been reupholstered with a fabric printed with replicas of old-fashioned library catalogue cards.

She sat and threw me a look chock full of daggers. Extra sharp deadly ones.

I hung up Dennis's coat on the rack near the door and tried not to feel guilty for subjecting Harper to Dennis's lack of a bedside manner. It was for her own good, I reminded myself.

"Are you staying?" Dennis asked me.

"I was planning to."

"Harper?" he asked.

"Darcy can stay. The sooner she finds out I'm fine, the better. I'm an adult and you're both acting like I'm a child."

Again feeling guilty, I sat on the couch, trying to blend in with the colorful afghan.

Dennis rubbed his hands together, warming them. "If you don't want to be treated like a child, do not behave as one."

Her jaw dropped. "How dare—"

He cut her off. "Save the indignation. It is clear you've neglected your health. I can tell by looking at you that you've not been eating properly. You've not been sleeping. You're dehydrated. I have little tolerance for people who don't treasure their health."

"You don't know what I've been—"

"I don't particularly care. There is no excuse for this long-term neglect. What's it been?" He looked her over, peering closely into her eyes. "Three months? Four?"

Her jaw jutted. "I don't particularly like you."

He smiled, a true smile. "Fair enough. The truth hurts."

Harper faced me. "He's dreadful."

I said, "His bedside manner could use a bit of work."

"A bit?" she scoffed. "That's like saying there's a bit of sand at the beach."

Dennis glanced my way, and I swear there was a sparkle in his eyes. Clearly, he liked his whole Dr. Dreadful persona.

"Let's see how deep this neglect has run." He slid a thumb across her forehead, then back again and frowned. "Stick out your tongue."

She did. He *tsk*ed at whatever it was he saw.

Her fists clenched and her back stiffened.

"I'll need you to undo your robe. I'm going to place my hand above your heart."

"Just get it over with." She slid her robe from her shoulders. She had on a long-sleeve formfitting tee beneath that did nothing to hide the way her shoulder bones protruded.

I had thought she'd lost five or ten pounds. Now I guessed it was closer to fifteen. I felt queasy.

Dennis set his hand gently beneath the point where Harper's collarbones met and closed his eyes.

The longer he stood there with his palm pressed to her chest and his eyes closed, the more the rebellion faded from Harper's expression. She wouldn't look my way, but I could see fear starting to creep into her eyes.

"Hold still," he instructed as he pulled his hand away. He rubbed his palms together again, whispered something under his breath, and then gently touched his fingertips to her temples. His left eye blinked twice—a sign he was using his Craft.

The color improved in Harper's cheeks almost immediately and her eyes looked brighter, but there was no denying she still looked ill.

He sat on the edge of the coffee table and faced her. "A little better?"

"A little," she admitted, slipping her robe back onto her shoulders.

"I used a calming spell because your anxiety is off the charts, and I did what I could for your nausea. I cannot cure what ails you, however, as it is a chronic condition that has gone on much too long."

He maintained eye contact with her the whole time he spoke. I noticed his tone had softened.

"What's wrong?" she finally asked.

Thank goodness she did, because I'd been biting my tongue to keep from asking the question myself.

"You have pernicious anemia, an autoimmune disorder. You've probably had low vitamin B_{12} levels most of your life, but your poor diet and other health changes over the past few months have caused it to bottom out. It explains a lot of what you've experiencing. Fatigue, weight loss, headaches, and pale skin. It most likely contributed to your depression. You need to start B_{12} injections immediately. Today. I'm going to go to my office, get some supplies, and come back here. I'll give you your first injection today. You'll need another tomorrow."

Harper was an information nut, so I knew she had been listening to him carefully. "What happens if I don't get the shots?"

"The progression of pernicious anemia is ultimately fatal if not treated. You're lucky Darcy called me."

Fatal. My god. My stomach was flip-flopping, and my palms had started sweating.

"I recommend reevaluating your depression once you've had several months of B_{12} injections." Dennis stood, studied her. "I understand you don't necessarily have the will to live right now. Your body and mind are tired, and you don't know if you have the energy to fight for yourself any longer."

A tear slid out of the corner of her eye.

Tears filled my eyes. I knew she'd been suffering but I hadn't quite known how much. She'd hid a lot, and I'd foolishly believed she was simply dealing with a breakup.

Dennis went on. "And all those feelings are reasonable given the way you're currently feeling. Since you have *me* fighting for *you* now, your burden in dealing with those ailments will be much lighter. But I have to ask how hard you're willing to fight for the child you're carrying. Because it's going to be a battle. One you might not win."

His words slowly registered through the thick haze of emotion clouding the room.

My jaw hit the floor, and Harper's mouth fell open. Had I heard correctly? Was he joking?

"The *what*?" Harper and I said at the same time.

"The child," he said as if we were both thick in the head. "It's rather a miracle you were able to achieve pregnancy, never mind carry this long. Low B_{12} is a notorious cause of infertility and miscarriage. And that's what you're facing now. The possibility of a miscarriage. It's a very real possibility. This is all assuming you want to keep the pregnancy?"

"Of course I do!" she cried, then held up a hand and started ticking off fingers.

Dennis sighed. "You're six weeks, three days along."

"Child?" I repeated, utterly flabbergasted. "Six weeks?"

Harper dropped her head into her hands. "Oh. My. God."

"Child?" I said loudly, standing up, then sitting down again.

Dennis put on his coat. "I'll be back soon. I'm going to give you the B_{12} injection, then I'm going to order you to bed rest for at least a week, and I do not want a single argument, understood?"

Harper stared at him blankly.

"Good," he said, then walked out, closing the door gently behind him.

She turned her dazed stare on me.

"*Child*?" I said again, unable to find any other words in my vocabulary.

Shaking her head, she stammered, "I—Marcus." She let out a long breath. "He came by one night, right after his father died . . . One thing led to another. It didn't change anything . . . It was just . . . One of those things."

Seemed to me it had changed quite a lot.

A child.

A baby.

Harper's baby.

Harper caught my eye. "Are you mad?" she asked softly. "About the baby?"

I snapped out of my fugue. "Why on earth would I be mad? I'm scared but not mad."

She swallowed hard, as though choking down emotion. "Because I know you've wanted to be a mom for a long time now. And here I am, not even knowing I was pregnant. This baby should be yours. I'm so sorry. I'm sorry about everything. I've been so . . ." She shook her head. "I've been so lost."

"Stop, stop right now." I knelt before her, taking her trembling hands in mine. "I'm happy about the baby. *Worried* but happy. You're going to be a great mom, Harper. Nick and I have always planned to have babies— we're just waiting until after the wedding. My time to be a mom will come. Don't worry another second about that, okay? Okay?" I repeated.

She backhanded tears away from her eyes. "Okay." She sniffled. "Darcy?"

"Yeah?"

Harper smiled and it brightened her whole face, and for a moment I forgot about how sick she was.

She said, "I think I'll have those crackers now."

I jumped up, more than eager to start plying her with food.

"And Darcy?"

Grabbing a bowl, I dumped a whole sleeve of crackers into it. "Yeah?"

"I, um . . . Bed rest." Her jaw jutted out, then shifted back. "Do you think . . . do you think I could possibly move in with you for the week?"

Harper valued her independence, so I knew what it had cost her to ask. I handed her the bowl. "Of course you can. You can stay as long as you want."

Staring at the crackers, she blinked furiously, then glanced up at me. Tears had pooled, blurring her beautiful golden-brown eyes. "Darcy?" Her voice cracked on my name.

I once again knelt down next to her. "Yeah?"

"Marcus is moving." The tears spilled over. "He's leaving town. He's leaving for good."

I swallowed over the lump in my throat. "I'm so sorry, Harper."

Chapter Ten

"Harper doesn't want Marcus to know about the pregnancy," I said to Starla as we sat cross-legged on my office floor. I had chicken stew cooking in the Crock-Pot and the scent of sage and thyme filled the air. "Not yet."

Her bright blue eyes filled with confusion. She set the mug of hot chocolate she'd been holding onto a coaster on the table. "But if he knows about the baby, it might make him stay. Isn't that what she wants? For him to stay?"

A laptop was set up on the coffee table in front of us, and I scanned the image on the screen. It had been taken at the starting line of the race this morning. Starla had done a great job capturing the determination in the faces of the Mad Dashers. I zeroed in on Ben's face. He wasn't standing in front but rather behind the first line of runners, and he wasn't facing straight ahead like the others and didn't share the same look of resoluteness. Instead, his body was angled to the right, and he looked angry, his focus on the area in front of the bookshop. Shoulders pulled back, eyebrows drawn low, eyes narrowed, and a scowl slanting his lips.

Unfortunately, I couldn't see what had caught his attention. Whatever it had been hadn't affected Lucinda, who stood next to Ben in the photo.

I kept scrolling through the pictures, hoping Starla had caught a different view of the same scene, and wondering what had triggered Ben's reaction. "Which is exactly Harper's reasoning for not telling Marcus. She wants him to stay because he *wants* to stay. Not because he *has* to stay."

It had been hours since I crammed as many of Harper's belongings as I could into a duffel bag, managed to get Pie into his carrier, and moved them here. Dennis had been his usual gruff self when I called and asked him to meet us at my house instead of Harper's, but had sounded relieved she was staying with me for a while. He'd come and gone, delivering Harper's first B$_{12}$ injection and also a sleeping spell, which was why Harper was sound asleep in the guest room upstairs, Pie and Annie flanking her like furry guardian bookends.

I clicked on another picture, scanned it, and closed it. None of the photos had confirmed Quinn's timeline. Nor had they discredited it either. I could check with Angela at Spellbound about Quinn using the restroom—and what time that would have been—but it wasn't looking like I could confirm Ben's whereabouts at the time Abby had gone missing.

The gas fireplace crackled as it filled the office with warmth, the delicate sound an accompaniment to Higgins' booming snores. It was quite the symphony. He slept on the love seat behind Starla and me, his body covering both cushions, then some. Missy was still at Ve's.

"All right." She unfolded her legs, kicked them out straight beneath the coffee table, and picked up her mug again. "I get that, but it doesn't seem fair to Marcus."

I tended to agree. "Nothing about any of this seems fair, but Harper's adamant. She doesn't want to tell him until she knows the pregnancy is out of the danger zone. Dennis said if the baby makes it to twelve weeks and if

Harper's B$_{12}$ numbers rise to safer levels, then there's a good chance she'll carry to term. Until that twelve-week mark, Harper insists only close friends and family know what's going on."

I clicked another picture. This one was a broader image of the starting line. I zoomed in on Ben, noted he was still staring toward his right, then zoomed out again. The area where he stared was crowded with onlookers who were there to cheer on the runners. I immediately picked out Madison and Aine among the faces. Madison was staring off in the distance, oblivious to Ben's glare.

Had Madison been the one who sparked his anger? It didn't seem likely, simply because I couldn't think of a reason why, but I didn't rule it out, either. I hit the print button and my printer purred to life.

A strand of Starla's golden hair slipped out of her top knot as she shook her head. She tucked the hair behind her ear as she said, "And at twelve weeks, Harper is going to call up Marcus and say what? Oh, by the way, I know you sold your house, closed your law office, and moved a thousand miles away recently, but you might want to move back if you want to get to know your child? It's not right, Darcy."

Eyebrow raised, I glanced at her. It wasn't the norm for Starla to be so vehement.

She laughed at my expression, and her blue eyes sparkled. "I'm sorry. I'm getting carried away. It's just that . . . they belong together, and I'm not just saying so because I'm a dopey romantic sap, because you know I'm off romance right now. It's about what's right and what's wrong. What's right is that those two belong together," she said again. "If there's ever a time Harper should fight for that relationship, it's now. Not just for her, but for the baby too."

After her split from Vince, Starla had considered starting a relationship with a local contractor who'd been wooing her, but ultimately she'd decided to take some time for herself. Time to heal. To grow. To discover herself. She was so dedicated to the notion that she decided to take a year off to travel. Instead of closing up her business, Hocus-Pocus, she had hired a manager and a few part-time employees to cover the shop here in the village, and she was taking her camera and hitting the road. She had launched a website and everything, and was due to leave on her first excursion—a four week trip to the UK, France, and Italy next week.

"I agree." I picked a piece of fuzz off the area rug and tried to ignore the ache in my chest. "At first, she thought he shouldn't have walked away from their relationship. That they were partners, and he shouldn't have excluded her from his struggles."

"She'd be right."

I absently clicked through a few more pictures, not really seeing them. "But he did exclude her. Instead of kicking up a fuss right when it happened, she let him have his time away from her, thinking he'd eventually come back. That he would realize what he had given up. That he would ultimately fight for what they had."

"Makes sense to me."

"But he didn't. So she gathered up the pieces of her broken heart and went on without him. Kind of. But there comes a time when you can't think too hard about who should have done what. It becomes about what *you* want. And how far you'll go to fight for it. That might mean having to set your pride aside or opening yourself up to more pain. It's all or nothing. Right now, Harper's choosing nothing."

"To avoid more pain."

I realized I wasn't paying the least bit of attention to the computer screen and picked up my coffee mug. "Exactly. And now I think she's more terrified than ever to go all in. Because what if she *does* tell Marcus about the baby? And he still decides to move? Imagine if he walked away from her and *their child*."

Starla whistled low. "That would be utterly devastating."

My gaze went to the painting above the fireplace. It was of a magic wand caught in midswirl. Done in cool silvers and blues, it was my one of my favorites. "Harper's playing a complex mental game to protect herself from more pain. But . . ."

"What?"

"I think she's unwittingly creating a scenario that will cause her only more pain in the long run. Honestly, they just need to talk it out. But neither can see the light from inside the stupid hole they've dug for themselves."

She bent a knee, rested her mug atop it. "We need to make them see it."

"Yes, we do."

She elbowed me. "You have a plan. I can tell."

I smiled. "I'm working on a plan. I saw Marcus today, from afar. He looked just as miserable as Harper. I think he's suffering too. He created all this pain and probably doesn't know how to fix it."

"*Men,*" Starla said, shaking her head.

"It will be weeks before he can move. Escrow takes time." I knew this from experience. Nick's farmhouse, which sold almost immediately, was finally closing on Tuesday. Three months after he accepted the offer. I had to concede the timeframe was longer than normal because there had been a snafu with the buyer's financing. But still. "I have some time. Not much, but enough, I think, to help Marcus get a clue."

"Harper's not going to like it if you butt in."

I stood and grabbed the photo I had printed. I couldn't stop staring at Ben's hardened features. He was fuming. "No, she's not. But I don't intend to tell her? Do you?"

Shaking her head, she smiled, then took a sip of her cocoa. "My lips are sealed." She motioned toward the photo. "Find something interesting? I'm kicking myself for focusing my shots at the starting line instead of incorporating the trailhead as well."

In my opinion she'd gone above and beyond with her photos. There were hundreds to look through.

"It's not like you could have known what was going to happen." I sat back down, stretched out my legs. "Look at Ben's face."

"Looks like he's royally ticked at Madison. Why?"

"I don't know because she doesn't seem to be paying attention to it, looking off in the distance like she is."

"Not in the least." I tapped the photo. "You know what I'm now realizing?"

"What?"

"Joe's not there."

She scanned the photo. "Where is he?"

We looked through the photos again. Joe was in none of them, except for those at the *finish* line. Where in the world had he been?

On the Aural bridge?

He'd been angry about those ledgers. If he'd been doctoring the books, it was entirely possible he was concerned Abby would figure out the truth.

But would he kill her over it?

My stomach knotted. "I'll add it to my list of things to find out."

"That's getting to be a long list."

"Tell me about it."

Higgins snortled, lifted his head, licked his lips, sending drool flying, and then settled back down again. He had a rough life, that dog.

Starla ducked out of the way of the drool. "Ben staring at Madison is just plain strange. Could it be he was still angry from his spat with Abby?"

"Could be, but I doubt it. According to Quinn, the fight was about Ben being mad at Abby for running the race. I'd think he'd be showing relief in his face that she wasn't at the starting line."

"Because he'd be thinking she took his advice not to run. *Hmm.*"

"Right. So this kind of rage doesn't make any sense. I need to talk to him, but tomorrow will have to be soon enough, since he's been talking to the police all day. Quinn gave him an alibi when she said she saw him going to the event tent, but I didn't see any photos right before the race started. Did you?"

"No." She shifted toward me. "You know . . ."

I waited.

"You might want to talk to Vince." She barely flinched at his name. "He has a surveillance system set up on the outside of Lotions and Potions. He probably has footage of the whole morning."

I wanted to thunk my head against the table. "I probably should have thought of that already."

"Don't worry—I won't tell your boss."

My boss. My mother. "I appreciate it."

"Did Quinn give you any hints as to why Ben would be so angry with Madison? Did they get along?"

I told her what Quinn had said about the family dynamics. "Beyond that, she didn't say too much about Ben. She did kind of freak out when I mentioned Duncan Cole's name, which was odd. I have no idea why though."

"Duncan Cole?" Starla set her mug down. "What's he have to do with anything?"

"He and Abby dated for a while. They broke up right around the same time he was let go from the Balefire Racing team. I was wondering if Quinn knew if Abby and Duncan had bad blood between them, since Abby doesn't seem to have any enemies."

"I had forgotten Duncan and Abby had dated. I didn't know him well, but it's just so odd to hear his name so soon after seeing him."

"You saw him? When?"

"Just now." She tapped the photo. "He's standing right behind Madison. Look."

I looked. Frowned. The man stood a head taller than Madison and wore a heavy sweatshirt with the hood up. A thick beard covered most of his face.

I suddenly realized he was the man who'd helped me with the banner this morning. Mr. Neon Green Sneakers. "I didn't recognize him with that beard."

Even now, knowing who he was, it was hard to see, but I couldn't miss the smug smile he was giving Ben.

"Are you thinking what I'm thinking?" Starla asked.

"That perhaps it wasn't Madison who'd captured Ben's attention? It was Duncan."

"Yep, you're thinking what I'm thinking."

But Duncan's presence begged the question of what he was doing in the village in the first place.

And if he had, in fact, had anything to do with Abby's death.

Chapter Eleven

"Do you know yet? Was Abby's death murder or an accident?" I glanced at Nick over my shoulder as I checked on the baguette in the oven. The loaf was still slightly pale, so I reset the timer for a few more minutes.

He'd been home only a little while. Just long enough to wash up, check in on Harper and Mimi, who were binge- watching *Survivor* episodes upstairs, play fetch with Higgins, and help set out dinner dishes. This was the first time we'd really had a chance to talk about the day's events other than through text messages or hurried phone calls.

And what a day it had been.

"What do *you* think, Darcy?" Nick placed a stack of colorful soup crocks on the island.

I wasn't sure whether he simply wanted my opinion, or if he knew I had seen or heard something during the day that would tip Abby's cause of death one way or the other.

A way that fell in line with his investigation.

After grabbing a stack of napkins and four spoons, I met his curious gaze. "Evan asked me the same question earlier, and I hadn't been sure."

"But now?"

I folded a napkin in half. "I've been thinking about it most of the afternoon." In the quiet hours between Starla leaving and Mimi getting home from her shift at the bookshop. Time during which Harper had spent catching up on some much-needed rest. I'd taken notes about what I knew so far, made lists, and asked myself questions that as of yet had no answers.

Questions like why was Abby on the bridge? Why was there wig hair on her backpack? Was Joe an embezzler? Why was Duncan in the village this morning? Did his presence have anything to do with Abby? Or something to do with the Bryants in general? What had Ben and Abby fought about the night before?

But at the top of the list had been the question I'd asked Nick. Murder or accident?

Because if it had been an accident, none of my other questions mattered much.

Except . . . if it launched a secondary investigation. One centering around the ledgers Abby had given me, and Joe's desire to get them back as soon as possible.

"And?" The top two buttons of his uniform shirt were undone, the sleeves pushed up. The muscles in his forearms contracted and released as he unfolded a breakfast tray table and went about loading it up to take upstairs. The small table would be pulling breakfast, lunch, and dinner duty for the next week or so.

"Murder."

I hated even saying it aloud, but it was the only conclusion I could come to that made any sense whatsoever.

"Interesting." He kept an impartial expression. "Is that your gut impression or do you have evidence to back it up?"

"You know, you could just tell me if I'm right or wrong."

He laughed and scratched the stubble along his jaw that had emerged throughout the long day. "I could, couldn't I?"

Yet he said nothing more. I rolled my eyes as I folded another napkin and said, "Fine, but I want every last detail of your investigation before the night is through."

"That's a deal I'll gladly make. Especially if it takes all night. And we're in bed and have the fire going." He wiggled his eyebrows.

"Nick Sawyer, are you flirting at a time like this?" I couldn't stop a smile—or my heart from beating just a little bit faster.

"I am. That's probably in bad form, isn't it? Considering the day we had?"

Maybe in spite of it. We'd investigated a lot of crimes together since I'd moved here—and we could either let the ugliness of the world interfere with our personal lives or learn to compartmentalize to save our sanity.

We had both opted for sanity. Though, to be perfectly honest, sometimes it was hard to separate completely. In those moments, I was glad to have a partner who knew what I was going through. Who could comfort and console and chase away the demons that haunted the memory, long after a case was closed.

"I just can't help it," he said. "You look so cute, standing there with your hair in that messy bun, looking all cozy in that oversized sweatshirt, and with flour on your nose."

I immediately reached up and rubbed my nose. I'd made the baguette from scratch, and I was anything but a neat and tidy baker. "As I talk about murder . . ."

"Just makes you that much more alluring."

"Flatterer."

He came around the island and pulled me into a hug, holding me close. I settled my head in the crook of his neck and simply breathed in the scent of him—which was even more enticing than the aroma of the baking bread that filled the rest of the kitchen.

I'd have happily let him hold me like that all night, but the sound of the electric dog door had us breaking apart as Missy raced inside.

"Stay," Nick said quickly to her.

She'd left little snowy footprints all over the house not ten minutes ago when she came in from Ve's—I'd already cleaned those up. She'd done her rounds about the house, then dashed back outside again not five minutes later. Now, here she and her footprints were again. If she was planning to come and go every five minutes, I was going to have to seriously consider turning off the automatic door for the night. It was possible we'd given her too much freedom.

For months, we'd been trying to teach her simple commands like sit and stay, but she was stone-cold deaf when it came to taking orders from us. Tonight was no different. She ignored Nick and ran full tilt into the kitchen. Once she reached us, she gave her fur a good shake, sending melted snow droplets flying.

Nick threw his hands in the air in surrender. "I'll get a towel. And the quick mop."

I laughed. "There's a towel by the back door. I'll get the mop."

Heading into the mudroom, I let out a scream as a face suddenly appeared at the back door. I put my hand on my heart.

Ve let herself in. "Have mercy! I didn't mean to scare you."

"Darcy?" Nick called out.

"I'm okay," I yelled back.

Ve wiped her boots on the mat, sniffed the air and said, "You've been making bread."

"And you're more than welcome to some." She followed me into the kitchen. "There's chicken stew, too, if you're hungry. Where's Archie?"

"Sleeping," she said. "Those piña coladas really did a number on him."

"On *him*?" I asked, amused.

She smiled. "I bounce back better than he does. Since, you know, I have youth on my side."

I grabbed another soup crock and set it next to the others. "I'll be sure to tell him you said so."

"Ruffled feathers will fly for sure!"

Nick looked up as he dried off Missy's paws. "Piña coladas?"

The oven timer went off. I said, "Long story involving Tom Selleck."

"Say no more," he said, laughing.

I pulled the bread from the oven and set the baking sheet on a rack on top of the stove.

Ve, I noticed, kept glancing upward.

When she caught me watching her she cleared her throat and said, "Well, I'm just going to come out with it. Did I hear correctly that Harper's staying here? That she's quite . . ." She coughed. "Ill?"

It was quite clear to me Ve knew exactly what was wrong with Harper, but I didn't know how she knew the information. "Where'd you hear that?"

She waved a hand. "Oh, you know how rumors are around here. Thought I'd verify this one myself."

I narrowed my gaze on her.

She squirmed.

"Have you been talking to Dennis?" After all, she knew him well since she'd once been married to his father.

Ve had been married four times. She loved to be in love, but had commitment issues, which made it all the more surprising she'd been dating Andreus Woodshall for almost a whole year now. I had the feeling wedding bells weren't in their near future, however. Both seemed utterly happy with their often long-distance relationship.

Missy barked, shook herself again, and leaped out of Nick's reach. She ran for the staircase.

Ve blinked rapidly then said, "Dennis? Yes Dennis! Called him for a hangover cure, but he was busy. With Harper. Now you know. I'm just going to . . ." She moseyed toward the front hall. "Check on Harper."

Nick and I watched her go. He said, "That was strange."

"She's lying about Dennis, but I don't know why."

"Is it possible your mother told her about Harper's pregnancy, and Ve's trying to protect her source?"

I ladled stew into the crocks. "I'm not sure. Maybe."

"Harper would have told her as soon as she saw her, so it probably doesn't matter how Ve knows," he said. "And as much as Harper would like to keep the pregnancy a secret, in this village, word is going to catch like wildfire. Just like the news that Abby was murdered."

As his words sank in, I let go of the ladle. "Oh no. So it was murder."

"Yeah." He wiped a spot off the butcher-block top with his thumb. "You were right, but you never said why you thought so."

"It was a few things," I said. "One being why she was on the Aural Gorge bridge when she was afraid of heights."

"Abby was afraid of heights?"

"According to Quinn, she was. She was deathly afraid of bridges in particular. She said there was no way Abby would have willfully been up there. Besides the fear of heights, Abby knew those woods inside and out. She would know to avoid the dangers of the bridge and the gorge in the bad weather."

"Even if she was dehydrated from being sick all night?"

I explained how Vince's hex had worn off, so that theory wasn't likely. "But ultimately, it was her hat that made me think she'd been murdered."

"The hat?"

"I own one just like it, and it takes some effort to pull it on and off. It's not likely it came off on its own. So either Abby threw it off, or someone else threw it off." I let out a breath. "And in that weather, it doesn't seem likely Abby would have done it."

Nick's deep brown eyes widened. "Well, I don't know why she was on the bridge—yet—but she was not alone. Someone hit her in the back of the head with a thick branch. Whether she was dropped, or pushed over the railing afterward, or fell because of the blow to her head, I don't know. There were splinters in her wound, and the branch was found not far from her body. I suspect there had been a struggle and that the hat came off *before* Abby fell. Because there's not a drop of blood on the hat itself, and there would have been if she'd been wearing it when she was hit."

As I processed what he was saying, all I could picture was Abby's face as she left for her warm-up run. Her smile. The twinkle in her eyes. Who could have done such a thing to her? Why? "What now?"

"Techs are combing the bridge and the area around it. The snowfall . . ." He sighed. "It's been a challenge. No footprint evidence, and sifting through the snow for fibers and hairs is near-impossible. Abby's clothes have been sent to the lab for analysis, but the storm may have destroyed any usable evidence. Her cellphone is locked, and without the code, we can't access it. The warrant for the phone records should be ready tomorrow, but it could take days for the phone company to get the information to us."

So he didn't have much to go on. It was disheartening to hear, but I'd investigated many cases where the killer's behavior, rather than the evidence, had led to an arrest. I hoped Nick and I would be able to find that potential error. Soon. "What did Ben have to say for himself?"

"Not much. He was . . . evasive. Told me a little about a lot. But not a lot about what I really needed to know. Then he lawyered up. Oh, one thing was especially interesting. He claims he and Abby didn't have a fight Friday night. Only the argument Saturday morning at the race."

"Have you found anyone who can verify there *was* a fight?" It was entirely possible the late night fight had been only village gossip—and had no merit whatsoever.

"Not yet, but I haven't looked too hard. I will now."

I had to remember the investigation was only hours old. "Did Ben tell you he and Abby were planning to elope on Tuesday?"

I'd called Nick earlier and left a message to let him know that particular piece of news, along with the news about Joe and the ledgers.

"He didn't say anything to me about an elopement, and I didn't get your call about it until after he left, so I couldn't ask him. We're trying to get him back in for more questions, but his lawyer is stonewalling."

"Did Ben give you an alibi at least?"

"Said he last saw Abby at the trailhead and confirmed they argued about her running the race. He said she ran off onto the trail, and he went back to the village."

"That jibes with what Quinn told me as well. Did you get any other corroboration?"

"Plenty of people claimed to have seen Ben around, but no one can pinpoint a specific time until seeing him at the race's starting line. But let's just say Quinn is right. That Ben did go back to the tent. He could have easily turned right back around again and gone after Abby."

"True."

"How long would it have taken to backtrack, find Abby, get her onto the Gorge Trail somehow, attack her, and get back to the starting line before the race started? Was there time?"

"You're forgetting how fast Ben is. If he put some effort into it, he could run a mile in less than four minutes. Which probably isn't likely with the conditions and terrain, so I'll give him six minutes just getting to the bridge and back. Abby left the tent about fifteen minutes before the race, so there's eight minutes or so to lure and attack. Plenty of time."

"I wish I found someone who could rule him out as a suspect. It would make my job a whole lot easier."

My skin tingled when he said "wish" but the sensation faded quickly. I couldn't grant Nick's wishes any more than my own. He'd once been mortal, but after he married Melina, a Wishcrafter, and she told him of the Craft, he'd been adopted into our culture, becoming a Halfcrafter. Half mortal, half Crafter. In his case, half mortal, half Wishcrafter.

The penalty for a witch telling a mortal of their powers was losing them. A large price to pay for falling in love, but a price Crafters deemed necessary so witches would take protecting their heritage seriously. Loose lips came with a big penalty, and usually a lot of thought went into the decision. Witches who told potential spouses were usually ones who would rather not keep such a big part of themselves from someone they loved. And keeping the secret took a toll. Most of those relationships failed quickly.

Nick didn't have any powers as a Halfcrafter, but he was allowed to know all the ins and outs of our ways, and that knowledge allowed him to raise Mimi as Wishcrafter. She was carrying on her mother's legacy.

"I'm going to check with Vince about surveillance footage. Starla's idea, and it's a good one. Because if anyone has an eye on the goings-on in this village, it's Vince."

"Very true."

I wanted to talk to him more about the case, the ledgers Abby had given me, Joe's anger, Quinn's dodgy behavior, and about Duncan, but when I heard steps on the stairs, I went back to ladling stew. There was plenty of time later tonight to nitpick every detail.

"Is dinner almost ready?" Mimi asked, striding into the kitchen. Dark spiral curls bounced around her face. "Because Aunt Ve is suggesting baby names to Harper, and Harper looks like she wants to jump out the window. We need a distraction, fast."

Most of the time Mimi seemed like she was thirteen going on forty. She was more mature than most adults I knew. She had an endless quest for knowledge that shone in her brown eyes, was whip-smart, had a quick laugh, and I loved her more than words could say.

I handed Mimi the tray with three crocks of soup on it and half the baguette. "Here you go. Ask Ve about piña coladas to change the subject. I'll be up in a minute with some drinks and to check the lock on the window."

Mimi laughed. "Gotcha. Can you even believe we're having a baby? A little Harper. She's going to be so cute."

We. It said a lot about our family. Harper wasn't alone in all she was going through. Not by a long shot.

"She?" Nick asked.

"It has to be a girl," Mimi said, heading for the staircase. "It just has to be."

I filled a crock for Nick and handed it to him, then put the last soup bowl back into the cabinet.

"Not hungry?" he asked.

"Lost my appetite."

"Because of Abby?"

"Because of a lot of things. It's been a long day."

"The longest," he agreed, watching me intently. "Tomorrow has to be better."

I was thinking it couldn't possibly get worse.

But then had the sinking feeling it just might.

Chapter Twelve

Early Sunday, I skipped my usual morning jog to enjoy a leisurely breakfast with Nick and to entertain a bored Harper. She wasn't used to downtime, especially not lately. I made a mental note to stop by her place to pick up some books. If there was one thing that would perk up her spirits, it was reading. Dennis Goodwin was due to stop by to see her in another few hours, and I hoped to be home by then. I had a few errands to run beforehand.

The first being a stop at the Witch's Brew for coffee before I met with Glinda Hansel at the Bewitching Boutique. It was half past ten when I headed out, and sunbeams set the village alight in sparkles as they danced across snowbanks and snowcapped trees.

Despite the cheerful weather, anxiety had taken root on my emotional state. Between thinking about Abby's case and worrying about Harper, I hadn't slept well. I'd been up early, studying the photocopies of the ledgers that Abby had given me, and trying yet again to see what had caused her to think she'd made an error. Everything looked fine to me. I was usually good with spreadsheets and accounting so I felt as though I was missing something obvious, especially given Joe's reaction to Abby taking the ledgers from the store. But for the life of me I couldn't figure out what it was. I'd left the ledgers with Harper in case she wanted to puzzle it out while I was gone, since she was itching for something productive to do.

Somewhere nearby a squirrel chattered loudly, and I picked up the *chick, chick* of a cardinal as well. Temperatures were on the rise as I crossed the village green, and at this warming rate it wouldn't be long before all the snow melted. As I walked along, I found I was actually looking forward to seeing Glinda and finding out why she wanted to hire me. Because sometime during my sleepless night I'd realized why her behavior seemed so odd yesterday.

She'd been happy.

Truly happy.

It hadn't been easy for her getting there. Especially with a mother like Dorothy, whose wickedness tended to exemplify everything Glinda had turned away from in the past year.

I jumped and let out a yip as snow toppled from a branch, plopping in front of me. Then I laughed at my reaction, hoping no one had seen me. But it just proved how on edge I was after yesterday's events. And as I crossed the street in front of the coffee shop, my thoughts went again to Abby Stillwell.

In these quiet moments, I kept picturing her fighting for her life. Had her attacker snuck up on her? Or had she met someone along the trail? Another runner? If she'd been alone, she might not have noticed anyone approach. After all, she'd been running, and every step of hers would have been loud as her feet hit the snowpack. Then there was her breathing and the pulse in her ears and the wind to take into consideration. Plus, she was wearing a hat. It was entirely possible someone could have taken her by surprise.

But she was a Vitacrafter. She should have been able to sense the danger around her, no matter the circumstances. And though she was no longer an Olympic caliber racer, she was still fast. She should have been able to get away.

"Darcy! Good to see you. Are you going inside?"

Noelle Quinlan had come up behind me, and I nearly jumped out of my skin yet again. My feet slipped on the slushy sidewalk, and I shot my arms out for balance.

Noelle grabbed my sleeve to help steady me. "Whoa, there!"

Her choice of words made me wonder if she knew how much she resembled a horse. I hadn't always thought so—not until Dorothy Hansel Dewitt had pointed it out last spring while ridiculing her. But now it was all I could see every time I bumped into Noelle. Curse that Dorothy. With Noelle's dark hair, which was usually pulled back into a ponytail, long face, wide smile with big bright white teeth, and strong jaw, she was beautiful, to be sure, but there was no denying an equine similarity.

"Are you okay?"

"Fine, fine. Thanks. Just lost in my thoughts." I stepped away from the door so someone could go inside.

"I can only imagine. It's probably impossible for Nick not to bring his work home with him. It's a shame about Abby. Truly terrible. A tragedy."

Little did Noelle know it wasn't just Nick who brought his work home. As a mortal, she had no idea I was a witch, let alone an investigator for the Craft. "Did you know her well?" I asked, not wanting to miss an opportunity to learn more about Abby. So I could figure out who might have wanted her dead.

"Only as a client," she said. "Sweet woman. I can't imagine who would want to hurt her. When I met with her last week she was all smiles, full of love and light."

Her sentence sank in, and I tensed. "Last week? Was she a *recent* client?"

Noelle was the top real estate agent in the village. She possessed boundless energy, a perpetually chipper attitude, an over-the-top work ethic, and she seemed to know *everyone*. All those qualities had launched her company, Oracle Realty, to the top of the best agencies in the state.

"Yes. We signed the paperwork to list her house last week. She'd requested holding the listing until the middle of this week."

After the elopement. That made sense, I supposed. But Abby selling her house was one more thing that had taken me by surprise. I'd spent a portion of every single day with Abby last week, and she hadn't said a word about listing her house for sale.

Why the intense secrecy?

Noelle lifted an eyebrow. "Do you happen to know who her next of kin is? I know her parents passed when she was younger and she didn't have siblings. But maybe an aunt, uncle? Did Nick say?"

Noelle was *always* working. "He didn't say, but since it's Quinn Donegal handling Abby's funeral arrangements, I doubt Abby had any close family. But you could ask Quinn. If anyone would know, it's her."

Noelle took out her phone and typed something into it. I presumed it was a reminder to check with Quinn. Houses in the village were a hot commodity.

But this news also made me wonder about Quinn. Had she known Abby was selling the house? And how soon was she now going to have to find another place to live? I figured she had time to find a new living situation. Even if Abby had a will, it could take quite a while to sort out her estate.

"Ladies," a male voice said from behind me, "is the quest for morning coffee so rampant the line is now forming outside?"

"No, we're just blocking the door." I shifted to the side so Vince could pass by and was grateful I hadn't jumped the way I had earlier. "How's your hand doing?"

"Still attached to my arm." His left hand was heavily bandaged from the base of his fingers to his wrist.

"Did you need stitches?" I asked.

"No need. 'It's just a flesh wound.'"

"*Monty Python and the Holy Grail*," I said, picking up that he was playing the movie quote game. And also that he was trying to change the subject. I tipped my head. "Did you even see a doctor?"

He rolled his eyes. "Don't be such a girl."

"Don't be such a stupid head. Get it looked at."

"Stupid head?" he asked. "That's the best you could do?"

"It's been a long day and a half."

Noelle cleared her throat as she put her phone away. "Sorry to interrupt your tiff, but I need to get inside. I didn't realize the time. I'm late for a meeting with Marcus."

Then her gaze cut to me as if she thought she'd said too much. Months later, and his and Harper's breakup was still the talk of the village.

I said, "Tell him hello from me."

"Oh, you can tell him yourself if you're coming in." She motioned with her chin. "He's right there."

I glanced over my shoulder. Sure enough, Marcus was sitting at a table near the counter, watching us. He still looked as miserable as he had the day before. I waved.

He waved back then quickly glanced away.

Vince said, "Is Marcus selling his house?"

Noelle gave Vince a once-over. "Are you in the market for a house, Vince?"

I wanted to know, too. Currently, he lived in the apartment above Lotions and Potions. Sure, it was small but it was plenty big enough for one person. And I noticed Noelle didn't mention Marcus's house was already under contract. She wasn't going to let a potential client slip out of her grasp so easily.

"I might be," Vince said.

Before I knew it, she'd whipped out a business card. "Do you have an agent representing you?"

"Not yet."

Out came Noelle's phone again, and I swear I saw dollar signs flash in her eyes, foreseeing a big commission in her future. And so much for being late to her meeting with Marcus. She seemed to have all the time in the world once she sensed a potential sale.

"You should give me your number too." She handed Vince the phone to punch it in himself. "So I can keep in touch. If you'd like to discuss me representing you, we can set up a meeting."

Vince looked like he was trying not to wince as he gripped the phone with his bad hand and said, "Why does this feel like some sort of covert way to get my number? I mean, if you want to ask me out, you should just go for it."

Confusion filled Noelle's eyes, briefly covering up the dollar signs. "What? Oh!" She laughed. "I get it. You're funny."

"But seriously," he said, handing the phone back to her. He grinned and gave an exaggerated wink.

Her cheeks flushed red and she chuckled. "I'll keep that in mind. Bye!"

She hurried into the coffee shop, but not before I saw her take another look at Vince. Assessing the potential, perhaps, in more ways than one.

I glanced at him once she was out of earshot. "Dorothy hates her, too, doesn't she?"

It wasn't really a question. I knew Noelle was on Dorothy's hate list—and had been since last spring when she considered Noelle competition for a TV host job that never materialized. It was right about the time Dorothy and I almost had a knock-down, drag-out catfight on the village green after she threatened to have my dog Missy put down.

"Can't I flirt without any hidden motivations?" he asked.

"I don't know. Can you?"

He laughed as he held open the door for me. "Probably not."

"Are you really looking for a house?" The scent of coffee, strong coffee, filled the air and my soul. I needed a heavy dose of caffeine if I was going to make it through the rest of this day.

"I could be," he said, stepping in line behind me. "One with a yard. I've been thinking about getting a dog."

"Big, small?"

"Why? You're not thinking about trying to pawn one of yours off on me, are you?"

"What? You don't like drool and tiny escape artists?"

"They're not high on my list, no." The line inched forward as he added, "A dog like Clarence, maybe."

A golden retriever. "Then yes, you need a yard. A big one. I'm meeting with Glinda right after this, by the way."

He adjusted his glasses. "So she finally got in touch with you."

"But she wouldn't say about what. Don't suppose you'd care to give me a hint?"

"Don't suppose I would."

I took another step forward. "Since I'm asking favors, I don't suppose you have surveillance footage of the village from yesterday morning, do you? From the cameras at Lotions and Potions?"

"Is this about Abby?"

He didn't beat around the bush in asking, so I didn't in answering. "It is."

"Something in particular you're looking for?"

"Not so much something as someone."

"Ben?"

"Mostly. Though footage from the whole morning would be good to have."

"I'll see what I can do."

The line was moving fairly steadily. As we neared where Marcus and Noelle sat with their heads bent over paperwork, I nudged Vince's arm and whispered, "Ask me how Harper's feeling. Ask me loudly." I motioned with little jerks of my head toward Marcus.

With a furrowed brow, Vince stared at me as if I had six heads that were all having spasms at the same time. "You're pressing your luck today."

"*Please*," I added.

I heard a low groan before he said, quite loudly, "How's Harper feeling today, Darcy? Any better?"

I almost laughed at his stilted kill-me-now inflection but managed to keep a straight face. I used what Evan, a theater buff, would call my "chest voice" to make sure my words would carry over to Marcus. "Sadly, no. It turns out she's really sick. The doctor's making her take a week off to rest. And she has to get daily injections for a while. She's staying with me until she's feeling better."

True concern flashed in Vince's eyes. "Really?"

"Really. Dr. Goodwin said it's a good thing she saw him when she did, because the disorder she has can be fatal if not treated." I lowered my voice so only he could hear me. "She's going to be okay."

"So, basically, that food poisoning she had *saved* her life?"

I frowned at him. It might actually be true, but still. "Only you could turn that around."

He grinned. "It's a talent."

"Next," the woman behind the counter said.

I stepped up and placed my order, feeling Marcus's gaze on me the whole time.

I waited for Vince to order and made sure I kept my gaze on him as we walked out.

Outside, Vince said, "I'm guessing Harper doesn't know what you're doing with Marcus?"

I glanced at up him and blinked innocently. "What am I doing?"

He laughed as he walked off.

My interference might be wrong, but it was past time someone lured Marcus back into Harper's life.

And that someone was me.

Chapter Thirteen

G linda was already seated on a love seat in the Bewitching Boutique when I arrived. Godfrey Baleaux waved me inside after I ignored the "Closed" sign on the door and knocked on the glass.

"Darcy, dear!" he said, coming toward me to give me a big bear hug. "Let me look at you."

The assessment wasn't because he hadn't seen me in a while. Or to gauge the status of my health. No. He was evaluating my outfit, judging whether it needed to be changed. Immediately. As a Cloakcrafter, he not only had the ability to swap out my clothes out for another outfit with the wave of a hand, but also felt as though it was his right to enforce his fashionable opinions. Proclaiming himself to be my fairy godfather, I'd lost count of all the times he'd altered my wardrobe.

"Look all you want," I said, handing Glinda a coffee from the tray I carried. It also held a skinny caramel latte for Godfrey and a bagged pastry for Pepe and Mrs. P, who lived in the walls of the shop. I glanced around, looking for them. The small arched door notched into the baseboard was firmly closed.

Glinda saw my glance. "They're actually at your place. Went to see Harper." She held up the coffee. "Thanks for this."

"Yes, do tell all about poor Harper," Godfrey said as he circled me while scratching the white hairs of his neatly clipped beard.

He'd slimmed down a bit over the last year but seemed to be happily holding steady at his current weight, which was probably more than his doctor wanted to see but less than Santa Claus territory.

I shrugged out of my peacoat and said, "What have *you* heard about Harper?"

"What haven't we heard?" Godfrey said, *tsk*ing as he eyed my utilitarian snow boots.

"Don't even think about it," I warned him. "They're warm and waterproof. The snow is knee-deep out there in most places."

Dismissing the boots' practicality with a huff, he continued his inspection. I was glad I'd taken care to choose items he'd given to me in the past—skinny jeans and a black sweater so soft I wished it were a blanket.

"I heard Harper was near-death. Days to live," Glinda said dramatically.

"I heard you carried her in your arms through the snow and wind to your house," Godfrey said with a gleam in his eyes.

Glinda snapped her fingers. "I heard that one, too, but in the version I heard, you were carrying Harper while she was carrying her cat, which was howling pitifully."

"This village," I said on a sigh as I sat next to Glinda.

"And," she said, her gaze meeting mine, "I heard Harper was pregnant."

"Pregnant? As in a *coochie-coochie-coo* baby? Oh my!" Godfrey's eyes widened. "Is that true, Darcy? Is any of it true?"

I took a deep breath—I should have been better prepared for the pregnancy question. I'd known the village would find out fairly quickly, but I hadn't expected it to be *this* quickly. I faced Glinda. "Where did you hear Harper was pregnant?"

She sipped her coffee. "Mimi texted me last night."

I should have figured that one out on my own. The two were close. Glinda had been a dear friend of Mimi's mom, Melina, and was like an aunt to Mimi. Practically family. But if Mimi had said something to Glinda about it, I figured she had to have asked Harper first. Mimi wouldn't have gone against Harper's wishes.

"Then it's true?" Godfrey asked, his hands over his heart. "Is that why Harper is ill?"

"She is pregnant. But . . ." In one drawn-out breath, I told them all about Harper's illness, the precarious nature of the pregnancy, and to keep the news under wraps until further notice.

There was a tremor in Glinda's hand as she set the coffee cup on her thigh. "I don't suppose you know if the baby is a girl?" she asked quietly, almost under her breath.

"It's too soon to know. Why?"

"Oh my," Godfrey said, holding his fingertips to his lips as though wanting to bite his nails. He sat down, then stood up again. "I didn't think of that. Oh dear."

I didn't know what to think of their odd reactions. I scooted to the edge of my seat. "Think of what? What am I missing?"

Godfrey waved a hand. "It is not for us to say. You must ask your mother."

I immediately stiffened and felt my eyes go wide. Did I have any memory cleanse in my tote bag? I couldn't remember. All I knew was that Glinda didn't know about my mother. Not that she was alive (well, kind of) and certainly not that she was the Elder. I had wanted to tell her many times, but it wasn't my place. Craft rules. Glinda was going to need a memory cleanse as soon as possible.

"Breathe," Glinda said, patting me on the back. "You're going to pass out if you hold your breath much longer. I know all about your mother."

I looked at her. "You do?"

"For a couple of months now."

"You didn't say anything . . ." No one had said anything. It would have been nice if someone could have mentioned something. For the love, as Harper would say.

"It's not an easy subject to bring up," Glinda said. "Oh, hey, Darcy, I know your mom, who died when you were a little girl, is the matriarch of the Craft."

Godfrey chuckled.

I shot him a dismayed look.

His chuckle turned into a cough as he focused on a piece of lint on his suit vest.

It suddenly occurred to me Godfrey knew Glinda was aware of the Elder's identity. It further bolstered my suspicion that he was one of the Coven of Seven. There had been many times he had knowledge of what was going on in the witchy world before anyone else.

I held up a hand. "I need a second to wrap my head around all this." I took a deep breath. If there was one thing I knew for certain: If Glinda knew about my mother, my mother had allowed her to know. And if she was okay with it, then so was I. A second later, I said, "Okay, so what's this about Harper's baby? What does it matter if the baby is a girl?"

Godfrey shook his head. "Talk to your mother. It's all I can say."

I hated knowing I'd been left out of the loop on something obviously quite important. "All right, I will."

I glanced at Glinda. "But right now, I'm here. I still don't know why."

The color was slowly returning to her face, and I tried my best to forget the way she'd appeared moments ago. The fear.

Over a baby.

I didn't get it.

Forcing the thoughts out of my head, I waited for an explanation from Glinda about why she'd asked to meet with me.

A smile slowly spread across her face. "I need to use you, Darcy."

"Use me?"

"As a cover."

"For?"

She beamed. "Wedding planning."

It took me a moment to understand. "You and Liam are getting married!"

She laughed. "Yes! We want to have a quickie wedding the day after Valentine's Day. Next Saturday. We want it to be a surprise ceremony, though. No one knows but you, Godfrey, and Vince. Oh, and Will. He'll be officiating."

Will Chadwick, Liam's brother. He'd officiated village weddings before. He had a theatrical flair that made his officiating feel more like a stage show than a solemn event. No doubt it was going to be an entertaining evening.

"I'd like to keep the ceremony a secret until the night of our Begin These Wood-Birds party."

She used air quotes around the name of the party.

"Begin These Wood-Birds party?" I asked.

Looking like a long-suffering partner, she said, "Liam's idea."

"Let me guess, something to do with Shakespeare?" His family was the one that ran the Shakespeare society.

"Good guess," Glinda said with a smile.

"It's from *A Midsummer's Night Dream*," Godfrey supplied. " 'Good morrow, friends. Saint Valentine is past. Begin these wood-birds but to couple now?' " He supplied a flourished bow when he finished.

Archie would have been proud of his rendition. I figured the quote had something to do with birds pairing up so it was appropriate, I supposed, for a wedding.

"Obviously, the wedding is kind of a spur of the moment idea. So, we tried to figure out what kind of party we could throw as a diversion. Neither of us have birthdays soon, and there aren't any grand celebrations on the calendar either. Valentine's Day was it. Unless we wanted to wait a month until St. Patrick's Day. And we don't."

"Is there a reason for the rush?" I asked, eyeing her up and down.

"What? Oh, no! No, no. Actually, we don't want to have kids." She glanced at me as though bracing to defend the decision.

While this was surprising news to me, she should have known I wouldn't judge her choice. "Clarence *is* quite a handful on his own."

Relief flooded her features, softening them. "That he is. And . . . I don't want to be a mother like mine."

"You wouldn't be," I said, suddenly feeling a depth of sadness for her.

"You don't know that. I don't know either. No one knows. I don't want to risk it." She added, "I *can't* risk it."

"How does your mother feel about the no-kids decision?" Godfrey asked with a pensive look in his eye.

"How does she feel?" She tapped her chin as if debating. "I'd say it straddles the line between rage and hysteria. *I* wouldn't have told her anything, but at Christmas she cornered Liam and asked him about potential grandkids. He made the mistake of telling her the truth. Which is why she's done everything in her power to break us up over the past two months."

Even though I knew all this—Glinda had already told me what was happening—I still felt a ripple of shock at her words.

Glinda took a sip of her coffee. "And it's only been escalating. She's all-out declared war on Liam. She's even asked Vince about hexes."

"No," Godfrey said.

"Impotency, baldness, genital warts. You name it."

Godfrey flinched and crossed his legs.

Glinda went on. "So far Vince hasn't acted on her behalf, and she hasn't taken the impetus to dabble in dark magic herself. But I can see the writing on the wall. It's only a matter of time before she does, because what Dorothy wants, Dorothy gets."

"So you're planning to cut her off at the pass by getting married," I said.

"Exactly. We'd been talking about getting married this summer, but now we don't want to wait. Maybe when we're married she'll get it through her thick skull that we aren't breaking up, no matter what she says or does."

"It's a brilliant plan," Godfrey said.

"Only if she doesn't find out," Glinda added. "My mother absolutely cannot know about this wedding or she will stop it from happening, one way or another."

"My lips are sealed," I said.

"Mine too." Godfrey made a zipping motion over his mouth.

"Thanks. Anyway," Glinda said with a deep sigh, "if there's anything good to have come of her trying to break up Liam and me, it's that Vince and I have bonded over her controlling nature. She hates his girlfriend, too."

Godfrey raised a perfectly arched eyebrow. "Girlfriend?"

"Stef from the Sorcerer's Stove," I said.

"Cute," he said approvingly.

"Why does Dorothy hate her?" I asked Glinda. "I mean, is there a reason? They haven't dated long, so it can't be about grandkids, can it?"

"Stef is mortal," Glinda said simply. "And Dorothy is as elitist as witches come. She doesn't want Vince getting attached. She's not overly fond of mortals as a whole."

Godfrey started laughing, great big bellows of laughter. "Poor, poor Sylar. The man had no idea what he was getting into, did he?"

Sylar Dewitt, Dorothy's husband, was mortal.

Glinda smiled. "She's had those divorce papers sitting in her lingerie drawer for nearly six months."

"Why hasn't she filed them?" I asked.

"Because then she might have to admit, even if it's only to herself, that Ve pulled her strings, manipulating her to take Sylar off her hands. There's nothing my mother despises more than looking foolish. Well, except maybe for your family. No offense."

"None taken. She does realize Vince grew up thinking he was mortal? And that by putting down mortals, she's essentially saying *he* wasn't good enough before he learned the truth about his Craft?"

"If she realizes, she doesn't care."

It wasn't a surprising statement. Dorothy cared little for anyone other than herself.

"Did I ever tell you how she once tried to burn down my house?" Godfrey asked.

"Yes," Glinda and I said in unison.

Dorothy had a bit of pyromaniac in her. She'd been lighting fires, figuratively and literally, around the village for years. Somehow she'd always gotten away with it.

He chuckled. "Just making sure." More seriously, he added, "Do you have a protection spell on your house, Glinda?"

It was a good question. If Dorothy found out Glinda was getting married at her home, I wouldn't put it past her to burn the place down to prevent the wedding from happening.

"I do. Do you?" she asked him.

"Ever since the first time she tried to burn it down."

He looked at me, and I in turn looked at Glinda. "I'm covered."

The protection on my house had come in the form of a beautiful besom Glinda had gifted me at Nick's and my housewarming party.

There were additional protections in place as well, courtesy of Andreus and my mother. My house was a veritable Fort Knox.

"Why not elope?" I asked. It seemed to me eloping would be a safer choice. For everyone.

Glinda said, "We considered it. But I want our friends and family there. I want the ceremony and the white dress and the cake and the flowers. Which is why I need your help, Darcy. It's too risky for me to go about this on my own. My mother's already suspicious that I'm hiding something from her," Glinda said. "Mother's intuition or something. So we'll need to be careful. I mean, if you agree to help you have to know there are risks involved . . ."

She and Godfrey both looked at me expectantly.

Laughing, I said, "I'll help. How can I resist? I'm guessing our first item of business is your dress since we're here?"

Glinda said, "I know it's short notice, Godfrey."

"Pshaw. I can create wedding dresses in my sleep. What do you have in mind? Come, come, we should go back to the workroom."

Her face lit again as she stood up. "Something ethereal. Long, flowy. Cap sleeves or sleeveless."

"Veil?" he asked, leading the way.

"I like the idea, but I don't know if I want the weight on my head all night," she said, then turned to look at me. "What do you think?"

"I think—"

I was cut off by a knock at the door. Quinn Donegal offered up a hesitant wave when we all looked her way.

"Just a second, my dears. Let me take care of this," Godfrey said as he strode to the door and pulled it open. "Quinn, this is a surprise."

Glinda and I sat back down as Quinn came inside.

"I'm so sorry to interrupt," she said, "but I was walking by, and I saw you in here, and I know that Abby was supposed to be meeting with you today to pick up her wedding dress, and . . . I couldn't stop myself from knocking. I'm sorry. I just hate the thought of leaving Abby's dress here, as if it's waiting for her to come back." Tears spilled down her cheeks.

"Ah," he said, handing her a handkerchief. "Sit, sit. Would you like some coffee?"

Quinn dolefully glanced our way and said, "Actually, I don't have much time. I'm on my way to a meeting. I just . . . What's going to happen to the dress?"

Quinn appeared to have wilted overnight. Her shoulders slumped, her face was pale. It was as though life was slowly draining out of her. I had called her this morning to set up a time later today to hand over the ledgers. I made a mental note to bring some soup with me. She looked in desperate need of nourishment.

Godfrey said, "Nothing like this has ever happened before. The dress is bought and paid for, so it technically belongs to Abby's estate."

"I didn't know Abby was getting married," Glinda said.

"On Tuesday." Godfrey wrung his hands. "It was a secret, but now that she's gone, I suppose everyone will know soon enough. The wedding was to be on Tuesday, at the Marblehead city hall."

Salem, I knew, didn't offer civil ceremonies at its city hall, so it was no surprise Abby and Ben had looked elsewhere. I was starting to wonder if quickie weddings were the going trend. As a soon-to-be-bride, I understood the appeal. A lot.

Godfrey walked over to a white garment bag hanging on a hook by the workshop door. He unzipped the bag as he brought it over to where Quinn stood.

Inside was a simple, yet elegant champagne-colored silk cocktail-length sheath with a sweetheart neckline and thin pearl-studded belt. It was lovely, and I suddenly teared up thinking about how Abby was never going to be able to wear it.

Silence lingered before I said, "Maybe it can be donated to a good cause?"

"Or perhaps she can be buried in it?" Glinda added.

We all stared at her.

"What?" she asked. "Too morbid?"

"No, no," Godfrey said. "It's quite romantic if one thinks about it."

"I don't kn—" Quinn started to say.

She was interrupted by the door being thrown open.

Drolly, Godfrey said, "I should have locked the door."

"What is going on in here?" Dorothy said loudly as she stomped over to us. "What is that?" She pointed at the wedding dress.

"Have you gone senile, old woman? It's a wedding dress," Godfrey said.

I thought he was pretty much asking for his house to be burned down by calling her old. There might not be a worse insult in her book.

Dorothy jabbed a finger at him. "Godfrey Baleaux, you did not just call me old. So help me."

Wisely, Quinn took a step away from Dorothy. Out of arm's reach.

"I did," he said. "So help you." He quickly zipped the garment bag and pushed it into Quinn's arms. "Whatever you decide, I'm sure Abby would agree with. Go on now, before you're late for your meeting."

Her eyes were filled with confusion and a tinge of fear as she glanced at a fuming Dorothy.

"Come back if I can be of any more service," he said, promptly ushering her to the door.

"I, ah . . . Thank you." She lowered her voice, but it still carried. "Do you want me to call the police?"

He chuckled. "No need. I have this under control." In a stage whisper, he added, "She's off her meds right now."

"Oh." Quinn glanced over his shoulder at Dorothy. "Okay, then." With one last look and a quick wave to Glinda and me, she walked out.

"*Meds*?" Dorothy asked, somehow turning the single syllable into three.

"What other explanation could there be for such an intrusion?" he asked. "Nay, *invasion*?" His arms flailed. "You come barging in here like a witch gone mad . . . There is no other explanation I can deduce for such behavior unless you've well and truly lost your mind. Which, sadly, has been a long time coming." He bowed his head. "Let us have a moment to mourn your sanity."

Dorothy fisted her hands and let out a guttural cry of frustration, then pointed a finger at him again, then shook her head as if deciding he wasn't worth the effort. Slowly, she pivoted, aiming her pointed finger—and her sights—on Glinda.

Uh-oh.

"What's going on here, Glinda? Explain," the finger wagged between Glinda and me, "*this*."

Dorothy's white-blonde hair framed her florid face, and her bright red lipstick oddly complemented her angry complexion. Beneath a long coat, a skintight dress hugged her hourglass figure, but if she kept hyperventilating the way she was, I was afraid she was going to a wardrobe malfunction of epic proportions, considering the way her enormous breasts were heaving.

I could feel the tension radiating off Glinda, so I spoke up. "This," I said, gesturing between us, "is us consulting with Godfrey about my wedding gown. Glinda's helping me decide on embellishments." I smiled brightly. "Like, do I really need crystals *and* beads?"

Dorothy opened her mouth, then held up a hand and took a deep breath. "Why is Glinda helping *you*?"

"It's what bridesmaids do. Harper and Mimi and Starla have already given their very vocal opinions. Trust me, those three in a room full of chiffon, organza, lace, and cotton is not a good idea. I really need Glinda to be the voice of reason."

Godfrey coughed. "Hello? That's why you have me. There will be *no* cotton. Mark my words." He shuddered.

Dorothy laughed, a high-pitched cackle. "Glinda? As your bridesmaid? I don't think so."

"I do think so," Glinda said, standing up.

"Well, I don't," Dorothy said, her gaze burning. "No. Nope. No way. Not happening."

"You don't get to decide, Mother," she said. "And you're embarrassing me in front of my friends."

"Friends?" She scoffed. "Since when?"

"For a while now," she said. "You've just been too busy fanning the flames of your hatred to see it."

"Flames." Godfrey laughed. "I see what you did there. Good one."

Dorothy glanced at Godfrey as though thinking about setting *him* on fire, then said, "It's time to leave, Glinda. Let's go."

"Darcy and I aren't done here."

"Oh, you're done. Come on."

Glinda didn't budge.

The redness intensified in Dorothy's plump cheeks, and I thought that maybe her head was about to pop off.

She stomped in her stilettos. "I. Said. Let's. Go."

I was starting to think perhaps Quinn should have called the police, because it felt as though bloodshed was imminent.

Slumping in defeat, Glinda turned to me. "I'll be in touch."

Dorothy grabbed her hand and yanked. "No she won't."

Glinda gave me a conspiratorial nod before allowing her mother to tote her out of the store.

Once the door closed behind them, I said, "What in the world was that about?"

Godfrey said solemnly, "Battle lines, Darcy. Battle lines."

It seemed to me Dorothy had been sketching those lines for a while now, but she'd just set them in stone.

I walked over to the window and was surprised—and utterly confused—to see Dorothy laughing it up, practically doing a jig, while clapping Glinda on the back. As if being congratulated for a job well done.

Glinda glanced back, caught me watching, and quickly looked away.

Battle lines.

Hmm. Opposition often used spies.

And just like that, I couldn't help thinking it was possible Glinda was using me in more than one way.

Chapter Fourteen

Stewing about Dorothy and Glinda, I walked along the village square on my way to Ben Bryant's apartment. So far he'd been ignoring my calls, which put me in the horrible position of having to drop in unannounced. It also made me wonder why he wouldn't want to get talking with me out of the way. He knew, as a Crafter, that he couldn't put it off for long. If he didn't speak with me soon, he'd have to appear before the Elder, where he'd not only have to answer all the questions I'd planned to ask but also face consequences for avoiding me. Which could be as severe as his powers being suspended . . . or even revoked.

I paused in front of Balefire, which occupied the retail space below Ben's apartment. There was a sign on the door that read "Closed for Death in the Family", but the lights were on, and I saw silhouettes in the storage room at the back of the shop.

I cupped my eyes and pressed my face to the door. I couldn't see who was in the storage area, but decided it ultimately didn't matter. I would need to speak with all the Bryants eventually.

With the hope that Ben was in there, I knocked on the door and waited. And waited. I knocked more loudly and was rewarded with a perturbed glance from Joe Bryant as he stuck his head out of the storeroom.

What looked like resignation crossed his face as he strode toward the door, flipped the lock, and let me in.

"Darcy," he said. "Wish I could say I was surprised to see you, but I'm not."

He was wearing a pair of dark athletic shorts, short-sleeve tee, a ball cap that covered hair cut military-short, and a look that said I wasn't welcome. My skin tingled at hearing wish, but there was no wish to be granted here. His wish hadn't been phrased in the proper manner of "I wish that" or "I wish for."

I stepped inside. There was a certain scent to the store, a mix of new clothing, rubber, and leather. One half of the store was dedicated to running. Apparel, shoes, nutrition. The other half was for all other sports—a small selection to be sure, but big enough for the basics.

"Who is it?" Lucinda called from the back room.

I recognized her voice, with its gravelly sound.

"Darcy Merriweather," he said loudly to her. He looked at me. "I'm just on my way out. Anything I can do for you before I leave?"

"I'll be right out," Lucinda yelled back.

"I do have some questions . . . about Abby's death," I said to Joe. "And about those ledgers."

"Can the questions wait?"

"Until?" I asked.

He glanced at his watch—one of those big round GPS models—all the Bryants seemed to wear them—then shook his head. "Today is jam-packed. Tomorrow morning might be better. Oh, wait, Aine has a doctor's appointment in the morning."

"How about the afternoon? After the appointment? It would be good if I could speak to Madison as well."

He rubbed a hand over his dark beard. "You should call her to set it up."

"Maybe you should just pick a time," I said, meeting his gaze.

Irritation sparked in his blue eyes. "Three o'clock? Here?"

"I'll be here."

"What did I miss?" Lucinda asked, coming out from the back room.

"Darcy has questions," Joe said. "But I need to head out."

"Where to?" his mother asked.

He said, "You know, that thing."

That thing. Right. "Before you go," I said. "One question: How come you weren't on the starting line when the race went off yesterday morning? Where were you?"

"Bathroom," he said, shrugging. "No big deal."

"So close to the start of the race?" He was an experienced racer, one who spent nearly half his life perfecting his timing. When to eat breakfast. When to warm-up. Top athletes prized their spot at the starting line and little deterred them from claiming a space.

His eyes narrowed. "It wouldn't have been an issue except the portable restrooms were broken. Whose fault is that? Who hired the company?"

I saw what he was doing—deflecting—and didn't fall for it. Nor did I throw Vince under the bus, though he deserved it. I also recognized that Joe *could* have been delayed by the restrooms and wasn't, oh, tracking down Abby in the woods. I needed to find someone who could verify his whereabouts. "It was the company you chose last year and recommended to Abby to use this year as well."

I was about to throw in a question about the ledgers when he said, "I don't have time for this. I need to get going." He pulled open the door and practically ran out.

Without a coat. Without looking back.

"Quite a rush he's in," I said to Lucinda.

She cracked a smile. "He doesn't want to talk to you."

I couldn't help laughing. "Really? I never would have guessed. But why?"

She watched him sprint away. "Part of it is that he's upset Ben is a suspect in what happened to Abby. The other is that talking about what happened to Abby . . . makes it real? Know what I mean?"

"I understand the Abby part, but not about Ben. Talking to me can only help Ben's case. Unless . . ."

"He's not guilty," she said adamantly.

For a second, I saw the fire in her eyes that was often present when she'd raced as a younger woman. A total commitment to a goal. It was clear she fully believed her son was innocent.

Yet, was he? Sometimes mothers were blinded by motherly love.

"But," she said, "I see your point. I'll talk to Joe."

"I'd appreciate that." I decided to press my luck where her motherly love was concerned. "I don't suppose you know why Joe was so angry at Abby for taking the accounting ledgers from the store?"

"It was foolish for her to have taken them," she said. "There are a stack of invoices on Joe's desk from vendors who are expecting payments. Without the ledgers, Joe is going to have to delay disbursements. It's put him in a bad position."

"Surely the vendors will understand, after what happened to Abby."

"Goodwill only goes so far," she said. "People have families to feed."

I hated that what she said rang true. For some reason, I was ready to pin Abby's death on Joe. Maybe because of what Quinn had said earlier—he wasn't a nice person.

Was that the truth? Or had she been feeding me a line?

I glanced out the door. Joe was a dot in the distance. "Does Aine really have a doctor's appointment tomorrow morning?"

Lucinda shook her head. "No. She doesn't go back for another month, when her casts are due to be changed."

With that, I sided with Quinn's opinion of Joe. He hadn't needed to lie to my face. And using his daughter's medical issues as an excuse? Vile.

"Is Aine's treatment working?" I asked.

"It is. She'll be up and running in no time. I can't wait until she's old enough to start training. But, I need to be patient." She smiled. "That's a few years off."

I had the feeling Lucinda was already picturing Aine on an Olympic podium. No doubt, Joe and Madison had pictured it too, though I wondered which of Aine's Crafts was more dominant. Technically, she was a Cross-Crafter, a hybrid. She had both Joe's Vincicrafting in her as well as Madison's Terracrafting. One power would outshine the other, but only time would tell which.

I glanced around. "Is Ben here?"

"He left for a run about half an hour ago." She looked at her own monstrous watch. "He should be back soon. I'm free until then if you have any questions for me."

"I do. Thanks."

She gestured to two chairs near the shoe display. "Have a seat. Coffee? Tea? Water?"

"I'm fine, thanks."

Lucinda sat across from me. She was dressed in workout wear. Sweat-wicking leggings, a zippered sweatshirt left unzipped to show a Balefire training tee underneath, and ankle socks. Her sneakers looked new, but I could see the worn tread when she crossed her legs. Her short hair was pulled back into a tiny ponytail that accented high cheekbones and a wide jaw.

She was in better shape at sixty-something than I was at half her age.

I made a mental note to beef up my exercising regime, pronto.

Looking around, she said, "I thought staying busy in the shop today would keep my mind occupied."

I followed her gaze around the store, past the shelves of clothing, bins of socks, the display of hand and ankle weights, jump ropes, foam rollers, and resistance bands.

Her gaze came back to me. "Busy work. But it feels like Abby is here with me. I see her in every corner, by the register, stocking shoe boxes."

Busy work. Like Harper had done with her heartache. "In my experience, there's no escaping grief."

"Sadly, no, there's not." She took a deep breath. "What do you want to know?"

I appreciated that she didn't try to stall. I pulled a notebook and pen from my tote bag and glanced at the questions I'd been jotting down as they came to me. "I have some general questions and then some that are more specific. Right now, I'm fact-gathering, because nothing makes sense if I look at this case as a whole."

"I can barely wrap my head around what happened. It doesn't seem real."

"I guess that leads to my first question. Do you know if Abby had any enemies?"

"True enemies? Not that I can think of. As a competitive athlete, she had rivals, but she hasn't been racing much lately. The stress fracture she had years ago never healed quite right, and she'd been dealing with ligament issues lately as well. Her career was winding down. She'd been talking about opening a training center and starting to meet with people to make that happen."

Lucinda shook her head again as if realizing Abby's plans were never going to happen now. I thought about what she'd said about Abby's rivals. It didn't make sense for a competitor to want Abby out of the picture if she wasn't a racing threat anymore.

"I can't think of anyone else," Lucinda said. "Everyone liked Abby."

"What about Duncan Cole?" I asked.

Her lips pursed as though she tasted something sour. "Duncan? What about him?"

"As you undoubtedly know, he and Abby were a couple before he was let go from Balefire Racing. I heard it wasn't the smoothest breakup."

"It was a mess, that's what it was. Abby was heartbroken to learn, as we all were, that Duncan had been using illegal performance enhancing drugs. Doping. He denied it, then accused all of us of cheating because we were witches. He caused quite the scene, and we ended up having to memory cleanse him and three customers. It was terrible."

So, that had been the ruckus Glinda had heard about. "How did he know about the Craft?"

"Abby had told him months before the incident, thinking he was the love of her life." Lucinda scoffed.

It sounded to me as though Lucinda hadn't lost much sleep over losing him as a member of the team. "You didn't like Abby dating him."

It wasn't really a question. Her scoff had told me what I needed to know.

"I'm one of those old-fashioned witches who believe we shouldn't interdate or intermarry. Even friendships are iffy. But romantic relationships with mortals are almost always a bad idea and often end disastrously for witches."

I wanted to argue that love was worth the risk, but she had a point. The majority of relationships between a witch and a mortal ended badly.

She went on. "Abby never thought Duncan would tell anyone of the Craft, but she also never thought he'd dope. His lab results—and his behavior—proved otherwise. We have strict standards here at Balefire—there's no room for cheating. Vincicrafters might have a slight advantage being born as natural athletes, but we do not cheat. We work hard. Harder than most, because we want to prove we *earn* our wins, even if we're only proving it to ourselves and other witches. We had no choice but to let Duncan go."

"How did Abby react to what happened?"

"She felt doubly betrayed," Lucinda said. "And broke it off with him. At Abby's core was a deep sense of right and wrong. She lived her life by rules, and she didn't waiver if she believed in a cause. She couldn't wrap her head around his cheating. She was understandably heartbroken. And when he spoke openly and publicly about the Craft, it was a painful lesson for her on who to trust. She should never had told him about the Craft in the first place."

It suddenly made sense to me now why Abby hadn't sensed she was in danger yesterday—she'd lost her powers when she shared the Craft with Duncan.

If a witch lost his or her powers due to a Craft infraction, other witches might not know, unless that witch openly shared the information. But when a witch lost their powers due to being in a relationship with a mortal, it was usually common knowledge in the village, simply from word of mouth. It helped in the mortal's transition to a Halfcrafter. Yet I'd heard nothing about Abby losing her abilities. I wondered if that was because Duncan had exited the picture early on.

"Where is Duncan now?" I asked.

"He's gone on to do well on another racing team. He's not top tier, but he's up there."

"Still doping?"

"There's no way to know. I haven't heard any gossip, so it's possible he's not. Perhaps he learned his lesson."

"Does he live around here?" I hadn't been able to track down an address for him. Nick had taken over that search, since he had broader databases. I hadn't yet heard if he'd found Duncan's current location.

"Not anymore. Last I heard, he was on the White Mountaineer team, based out of New Hampshire."

I wrote that down. "Do you know why he might have been in the village yesterday morning?"

She paled. "He was *here*?"

"At the race." I pulled the photo of Ben making eye contact with Duncan out of my tote bag. "Ben didn't tell you?"

"No, he didn't."

She didn't sound pleased that she'd been left out.

She kept staring at the picture, then abruptly handed it back. "I have no idea why he was here. Do you think he had something to do with what happened to Abby?"

"I don't know yet. Has he been in contact with her that you know of?"

"No. As far as I know, no one's heard from him since the day he left the village."

I jotted a note, then asked, "What do you know about the fight Ben and Abby had the night before the race at the Sorcerer's Stove? Any idea what it was about?"

"At the pre-race dinner?"

I nodded.

She shook her head. "I didn't know they had an argument there." Lucinda absently added, "It's not like them to fight. They were an agreeable couple. Too agreeable sometimes, I thought."

Had the fight really taken place? Ben had denied it, yet it was hard to dismiss the gossip. If an argument had occurred, someone had to have seen it since news of it had made the rounds of the village. I wrote down the word "fight" then circled it. "How so?"

"Theirs seemed more of a friendly relationship." She twisted her hands. "What's that quote? There's always some madness in love? I didn't see the madness between them."

Madness. I'd understood the quote—about how being in love sometimes felt like you were losing your mind. Willingly. Love was quite the ride, one I was personally grateful for.

"But," she added, "there was no question they were happy. Content."

Contentedness was certainly enough to sustain a relationship, but now that I thought about it Abby had never shown that madness around me, either. It didn't mean they lacked the madness of it all, but were perhaps better at hiding it from those around them.

It didn't seem to me Lucinda knew Ben and Abby had planned to elope so I chose my words carefully. "I don't know Ben well, but Abby definitely seemed happy in the relationship." I tapped my pen, letting the ink bleed into the paper. "She even mentioned marriage potential once or twice," I lied.

"She did?" Lucinda let out a light laugh, as though she found the idea humorous. "As far as I know, they weren't that serious. It was more of a casual relationship. Companionship, really. When they started dating, Abby was just coming off her breakup with Duncan and made it clear she was still healing, and Ben's always been more focused on running than committing to a deep, long-lasting relationship."

It was an interesting assessment, but one that didn't hold water considering what I knew about the planned elopement. "I think it was more than that," I said as gently as I could.

Her eyebrows dipped, her forehead crinkled. "What exactly are you getting at, Darcy?"

I tapped my pen again, then met her gaze. "It's become apparent Abby and Ben had plans to elope this week. On Tuesday."

"No." She shook her head. "That's ridiculous."

"I saw the wedding dress myself when Quinn stopped by the Bewitching Boutique this morning while I was there. She confirmed their elopement plans. Abby had also ordered a cake from the Gingerbread Shack."

"I don't believe it," Lucinda said firmly.

"Maybe you should talk to Ben about it," I suggested.

"Oh, I will."

I looked at my notes and switched topics. "This is kind of a strange question, but do you know if Abby wore a wig sometimes?"

"A wig? Really?"

"It's one of those loose ends."

"Not that I know of." She rubbed her temples.

I looked up when I heard the bell on the door. I swiveled in my chair in time to see Ben come in, spot me, then head back out again. He looked like he was breaking land-speed records as he ran off.

I sighed.

Lucinda said, "I'll talk to him, too." She stood up. "Can we continue this another time, Darcy? I suddenly have a bit of a headache."

I gathered up my belongings. "I think I have enough for now. I'll let you know if I need anything else."

It took her a moment to respond, and I had the feeling she was lost in thought.

She finally said, "You know where to find me."

I circled around a display of high-energy running snacks. "Yes, but you're still faster than I am if you decide to run off too."

With a smile, she said, "Not that much faster on these old legs."

She was being modest. And kind, even after I'd ticked her off, so I didn't argue the point that she could probably lap me three or four times if we raced around the square. She walked me to the door.

I said, "Do you know yet when Abby's services will be?"

She said, "As of right now, a memorial service is being planned for tomorrow night here at the store, and a private funeral service will take place as soon as the medical examiner's office releases Abby's body."

"What time is the memorial service?"

"Five?" She rubbed her temples. "Six? I need to double check the time. Quinn has taken charge of everything, but . . ."

I waited.

"If you don't mind, Darcy, could you offer to assist Quinn? She volunteered to take on all the planning, but

I think she's in over her head with all the details. If she accepts your help, I'll cover your fees of course."

I wanted to ask why Lucinda didn't offer to help herself but held back. After her earlier comments about mortals, I had the feeling she probably didn't want much to do with Quinn.

"I can ask her." I was seeing her later today—to hand over the ledgers. Photocopies, of course. I had wanted to talk to her again, and they had been the perfect excuse. "I take it you don't want her to know you hired me?"

"Let's keep it between you and me. Our little secret."

"I'm meeting her later on, so I'll let you know her decision."

"Thanks, Darcy." She went to pull open the door, then stopped and faced me. "About Quinn . . ."

I tipped my head, waiting for her to finish. When she didn't say anything more, I prodded. "What about her?"

She took in a deep breath. "She and Abby were close. Very close. I'll tell you the absolute truth—Abby is the only reason Quinn has a job here. If it was up to me, she'd never have been hired in the first place."

"Because she's mortal?" I guessed.

"Yes. It's utterly stifling to have a mortal around constantly. But Abby hired her out of compassion, and how could I argue that? I've looked and looked for a reason to let Quinn go, but if I'm still being honest, she does a good job around here."

"Stifling aside."

"Yes," she said with a spark of humor in her eyes.

I wanted to ask how Quinn had come about being hired, but I didn't want to sidetrack Lucinda, since it seemed like she had something important to say. I could ask Quinn about the topic later on.

"Anyway, like I said, they're close." Lucinda rubbed her temples yet again. "But I've noticed, especially lately, moments when Quinn has looked at Abby with envy. Jealousy. She hides it well, but it's there. I even mentioned it to Abby once, but she laughed it off."

"Jealousy over what?" I asked.

"I don't know. Abby's athletic talent? Her looks? Quinn is so plain, after all. Abby's relationship with Ben? All the above? She's mortal, so I have no idea how their minds work."

"You think Quinn is interested in Ben?"

Her brow furrowed. "I felt as though the jealousy stemmed from Abby being in a relationship whereas Quinn was not. She's a bit of a loner. Another thing . . ."

I waited.

"She quit today, effective immediately. Said she was moving away. The timing seems strange to me, so soon after Abby's death. It's as if she's in a rush to get out of the village as quickly as possible when she's not breathed a word about moving before now."

I wasn't nearly as surprised at Quinn quitting as Lucinda seemed to be. Not after hearing how she felt about Quinn. It was more surprising to me why Quinn had stayed so long—she had to have sensed the tension when the older woman was around. But leaving the village was another matter altogether. "Thank you for letting me know."

She waved a hand and pulled open the door. "Thank *you* for letting me get that off my chest. It's probably nothing."

"Probably," I said.

Or it could be something.

Something big.

I needed to ask Angela Curtis about Quinn's alibi as soon as possible, and I was glad my next destination was Spellbound. "I'll look into it."

Lucinda acknowledged my statement with a bob of her head, and I stepped out into the cold and turned toward Spellbound.

While I was concerned about the information Lucinda had given me about Quinn, as I walked along, it was Duncan Cole who was foremost on my mind. I left a quick message on Nick's voicemail about the new lead.

Duncan had been furious the day he'd been kicked off the team. He'd lost everything in one fell swoop. His reputation, his team, and the woman he loved. Did he blame Abby for everything? Or the Bryants? Or all of them?

If so, it seemed like a powerful motive for revenge to me.

Except . . . Duncan shouldn't remember the details of that day because of the memory cleanse. Or *anything* about the Craft. Frankly, he should be glad he hadn't been turned into a frog—which used to be a common punishment for a mortal blabbing publicly about the Craft.

But what *did* he remember about that day? And about his life with Abby?

Unfortunately, those were questions that couldn't be answered until we found him. And if he had anything to do with Abby's death, I had the feeling he wasn't going to make that easy.

Chapter Fifteen

"How is Harper feeling today?" Angela Curtis asked as soon as I walked into Spellbound.

Harper had called her yesterday afternoon to ask if she could take over the bookshop for the week—and told her why she needed the help. Angela hadn't hesitated to accept the challenge. Mimi had stepped up as well, offering to take on more shifts. Between the two of them, the shop was in good hands.

"She seems a bit better. Well, she seems a bit less . . . pitiful."

"Poor thing." She pushed up the long sleeve of a shirt with the words "The book was better" printed on it. "It must be killing her to sit still. Especially after these past few months of running herself ragged."

Anyone close to Harper knew exactly how ragged. "She was okay for the first few hours. Mostly because she was asleep. Now she's getting twitchy."

"I bet. Does she want visitors? I can sit with her for a while. Entertain her with Spellbound tales. Like the woman who was in here yesterday using her phone to photograph all the recipes out of a dessert book. Or the guy who spilled his coffee on a new hardcover release, then tried to get a discount because the book was stained."

"Oh, no."

"Oh, yes," she said, smiling.

"It's probably best you save those stories until Harper is back at work. Otherwise she'll be tempted to move her bed into the shop to keep an eye on things."

"That's true. But you know she's probably already watching." Angela pointed to a camera tucked discreetly into a high corner.

"I'd forgotten she added cameras." I waved at the one facing me, then took the opportunity to ask about Quinn's alibi. "I bet the camera captured Quinn Donegal yesterday morning. She was in here, right?"

"Yeah, not long before the Mad Dash started, to use the restroom. You should get a refund from the porta potty company, by the way."

I couldn't tell her it hadn't been the company's fault. Angela, as far as I knew, was mortal. There was no talking magic around her. Not even Vince's black magic. "I'll look into that. Did you happen to see which direction Quinn went when she left?"

"No, she actually asked if she could go out the back door—to avoid the crowd out front. It was crazy out there yesterday."

The alley that ran behind the shops had paths leading to the square between Spellbound and Lotions and Potions, near the Pixie Cottage, and at the far end of the square, near the Gingerbread Shack. Which also just happened to be near the trailhead Abby had taken into the Enchanted Woods. Which way had Quinn gone? Back to the square? Or into the woods? "An understatement," I finally said.

"I heard the news about poor Abby Stillwell. I can't imagine who'd want to hurt her. Does Nick have any suspects?"

"Not really. Right now, he's questioning everybody."

"I just keep thinking about the last time she was in here. She bought a stack of wedding magazines. She was practically glowing. I thought I'd be hearing about an announcement soon."

"When was that?" I asked.

"Let's see." She tapped her chin. "A week ago?"

I wondered *when* Abby and Ben had decided to elope. Was it a spur of the moment idea, like Glinda's wedding? I added it to my list of questions to ask Ben.

As I thought about what Angela had said, I realized that for someone who planned on secretly eloping, Abby hadn't exactly been hiding her trail.

She'd been to the bakery to buy a cake.

She'd been to the Bewitching Boutique for a dress.

She'd been here, buying wedding magazines.

"It makes what happened that much more tragic," Angela said. "And I swear if I hear Ben had anything to do what happened, I'll have to start questioning my instincts. Because the day Abby was in here, all I kept thinking about was that Ben must be one heck of a good guy. She was clearly head over heels."

It was interesting to hear Angela's take. Because I'd never seen Abby act gaga over Ben. And neither had Lucinda, apparently. It was one of those discrepancies that stuck like a thorn in my investigation.

We chatted for a few more minutes about Abby before I said, "I should get going. Harper has an appointment with Dr. Goodwin in a little bit, and I'd like to be there. I'm just going to run upstairs and grab a few books for her before I head out."

Angela dropped her voice. "Do you think she'd like any pregnancy books? I know how she loves to learn everything she can about absolutely everything. I can gather some up. I hesitate to ask only because of how tenuous the pregnancy is . . ."

It was sweet of her to consider it. "I think Harper would like that."

She reached underneath the counter and pulled up three books. "I already put them on my account, so they're good to go." She slid them across the counter.

"I'm not sure what Harper would do without you."

"Well, she doesn't have to find out anytime soon. I'm pulling for her little peanut. And I know it's none of my business, but it didn't escape my notice that Marcus has walked by the storefront at least four times in the past hour."

"Really?"

"That has to be a good sign, right?"

A lot of us were rooting for Harper and Marcus to kiss and make up. "I sure hope so," I said as I headed for the stairs. "I'll be right back."

A few minutes later, I had a heavy tote bag full of books to haul home. I was saying my goodbyes to Angela when she motioned outside with her jaw and said, "Heads up on your way out."

I glanced over my shoulder. Marcus was across the street on the village green, pacing a pathway between twin snowbanks. Every few steps, he threw a glance toward the bookshop.

"Do you think he knows about the baby?" Angela asked.

"I don't know," I said. "Despite Harper wanting to keep the news on the down low for a while, it's not going to be long before the whole village knows. People around here talk."

"And talk."

And were lousy secret keepers. Which again reminded me of Abby and the Bryants and all the secrets between them. I shoved thoughts of them out of my head for the moment. "He knows Harper is terribly ill, though."

"Did Harper tell him?"

"Are you kidding? She'd be the last one to let him know." I zipped my coat. "I might have let it slip in his earshot this morning."

Angela laughed. "Good for you. Go talk some sense into him, will you? Work a little magic?"

I glanced at her, wondering if perhaps she *was* a witch. I couldn't tell by looking, unfortunately. I pulled open the door. "I'll do my best."

A thin coat of salt and sand dusted the cobblestone road and crunched slightly beneath my boots as I made my way to the green.

Sunbeams glinted off Marcus's glasses as he looked up when I neared. He stopped pacing.

"Hi, Marcus," I said, trying to pretend everything was normal.

"Hi, Darcy. Nice, uh, day for a walk, isn't it? Weather's warming up." He looked around—everywhere but at me. "The village maintenance crew sure does a great job clearing the paths quickly, don't they? It's hard to believe we had blizzard conditions yesterday."

He abruptly cut himself off, as if realizing he was rambling.

Clearly, he wasn't as adept at pretending as I was.

His hair was longer than usual and barely combed. He ran a hand through it, pushing it off the side of his face before jamming fists into his coat pockets. Finally, he looked at me, and it was easy to see the sadness in his green eyes.

"How's Harper? I overheard some of your conversation with Vince this morning in the coffee shop."

I adjusted the strap of the tote bag. "Not well. She's staying with me until she's feeling better."

"Shouldn't she be in the hospital?"

"It's a possibility if the treatment doesn't work, but for right now Dr. Goodwin is taking good care of her."

"What's wrong?"

As I explained about her condition, I held the tote bag tightly to my chest so he couldn't accidentally see the spines of the pregnancy books. I didn't want him learning the news from me. I'd made a promise to Harper.

He said, "I knew she hadn't been feeling well lately, but I never thought it was that bad."

"None of us did. Not even Harper."

He glanced toward my house, on the other side of the green. I wanted to give him a shove in its direction but managed to keep my hands to myself.

"She is pretty stubborn," he said.

"She's not the only one," I said steadily. This time I wanted to hit him upside the head with the heavy tote. I gripped its straps even more tightly before I acted on the impulse.

He looked at me.

I looked back.

"It's . . . Things are out of my control."

"Did you sell your house? Because that seems like it would be in your control."

Slowly, he began to straighten, standing upright. Jaw up, shoulders back. This was the Marcus I knew. The one who'd fight for truth and justice, who'd righted wrongs. He might look boy-next-door, but deep down he was a take-charge kind of guy.

"It's complicated. My mother . . ."

"Shouldn't be making you choose."

"And my father . . . What he did."

It suddenly occurred to me that he and Harper were more alike than I ever realized. He'd been too immersed in his parents' pain to deal with his own. He'd thrown himself into trying to help them emotionally and physically, while Harper had occupied herself with every activity under the sun.

Neither had dealt with their own pain.

Their own grief.

I again adjusted the strap of the tote bag that was cutting into my shoulder. "I know you've had a lot to deal with, but no one in this village is judging you for what happened before you were even born. You are as much a victim as anyone in that case."

"You're nice to say so, but I feel the stares."

"People stare because they're nosy. This village is the nosiest place on the planet."

That, at least, elicited a half smile out of him.

"Marcus, there's nothing you can do about other people. You can only be who you are. You love your parents, the good and the bad. That's nothing to be ashamed of or to hide from. There's not a person around who doesn't understand that kind of unconditional love."

He broke eye contact to look once again at my house.

I added, "Look, you're a grown man. At some point, the decisions you make need to be yours. Not someone else's. Not Harper's. Not your mother's. *Yours*. I shouldn't have to tell you that, but it seems to me you need to hear it. What do *you* want to do with your life, Marcus?"

"It's not that easy, Darcy."

"Life isn't easy, Marcus. For any of us."

He reached into his pocket and pulled out a small, wrapped package. "Will you give this to Harper for me?"

"You should give it to her yourself."

He continued to hold it out, and with a sigh, I took it, and started walking away. Then, I stopped and turned back to him. "Come with me. See her. Talk to her. Really talk."

"She probably hates me. After everything . . ."

All I could do was stare at him for a moment, fighting the urge to shake him until he came to his senses.

"If you truly think that," I finally said, choosing my words carefully, "then you're right, you shouldn't see her. You *should* move far away and never think twice about who you left behind here in the village. Because she deserves better than someone who obviously doesn't know her at all."

I strode off, determined not to look back at him to see if had taken my words to heart.

If what I'd said didn't get Marcus to reconsider his life choices, nothing would.

* * *

"What was that all about?" Harper asked as soon as I walked into the house.

She was sitting on the lower landing of the staircase in her fluffy robe, and had evidently witnessed my conversation with Marcus.

"What are you doing out of bed?" I glanced around for Higgins and saw he was outside with Missy. No sign of Annie, but she tended to sleep most of the day.

"Dr. Dreadful came by early. He said I could move about the house as long as I took it easy."

"What else did he say?" I hated that I'd missed the appointment.

"He's pleased with my progress."

I set the tote bag on the hall table and took off my coat to hang in the closet. "Did he really say pleased?"

"Well, he said I was making progress. I inferred the pleased part. I'm not sure he's ever been pleased in his life."

"Progress is good." Although she still looked like death warmed up, color had returned to her face. "Did you have lunch?"

"Ve and Archie came by with enough food for the whole village."

"Did you eat any of it?"

"Some," she said, picking at the carpet runner. "There was no way I was touching the spinach smoothie."

I made a face. "Don't blame you. Anyone else here?"

"Nick's been here and gone again. Mom's been here and gone. Pepe and Mrs. P have been here and gone. Ve and Archie have been here and gone. Mimi's still sleeping. Did I ever sleep that long as a teenager?"

"Every chance you got."

"Did you tell Mom everything?" I asked.

"Yes," she said with a roll of her eyes. "And I had to listen to a lecture for a good ten minutes about taking care of myself. She's worse than you are."

"What did she say about the baby?"

"Oh, I didn't tell her that part."

"What? *Harper* . . ."

She laughed, and I forgot I had been briefly annoyed. She hadn't laughed much lately, and I took a moment to appreciate the sound.

"I'm kidding," she said. "Mom was ... happy because I am happy about it. But, I could tell she's worried. I don't like worrying her."

"She's a mother. It's what they do best."

She met my gaze. "So I'm learning."

I didn't want her focusing on all the worries, so I motioned to the tote bag and said, "I brought you some books to help stave off death by boredom. Oh, and before I forget, can you access the cameras in the bookshop?"

"Yeah, from my phone or my tablet. Why?"

I told her about looking for the footage of Quinn. An exact time stamp of when she was in the shop would be nice.

"I'll see what I can find. Oh, and before *I* forget, I found something strange in the ledgers Abby gave you. I already talked to Nick about it, but I also left a report on your desk."

I glanced behind me. The double doors leading into my office were closed tight. "A report?"

"I was bored."

I smiled. "I'm impressed, Harper. I stared at those ledgers for hours and didn't see a thing. What did you find?"

"Creativity at its finest. In last year's ledger, there are many instances of transactions for the same expense but named differently. For example, there was a debit listed for 'medals' but another for 'race hardware.' Same thing, right?"

"Yes." And so much for Joe wanting those ledgers back so he could pay vendors.

Had Lucinda lied to me, too? Or had she just repeated something Joe had told her?

I was beginning to dislike the Bryants.

A lot.

"And," Harper said, "another entry for 'timing chips' but also one for 'services' of the timing company itself. The company fee should have covered the timing chips, no?"

"The chips were included in the fee." I knew, because when I called the timing chip company on behalf of this year's race, I'd asked for the same package used last year.

"That's what I thought. There are six or seven instances of duplicates. Not to mention questionable expenses like 'post-race snacks and beverages.' Those items were donated, weren't they?"

It was no wonder Abby thought she had messed up somewhere. Her columns didn't include half of what had been listed last year. She probably thought she was missing receipts. "They were. I should have caught that. How much did all these extras amount to?"

"Well, I'm not sure which itemizations were the legitimate expense—you'll need to check the receipts. But ballpark? Around five thousand dollars. The question is, where did the money go?"

Into Joe's pocket was my guess. "Thank you. I was too busy looking at the numbers on the page to focus on where the money was going."

She waved away my gratitude. "You're welcome. Bed rest pays off sometimes."

"Speaking of . . ." I held up each book as I emptied the tote. All but the pregnancy trio were about witchcraft, her preferred reading material as of late. "All these books are guaranteed to keep you occupied for at least an hour or two."

She scanned the titles. "I'll take the baby books—that was nice of Angela to think of them.

You can either keep the others for yourself or donate them."

I stared. "What?"

"I don't want them."

"What?" I said again.

"I. Don't. Want. Them."

I took a deep breath and counted to ten in my head. "Why?"

She shrugged. "I'm done with them. Done with the Craft, too."

"I don't understand . . . I thought you were past that? I thought you had fully accepted the Craft?"

Harper hadn't moved to the village in full acceptance of being a witch. She had been slow to warm up to something she could not scientifically explain. But when she had finally started using her magic a few months ago . . . I thought she finally saw magic the same way I did.

"I changed my mind. What has the Craft done for me, really? It can't cure me completely. It certainly didn't help Abby Stillwell, did it?"

My gaze lingered on the birch besom hanging next to the front door. Magic was reflected in every corner of my world, inside and out. It shook me to my core that Harper was willing to walk away from it. "The Craft helped find Abby, and it *has* helped you feel better, whether or not you want to admit it."

"All the fancy magic in the world, and it can't guarantee my baby will be okay, can it?"

Ah, the heart of the matter. My anger deflated. "I see."

"See what? And please stop looking at me like that."

I set my hands on my hips. "Like what?"

"Never mind. I don't want to talk about it. Are we done yet?" she asked.

"With?" I said, trying not to lose my patience. I understood why she was lashing out. Fear often led to anger.

"Ignoring my initial question? What was that all about?" she asked, motioning toward the village green with her chin. "What were you and Marcus talking about?"

I handed her the pregnancy books, then put the wrapped present on top. "The package is from Marcus. If you want to know what we talked about, you should ask him yourself."

Jutting her chin, she hugged the books and gift to her chest, then stood up. "I'm going to go take a nap. Dr. Dreadful's orders. I wouldn't want to disappoint him."

Stubborn, just like Marcus had said.

I watched her go up the steps, then went up to my bedroom and grabbed my Craft cloak from the closet. Back downstairs, I made more copies of the photocopied ledgers and packed my tote bag. As much as I wanted to stick around the house, I had work to do. But first things first. I let the dogs in, then put on my Crafting cloak and went out the back door, and into the Enchanted Woods.

I needed to talk to my mother.

Chapter Sixteen

As beautiful as the Enchanted Woods were in every season, there was something breathtaking about them after a snowfall. The artist in me took mental notes on how the snow balanced delicately on outstretched branches. The way flakes stuck to the north sides of the tree trunks. The way drifts settled against fallen logs. I memorized textures and shadows, entranced by the loveliness around me.

Although the path was covered with fresh snow, I knew my way by heart. I recognized certain landmarks, like fallen trees, arched or gnarled branches, and lichen-covered boulders.

I'd walked this trail many times since moving to the village. At first this trek had brought trepidation as a visit to the Elder's meadow was usually a result of me breaking Craft laws.

I'd learned a lot since then, about the rules witches lived by, and the Craft itself, and about the Elder.

My mom.

I didn't visit the meadow often anymore—my mother tended to drop by my house most mornings, and I found as I walked along that I'd missed the journey through these woods.

I took my time walking along, noting changes in the trees like they were friends I hadn't seen in a while. I was startled out of my reverie when my cell phone rang, its tone jarring in the relative silence of the woods. I fumbled under my cape to find my phone in my pocket, then silenced the call as I glanced at the readout: Glinda.

The enchantment of the woods, and the measure of peace it had brought me, vanished instantly. I didn't particularly want to talk with Glinda right now. I hadn't had a chance to sort through my feelings where she was concerned, and until I did, I'd let her calls go to voice mail.

Was she friend or foe?

I hated that I was even thinking the question. Only because I thought we were past the foe stage of our relationship. It hurt to consider I might have been fooled. Again.

My phone blipped, alerting me to a voice mail. I listened as I walked.

"Hi Darcy, it's Glinda. I was just wondering if you had time for cake testing tomorrow afternoon, and if so, could you set that up? If not, maybe Tuesday? Or Wednesday? My schedule is flexible. Let me know. Thanks. Bye."

I wasn't only reevaluating our friendship, but now also my decision to help Glinda plan her wedding. For some reason, I couldn't help thinking I'd walked into some sort of trap.

My phone rang again almost immediately, and I was pleasantly surprised to see it was Nick.

I answered, keeping my voice low, "I feel like it's been three weeks since I've seen you."

He laughed. "We had breakfast together this morning. Why are you whispering?"

"It still *feels* like three weeks. And because I'm in the woods. It doesn't seem right to use my full voice."

As I finished the words, I noticed the woods had hushed around me. It was eerily quiet. Even though my cloak made me invisible to mortals, my voice could still be heard by all.

"Tough day?" he asked.

"Not as tough as yesterday, but I'm one thousand percent done with it."

"Bold statement since it's not even one o'clock yet."

"By one o'clock, I might be two thousand percent done." I brushed some snow off a log and sat down. "It's been one of those days." I told him what Noelle had said about Abby moving, plus what had happened at the Bewitching Boutique and about running into Marcus.

"And now you're in the woods?"

"Yep." He knew what that meant. "I need to know why Glinda and Godfrey are so concerned about Harper's baby."

"I hope you get the answers you want."

"Me, too." Whether I would wasn't guaranteed. There were some things about the Craft my mother thought I should learn on my own and others that she simply *couldn't* share due to various Craft laws. However, since both Glinda and Godfrey knew, I thought there was a good chance she would tell me as well. "Are you home?"

"Not yet," he said. "I wanted to let you know I checked out the lead on Duncan Cole."

"And?"

"One of the reasons he was so hard to find is that the New Hampshire racing team provides its runners with room and board. He was living in one of their houses."

I picked up on the past tense. "Was?"

"He resigned a couple of months ago. The director of the team said Duncan had been struggling with injuries and opted to retire."

I wondered what kind of performance enhancer he'd been caught using. If steroids, they could certainly lead to a body breaking down—and could also lead to personality changes, like being easy to anger. But blood doping didn't carry those kinds of side effects. "Did the team director have a forwarding phone number or address for him?"

"The phone number's been disconnected. The address is an apartment in Wakefield."

"Wakefield, as in twenty minutes away Wakefield?"

"The very same. I'm heading over there now."

As much as I wanted to go with him, I knew I couldn't. There was no explaining why the chief of police brought his fiancée along on official police business.

"Be careful," I said.

"Always."

We said our mushy goodbyes, and I hung up.

I sat for a moment, simply enjoying the beauty of my surroundings. Slowly, the birdsong returned, and I heard scampering all around me. Squirrels ran from branch to branch, kicking off snow in their wake.

I switched my phone to vibrate before tucking it back into my pocket. The digital noise of its ringtone didn't belong out here where the loudest sound was a woodpecker's knocking.

After taking a moment to just be, I pressed onward, toward the Elder's meadow. I soon spotted a familiar cake-shaped rock, which marked the turnoff I needed to take. I veered off the path, into a vast meadow covered in glittery snow. In its center stood a gnarled tree, its weeping branches weighted with snow and nearly touching the ground.

"Hello?" I called out.

In a blink, the meadow transformed from winter into summer, bursting into bold colors as snow melted away. Wildflowers bloomed. The tree shook off its wintry coat and leaves unfurled as the branches lifted upward as though stretching toward the sun.

The air warmed, and I unzipped my coat as I walked toward the tree. A mourning dove flew out from the tree top, swooped downward, and my mother appeared in front of me, her bare feet not touching the ground. Dressed in a flowy long-sleeved white dress with a cowl neckline, she gave me a hug as she motioned toward two tree trunks rising out of the ground.

"This is a nice surprise," she said as we sat. "But I have the feeling you're not just here for a cup of coffee and a chat."

"What? I could have just been in the neighborhood and decided to drop in. Plus, you do make the best coffee."

"I do, don't I?" She waved a hand, and a coffee cart appeared next to us. Pushing up her sleeve, she reached over, picked up a steaming carafe, and filled a mug.

How Harper could even think of giving up magic was beyond me.

My mother filled another mug, and cupped it between her hands as tendrils of steam rose up. "So you're not here about Abby or Harper?"

I reached over to the cart and picked out a shortbread cookie from a platter mounded with tasty offerings. "Well, now that you mention them . . ." I eyed her. "Harper said you stopped by the house earlier. So you know everything that's going on with her?"

"Everything, Darcy. Everything. Including her decision about the Craft."

"She doesn't mean it," I said. "She's terrified of losing her baby and is lashing out. That's all."

She stared into her coffee.

I ate another cookie, then said, "I need to know. It's time I know."

"Know?"

"Whatever it is about Harper that's been worrying you. You've been concerned for a while now. I've seen the looks you give her when you think no one is watching. I've seen them for months and months now, even before what happened with Marcus. This goes beyond Harper's health and the baby's health as well. What is it? And in that vein, why are Glinda and Godfrey worried Harper will have a baby girl?"

Her head came up. "They shouldn't have said anything."

"I agree. *You* should have been the one to say something."

For a long moment, she remained quiet. It was as if I could see the debate raging in her head. The fire in her eyes, then the softness.

Finally, she said, "You're probably right. I should have told you, but I didn't want to put you in the middle of a battle that is not yours to fight. And more than that, I wanted to protect you. But now here you are, and I should send you on your merry way, but I . . . I'm going to need your help after all."

"You have it," I said without hesitation. "Now, what is it we're fighting?"

She glanced around. "Let's walk."

I had to smile since she didn't walk at all. She floated. I set my mug on the cart, stood, and left my coat on the seat. Mom linked her arm in mine and started forward. The wildflowers parted, revealing a grassy path for us to follow.

"You know the Eldership is matriarchal," she began. "But what you do not know is that it is a hereditary monarchy."

I stopped in my tracks. Surrounded by the scent of lavender, I said, "A hereditary monarchy? You mean . . ."

"Yes. The Eldership has been in our family for generations. My mother was the Elder before me, and the one before her was her aunt."

I was trying to wrap my head around the monarchy part of her explanation when she started floating off, and I nearly tripped over my feet as she tugged me along.

"Every twenty-five years, there is a renewal ceremony," she said. "My renewal is coming up in June."

"On Midsummer's Eve." Harper had uncovered information on the renewal in one of her dusty old books not too long ago.

"Correct."

"It is possible on that night I will have to relinquish the Eldership and the line of our rule will end with me."

"Why? If it's hereditary . . . I mean, I know Harper and I aren't dead yet but some day we will be." Elders, after all, were always witches who'd already passed on and became familiars. "If it's a monarchy, you should be able to reign until one of us . . ."

"I don't even like thinking of such," she said with a small shudder. She patted my hand. "But the rules are clear. The reign is passed down to the *youngest* woman in the family. It has always been that way. On the day of her twenty-fifth birthday the heir apparent will be asked to make a vow that, upon her eventual death, she will claim the role of Eldership with a pure, willing, and voluntary heart. If she makes that pledge, I will continue to reign until the day she crosses over."

I barely had time to process what she had said before she continued on.

"But if that young woman is a witch who does not want to be a witch, she is unlikely to take such an oath. And no one can force or entice her."

Harper.

My heart sank.

I stopped again. "If you just told her all this . . ."

But my mother was shaking her head before all the words were even out of my mouth. "Impossible. And it's one of the reasons I didn't want you to know. I didn't want you to try to influence her. Not on purpose, of course, but subconsciously. As heir, she is not to know about the monarchy until the day of her twenty-fifth birthday."

"That is a lot to spring on someone all at once."

"One would think so, but if I said to you right this minute, Darcy, when the time comes, would you take over my role as the Elder? Would you govern our community with courage and strength, dignity, and fairness? Would you protect our heritage, our way of life? What would you say?"

I didn't have to think twice. "I would say yes, of course."

"That's because you have the love of the Craft in your heart. You feel it beating within you. Harper does not feel that way quite yet, or if she does, she has not accepted it and openly embraced it. She had been taking immense steps forward, and I was so hopeful, but I fear her recent troubles have set her back."

My head spun with questions as we walked a loop around the meadow. The scents of the flowers were at times subtle, at other times overwhelming. Mint. Orange. Marigold. It smelled of summer and sunshine. Of happiness. Which seemed wrong, considering the anxiety racing through my body. "You're Elder. There must be something we can do. We can lobby the Coven of Seven for more time. Something."

The special coven helped create and amend Craft laws and advised the Elder on important matters. They, as a group, had great power.

"While the Coven of Seven is loyal, most of them at least, I cannot ask them to change a rule simply to benefit my family. It goes against everything I stand for."

A disloyal witch? I immediately added Dorothy to my list of possible Coven members. "Is it possible they'd do it on their own?"

"Unlikely."

My heart beat hard and fast. "So what happens on Harper's birthday if she says no? What happens to *you* on the night of the renewal? Who takes over as Elder?"

She patted my hand. "I'm getting there. Patience."

I took a deep breath and tried to calm down, but I could feel my hands shaking.

She said, "From time to time, there have been coup attempts. Families who feel they could better govern the Craft. So far all those coups have failed, because our laws are strong, our family stronger. But that is not currently the case. The future of the Craft is in question, and though our family is strong, its ties to the Eldership are in question. Trouble has been brewing for some time now."

"This is about Dorothy, isn't it?" As soon as I said the words, I knew it was. I could feel it in my bones.

"As you already know, Dorothy believes our ancestors stole the Eldership from hers and feels it is *her* family who should be governing, not ours. Over the years she has gained supporters, mostly witches who have at one point or another felt slighted by an Elder's ruling."

Ooh, I despised that woman.

"For years, she has been biding her time, waiting for an opening to push for broad changes. That opening came with Harper, when she moved here. When she arrived in the village and didn't embrace the Craft straight off, Dorothy began plotting a new plan of attack for the next Renewal. Dorothy's plans, however," Mom added, "were abruptly derailed last fall when she learned Harper had started using the Craft."

"That explains her uptick in hostility in the last few months."

"Yes. She's been seething with rage." She turned back toward the weeping tree. "When Dorothy finds out about Harper's latest disavowal of the Craft—and she will find out—she will renew her plans with vigor. Full steam ahead."

"What are her plans exactly?"

"She wants the Coven of Seven to approve a massive overhaul to our ancestral laws, allowing a change for a *living* witch to become Elder once I am forced to resign. A living witch whose identity is known to one and all."

I froze, looked at her. "Let me guess. Dorothy wants to become Elder?"

"Not possible," she said. "With her reputation, she would never be approved by the Coven of Seven. She's burned too many bridges."

I wondered if that phrase was literal in Dorothy's case, considering she was a firebug.

"Dorothy knows the best approach with the Coven is to adhere to Craft heritage as much as possible. Too much change all at once will throw our world into turmoil. Her plan for a takeover aligns with the Craft's current form of government—a monarchy. One where the Eldership is passed down to the youngest female witch in the family. She simply wants to change the family to hers."

The youngest female witch in her family . . . My heart sank. "Glinda."

"Yes."

"Does she know what her mother is planning for her?"

"Yes. Dorothy informed her a few months ago, before Harper started using her magic. Back when she fully believed my Eldership was not going to be renewed."

"Is that when Glinda learned your identity?"

"It is."

I was rattling off questions as fast as I could think of them. "Isn't it against Craft law for Dorothy to tell people who you are?"

"Dorothy was not the one to tell her, Darcy. I summoned Glinda and told her myself."

"Why?"

"I wanted her to know the whole story. I did not want Dorothy to paint the Eldership—and our family—with one broad, bitter brush."

My mind raced. "Whose decision is it to choose the next Elder if you're forced to resign? Is it only the Coven of Seven? Or is there a global vote among witches?"

"It would be the decision of the Coven of Seven. There is no modern precedent for replacing an Elder. It's been hundreds of years since there's been a situation such as this. The Coven has been meeting regularly to discuss how to handle the matter."

"If Dorothy is in the Coven of Seven, isn't that a conflict of interest?"

Mom lifted an eyebrow. "Is she in the Coven?"

"Is she? You tell me."

She smiled. "I cannot reveal the Coven's members."

I sighed. "Well, I might not know who's in the Coven, but most of the witches I know aren't going to do what Dorothy says just because she says so. I can't imagine they feel especially indebted to Dorothy . . . and therefore Glinda."

"This is true. But they feel tied to our ancestry, and if there is a link to the Eldership and Dorothy's family as she has always claimed, then they would honor that."

"But this . . . that . . . It isn't right."

"Right or wrong is not up to us. If the time comes, it will be up to the Coven. They will decide."

As we continued walking, I said, "Then there's really not much of a battle to fight, is there? It's out of our control. Either Harper will decide, yes, she wants to be Elder, or the Coven of Seven will decide on a replacement."

"All of that is true. However, there's been a development of sorts that changes everything. And it's why we might have to fight harder than we've ever fought for anything ever before."

Her tone scared me. "I don't understand. What development?"

"Harper's baby," my mother said.

Suddenly it all made sense as to why Glinda and Godfrey had been concerned the baby might be a girl.

"If Harper's child is a girl, as the youngest female witch in our family *she* would then become heir apparent, not Harper," my mother said, confirming my thoughts. "I would remain as Elder for the foreseeable future. When that child is of age to consent to continue our family's reign, we go through this all over again."

"And the decision is made on *her* twenty-fifth birthday."

"Correct."

Feeling a little dizzy with all this information, I slowed to a stop. "But even if the baby is a girl, she wouldn't be due before Midsummer's Eve. Your time as Elder will have expired."

"It does not matter when the baby is *due*. If the baby is a girl, she was conceived before the renewal. It's all that matters. She already exists. We are simply waiting for her arrival."

"Mom?"

"Yes, Darcy?"

"Do you *know* if Harper is having a little girl?"

My mother took my hands in hers and faced me. There were tears in her eyes. "I do not know yet. It's too soon. We'll need to wait along with Harper for a blood test or ultrasound."

"There's no magic we can use?"

"Sadly, no. Until then, we need to keep a close watch on Dorothy. And an even closer watch should the child be a girl."

"And if it's a boy?"

"Then the future of the Craft as we know it rests in Harper's decision on her twenty-fifth birthday."

Good heavens.

"We need to be prepared for anything, Darcy. Because no matter what, Dorothy is going to do everything she can to make sure power changes hands from our family to hers come June. She is not going to go down without a fight."

No, she wasn't.

Forget battle lines.

There was going to be a war.

Chapter Seventeen

I stayed with my mother for a long time, brainstorming ways to keep Dorothy in check and Harper and the baby as safe as possible in the coming months.

It wasn't going to be easy, on either count.

Dorothy was wily, and Harper was both stubborn and fiercely independent. She wasn't going to welcome any kind of benevolent smothering. Adding to the issue, we couldn't tell her why we were being extra protective.

It was late afternoon by the time I left the meadow and speed-walked toward the village, taking a different route than I'd come. I wasn't going straight home.

As I neared the Enchanted Trail, the paved path that looped around the village, I took off my Craft cloak and folded it until it fit inside my tote bag. I took the trail around the square, headed for the second-floor apartment above Balefire.

I wanted to try to catch Ben Bryant at home, where he couldn't sprint away. Then I needed to stop by Abby's house to see Quinn.

The village was fairly busy for a Sunday afternoon. Drivers searched for parking spots along the square. A stream of people were standing in line on the steps of the playhouse for the matinee. I was more than a little amused to see Vince Paxton and Noelle Quinlan together in the crowd. That was quick. I guessed she'd taken him up on his offer to call him—and wondered exactly how long she had waited. An hour? Two? It made me wonder if she was truly interested in him . . . or only in making another sale. I kind of hoped for the latter since Vince wasn't interested in long-term commitments at the moment.

The lights were off inside Balefire when I arrived at the building, and my gaze went upward, to the second floor. I couldn't tell if Ben was home or not, but wished with all my might that he was. The sooner I could question him, the better.

I detoured around to the back of the building, where there was an exterior staircase. I trudged up the first flight of steps, hoping I could gather my wits about me enough to concentrate on the job I had to do. My thoughts were scattered, but I had a few set questions to ask Ben.

I wanted to know what he and Abby had fought about; whether he thought she had any enemies; who was responsible for the creative bookkeeping; why Abby was selling her house; and if he thought Duncan was dangerous.

I stood on the landing outside his door and knocked. Up here, I could see a light on inside his apartment. I heard footsteps and a moment later, Ben opened the door and groaned when he saw me. "Go away, Darcy."

I should have expected hostility after the way he'd behaved earlier, but I'd hoped his mother would have talked some sense into him. "I have a few questions. Talking to me can only help you, Ben."

With a weary sigh, he said, "I have nothing to say to you right now." He slammed the door in my face. I heard the click of the dead bolt.

Stunned, I stared at the door for a moment.

I debated knocking again but ultimately back-tracked down the steps and turned toward the neighborhood where Abby had lived.

As I walked away, I glanced back at Ben's apartment. I saw him looking down on me, but he quickly closed the drapes, blocking me out.

Hmmph. He could tell me to go away all he wanted, but I wasn't giving up so easily.

I'd be back. Maybe not today. But soon.

If he didn't talk to me then . . . he'd be summoned to see the Elder.

And I had the feeling that wouldn't turn out well for him. At all.

* * *

Abby had lived in a quiet village neighborhood a few blocks from the main square. The sidewalks had been cleared of snow and liberally sprinkled with sand. Tall oaks cast thin shadows over yards filled with small footprints and lopsided snowmen.

The driveway and front path of Abby's one-story cottage had been cleared. A small SUV was backed up to the single garage door, which was open, revealing Abby's sporty hatchback parked inside. The SUV's engine was still ticking—apparently Quinn had just arrived home.

I'd been here only a couple of times before, while dropping off paperwork for Abby regarding the race. Painted a lemon yellow with white trim, the house gave off a cheerful energy that seemed extra depressing considering the circumstances.

I'd completely forgotten to bring some soup with me and was chastising myself as I pushed the doorbell.

Quinn pulled open the door almost immediately. Her hair was piled high on her head in a loose top knot, and mascara was smudged under her eyes as though she'd been crying. She wore a heavy, hooded sweatshirt, loose sweatpants and sneakers.

"Darcy, hi." She looked surprised to see me, but stepped back to let me pass by. "I forgot you were coming by. Come on in."

She seemed so flustered, I believed she *had* forgotten and wasn't just feeding me a line. After I brushed past her, she stuck her head out the door and looked left, then right. Seemingly satisfied with whatever she was looking for, she closed the door and flipped the lock.

She caught my worried gaze and said, "I've been hearing noises and they're freaking me out. Come on in. Excuse the mess."

She wasn't kidding about the mess. There were clothes and books and shoes littering the living room, along with DVDs, picture albums and kitchen ware. Cardboard boxes were scattered about, some already taped closed while others waited, flaps open, ready to be filled.

"What kind of noises?" I asked.

Waving a hand, she said, "Just creaks and things. Undoubtedly, it's the wind. I'm just being a little paranoid after what happened to Abby."

As I moved a wool coat aside and sat on a chair, I noticed the garment bag holding Abby's wedding dress hanging on a hook near the coat closet. I fought a wave of sadness and said, "I'm surprised you're moving so soon."

Quinn crouched down and shoved a handful of clothing items into a box. Leggings and tees, sweatshirts and shorts. "This is Abby's house, not mine. It doesn't seem right to stay. And . . . it hurts to be here."

I understood her grief. "Do you know what's going to happen to the house? Did Abby have a will?"

"Not that I know of," she said after thinking about it for a moment. She loaded her arms with shoes, then dumped them all on top of the clothes she'd just loaded into the box. "She has no family that I know about, either. Maybe there's a long-lost cousin or something somewhere. She never mentioned anyone, and I think she would have."

It took everything in me not to visibly wince at her packing methods. I itched to take over the task. "Do you need some help?"

"Thanks, but I'm almost done. I've been running boxes to a storage unit all afternoon—I'm just taking the essentials with me for now. I should be fully out of here by tomorrow afternoon, before Abby's memorial."

"Where are you planning to go?" Lucinda's suspicions were echoing in my head, and I didn't like the thought of Quinn leaving town. But unless she was under arrest, she was free to go wherever she chose.

"Short-term? I'll find a hotel. Long-term? I'm not sure yet. It's something to figure out later."

"A hotel? Is there no one you can stay with here in the village for a few days?"

Reaching behind her, she grabbed a packing tape dispenser and sealed the box, then pushed it aside. She dragged an empty box closer and dumped in a load of books and more shoes. "Not really. I don't want to impose on anyone. And honestly, I'd rather be alone."

Glancing around, I noticed a framed picture of Quinn and Abby on the mantel. It looked like it had been taken at one of the local fairs. They appeared . . . happy with twin goofy grins.

"How did you and Abby meet?" I asked.

Quinn paused in her packing and gave me a wistful smile. "Balefire, a little more than two years ago. I was fresh out of college and working as a running shoe representative. Balefire was one of my accounts."

"A running shoe rep even though you don't run?"

"And I was a horrible salesperson, too," she said with a light laugh. "I was probably the worst person for the job. Although I had been a communications major in college, I wasn't comfortable in a sales role. Abby took pity on me and pretty much kept me afloat. We became friends. Every time I came to the village, I stayed a little bit longer. I love it here. There's just something so . . . magical about this place."

The cautious way she said magical had me on alert. It was as if she *knew* there was magic here. But she was a mortal. Wasn't she?

I had no way of knowing if Quinn knew about the Craft unless she volunteered the information. And I couldn't risk asking her without putting my own powers in jeopardy.

But if she did know . . . who had told her? Abby?

I silently berated Craft rules.

Quinn went on talking and whatever was in arm's reach went flying into the box. "One day when I went into Balefire Abby mentioned the store was looking for a social media and website coordinator and said the job was mine if I wanted it. But I knew I couldn't afford to live around here, especially on an entry-level salary. That's when Abby mentioned she'd been looking for a roommate. I didn't find out until later that the Bryants hadn't known Abby was hiring me. They weren't happy about it."

"Why?"

"They didn't really like me much. Still don't, honestly. Ben's nice enough, but everyone else is dismissive."

"I'm sorry," I said, because I knew it was true.

"It's okay. It's only because I'm not one of . . . them."

I bit my tongue to keep from saying "a witch?" and instead said, "One of them?"

"A runner."

I smiled, though I knew Quinn being mortal didn't help her cause with the Bryants. Especially after the disaster with Duncan Cole outing them all as witches in a fit of temper. With a mortal among them, they would have to watch their every word.

"I have two left feet and prefer to do yoga." Without missing a beat, she popped into a pose that made my body ache just looking at it. Using only her arms, she held up her whole body while twisting her legs. She let herself down. "But the Bryants don't really consider yoga a sport. You should hear the way Madison and Lucinda mock it."

I could imagine.

Sighing, she picked at a piece of lint on the carpet. "I quit my job today. I should have quit a long time ago, but I liked my job, and Abby more than made up for their indifference. Without her there as a buffer, they will be unbearable." Her eyes filled with tears. "There wasn't a better person around than Abby. She was funny and sweet and so selfless. I always told her that when I grew up I wanted to be just like her. But even if I hadn't been joking, that wouldn't be possible. There was no one like Abby."

"No, there wasn't." I wasn't picking up on any jealousy in her tone, just love. But to test the waters, I added, "I was often envious of how she could defuse a situation with her calm, yet happy demeanor. She had every Mad Dash vendor wrapped around her finger."

"I know just what you mean. I experienced it first-hand. And I envied that, too. Her easygoing nature. I envied a lot of things about her, actually."

"Oh? Like what?"

She sat back, bent her knees, pulling them close to her chest, and wrapped her arms around them. "I don't even know where to start. Her sense of humor? The way her laugh could make the crankiest person smile? Her morals. How she never met a stranger." She sighed. "I guess I was most envious of the way she could fit in anywhere. I told her that all the time, too, especially at work."

"Where you felt you didn't fit in." Had that been the jealousy Lucinda picked up on? I suspected it was.

Her eyes filled with tears. "I didn't just feel it. I knew it. Despite how hard I tried, how hard I worked, Joe, Madison, and Lucinda were never going to treat me like anything other than a nuisance." Suddenly Quinn's head snapped up. "Did you hear that?"

I listened but heard nothing out of the ordinary. "What?"

Shaking her head, she said, "I thought I heard something." She went back to packing, tossing items even more fervently than before. "My mind must be playing tricks."

Her anxiety was giving me anxiety. "Do you have any reason to think the person who hurt Abby would come here?"

"I don't know, do I? I don't know why she was killed."

I was at a loss at what to say. I didn't know why either.

When her phone rang, she lurched for it, then frowned after glancing at the screen. "Sorry," she said to me. "I need to take this."

I studied her as she answered. She looked on the verge of a nervous breakdown, and I wondered why. Sure, she was grieving, but it felt like it went deeper.

"No, no," Quinn said into the phone. "That's not going to work. The memorial is at five. I'll need you there by four at the latest to—" She looked over at me. "I'm going to have to call you back in a couple of minutes, okay? Yeah. Got it. Bye."

She dropped the phone in her lap, then tilted her head back and stared at the ceiling for a long moment.

"Everything okay?" I asked.

When she glanced my way, I saw the tears in her eyes. "Catering problems. Seems it's extra hard to do anything at the last minute. Flowers, food, printing . . ." She fisted her hands, then abruptly released them, spreading all her fingers wide. "I still have to find a pastor and figure out music. I didn't realize what a huge task I was taking on, but I . . . I have to do it for Abby. She's . . . family."

"Maybe I can help," I said, taking the opening she'd presented. "I have contacts with most everyone in the village. I worked with Stef at the Sorcerer's Stove for the race catering. I'm friends with the owner of the Black Thorn, too." It was the only floral shop in the village.

"That *was* Stef on the phone. She says she doesn't have enough staff to set up when I need her to."

"I can help with that," I said. "With my job, I'm used to hiring crew on a moment's notice. I have a long stand-by list."

She looked like she wanted to argue but then thought better of it and slumped in relief. "Okay, thanks. I'd appreciate the help. I'll let Stef know you're taking over. And if you can handle the flowers, too, that would be great. I couldn't even get a call back today. A call back would have been nice."

She obviously hadn't planned many events. Vendors were notorious for not returning calls in a timely matter.

"Lydia Wentworth doesn't usually work Sundays, but it'll be okay. It's short notice, but I know she can work magic."

Literal magic. She was a Floracrafter.

"I know I'm asking a lot, but tomorrow was the only day that worked best for the memorial service. Ben and Joe are leaving with most of the Balefire team on Wednesday for the Auckland Grand Prix, a big race in New Zealand. They won't be back for a couple of weeks."

I knew Joe and Ben had been training for an international race but didn't know it was so soon. I filed away that tidbit to share with Nick, then the date clicked. Wednesday? "Was Abby supposed to go to?"

"No, she hadn't qualified for the races, and the Bryants needed her help at the store."

"But she and Ben were supposed to elope on Tuesday? He was just going to leave her here? Doesn't that seem strange to you?"

She shoved more belongings into a box. "Elite athletes don't exactly live normal lives, with their training and race schedules. But what do I know? I just do yoga." She slammed a boot into the box.

On that note. "I have those ledgers for you." I reached down for my tote bag at my feet and let out a squeal when something furry brushed against my hand. "What is that?"

Quinn reached beneath the chair. "Sorry. It's just this old thing." She tossed the wig into the open box.

A wig made of long brown hair. "Was that Abby's?"

"Abby's?" Confusion filled her eyes. "No, it's mine. From an old Halloween costume." She set a stack of towels on top of it in the box.

"Did Abby ever borrow it?" I asked. "Or have one of her own?"

Quinn looked at me as if I had taken leave of my senses as she put a red leather photo album on top of the towels. "It's possible, I guess. We do share a lot of stuff. Usually clothes, since we're the same size. Why do you ask?"

I was having trouble coming up with a single excuse. "Just curious," I said lamely as I sought a change of subject. Then I remembered. "I almost forgot again. The ledgers. Photocopies, since Nick has the originals. I managed to talk him into letting me photocopy the books for you since Joe seemed to want them back so badly." I pulled the photocopies from my tote and held them out.

She didn't reach for them. "I don't want them. I forgot you were coming by, or I would have canceled. You can give them to Joe or Madison."

"Oh," I said. "Okay." I tucked them back into my bag and kept digging for more information. "There were, in fact, some discrepancies with the accounting. But not on Abby's end. The discrepancies happened last year." I explained about the vendor disbursements.

She started tucking smaller items in around the towels. Measuring cups, candles. She reached again for the tape dispenser. "Like I said before, I'm not surprised. They don't play fair."

"Who? The Bryants?"

"Ben's a good guy. Lucinda's cold but okay. But Joe and Madison . . ." She shrugged. "They think only of themselves. What they want. What they need. They don't care about hurting others."

It seemed to me she was talking about more than feeling like an outcast. Or even about creative bookkeeping. "How so?"

Her chin came up, and there was fire in her eyes when she said, "Take Duncan Cole for example."

"Abby's ex-boyfriend?"

"Abby adored him, and he adored her. It about killed them both when they broke up."

"Lucinda told me about what happened, the doping."

"But that's what I mean, Darcy. There was no doping. I found his original lab results months after he was kicked off the team. His tests were normal. Someone doctored the report on the Balefire end."

"But why would they do that?"

She looked at me. "To get rid of Duncan. They didn't like him dating Abby. They didn't think he was good enough for her."

Instantly I knew it was because he was *mortal*. Have mercy, as my aunt Ve would say. No wonder he'd flipped out on them, if he hadn't really been cheating and thought one of them had set him up.

"Did you know Duncan was in the village yesterday morning?" I asked.

"You . . . you should go, Darcy. Thanks for coming by. And thanks for your offer to help with the memorial, but I can probably handle that on my own."

I was dizzy from her one-eighty. What was she hiding? What was she so afraid of?

"Quinn, if—" A crash came from down the hallway. It sounded like breaking glass.

She spun toward the sound. "You heard that, right?"

"I definitely did. Do you have a cat? A dog?"

"No."

"Come on," I said, quickly grabbing the coat I'd moved off the chair earlier. I pushed it into her arms and rushed her outside. I slammed the door behind us.

I called the police as we huddled on the sidewalk in front of the house. Quinn was shaking, so I kept an arm anchored around her.

It didn't take long for two village police cars to roll up—along with half the village it seemed. There was never a lack of rubberneckers around here.

As we waited for the police to search the house, I said, "Do you really want to be alone tonight?"

She shook her head. "But I don't have anywhere . . ."

"Let me make a call."

"I can't ask you to do that."

"You didn't."

Tear brimmed in her eyes. "Thank you."

Aunt Ve was giddy with the thought of another houseguest for Archie to entertain. I'd stepped away from Quinn and the crowd when I called to make sure Ve knew that I hadn't yet ruled Quinn out as a suspect in Abby's death.

My gut instinct was that Quinn hadn't killed Abby. She was too skittish, too scared, to be a cold-blooded murderer. But that didn't stop me from thinking she knew more than she was letting on. Ve had assured me her house was under a top-notch protection spell, a gift of Andreus, but promised to be extra careful. She also mentioned something about how piña coladas tended to loosen tongues.

I warned her that could work both ways, and she'd just laughed.

I'd hung up, hoping she had plenty of memory cleanse in the house.

Just in case.

When I turned back toward Quinn, my gaze caught a familiar face on the fringe of the crowd. I did a double-take, but when I looked again the person was gone.

My mind could have been playing tricks on me, but I didn't think so. Madison Bryant had been in the crowd. Yet, she hadn't come over to Quinn to ask what had happened.

It made me wonder if that was because she already knew . . .

Chapter Eighteen

"So nothing was taken?" Mimi asked later that night. She slipped a piece of pizza crust to Higgins as we sat around the kitchen island.

"No," I said. "Nothing was missing."

Despite having a perfectly functional and lovely dining table, around this island was where we usually ended up eating most every meal together. It was a small island, custom made with a butcher-block top and a navy blue cabinet—the only color in the primarily white kitchen. Separated by two pizzas, a bowl of Caesar salad, plates, and a lot of napkins, Mimi and Harper sat on one side of the island, Nick and I on another. Higgins and Missy had parked themselves at Mimi's feet and Archie was perched near my elbow—as far away from Higgins as he could manage.

It was cramped yet cozy. Loud yet calm.

It was *home*.

Higgins happily licked his lips as he chewed the crust and drool flew. Missy patiently waited her turn and was rewarded with a piece of pepperoni.

"*Mimi*," Nick said from his spot next to me.

She blinked at him innocently. "But they're hungry."

"Hardly," Nick said with a smile. "No more, or soon Higgins will be need to go on another diet, and do I need to remind you how well that went over last time?"

It had been at their old house, and Higgins had howled so long and loud the neighbors had finally called to make sure everything was okay.

Archie huffed. "I heard the caterwauling all the way from my cage. Off-key as well. Mimi, do not subject us all to such misery again, I beg of you."

I had no doubt Archie's comparison of Higgins' yowls to a cat-cry had been on purpose—a subtle insult that was, alas, completely lost on Higgins. The two had a love hate relationship. Higgins loved Archie, and Archie loved to hate Higgins.

It didn't help that Archie was in a mood, so his patience was worn thin. He'd been uprooted from Ve's while Quinn stayed with her, due to Quinn's allergy to feathers. No one knew if that included *familiar* feathers, but we didn't want to take the chance. The last thing she needed right now was an allergic reaction.

In the short time span that he had been here, Archie had complained about his dinner (mixed fruits, vegetables, and seeds), our lack of a decent sound system, and that there was no rum in the house.

I was ready to stuff a rag in his beak.

Harper added, "I remember that. I had a customer at the time who wanted to call the police because she thought someone was being attacked."

"It wasn't that bad," Mimi said, glancing around the table.

We all nodded.

"Sorry, Higgs," Mimi said to the dog and patted his head. He slurped her arm up and down, probably searching for a stray morsel. "The tribe has spoken."

Harper grinned at the big dog, then wiped drool splatter off her arm with a napkin and said, "Why break in to someone's house and take nothing? Was someone lying in wait to harm Quinn?"

Leave it to Harper to turn the conversation back to the investigation. She loved being in the thick of things, and it showed by the glow in her eyes. Or maybe that was Dr. Dreadful's treatment. Or the fact that Marcus had called her earlier this afternoon. She hadn't answered—and he hadn't left a message—but still. Maybe my speech got through to him, and he was finally starting to come to his senses where she was concerned.

His gift to her had been a bookmark made of filigree silver. At one end, a charm of entwined hearts so twisted together it was hard to distinguish where one started and the other ended, dangled from a small chain.

A charm quite fitting of their relationship, I thought.

Harper hadn't tossed the gift straight out the window, so maybe she was starting to come to her senses too.

Nick reached for another slice of pizza. "Thousand-dollar question. Could be someone heard about Abby's death and decided to rob the place, not knowing someone was still living there. Or maybe someone was searching for something they hadn't been able to find."

Like those ledgers? Did the Bryants know that I, and now Nick, had them? Had Madison broken in, looking for them?

Archie cleared his throat. " 'I know how to search your mind and find your secrets.' "

I racked my brain trying to place his quote but came up empty. "No idea."

"You're not even trying," he accused.

"Don't make me pluck you."

"I am unafraid, Darcy Merriweather. You threaten to pluck me at least once a week, and yet here I sit with full plumage. The correct answer is *Inception*."

He was standing on a tall driftwood perch I'd bought a couple of months ago for when he visited. The local pet store, The Furry Toadstool, touted the stand as a place for parrots to roost and play. I hadn't seen a thing on its description about it being a place for grumpy macaw familiars to sling acerbic taunts.

"Higgins, do you want to kiss the birdie?" I asked in a singsong voice. His fluffy tail thumped the floor as he looked at Archie with bright, hopeful eyes.

Archie squawked. "Not the drool! You cruel, cruel woman."

I tore off a piece of my pizza and held it out to him. He eyed it for a moment like he'd rather eat straight-up hemlock, but eventually gave in to the inevitable. His love for cheese outweighed his irritation with me.

"Does Quinn feel like she's in danger?" Harper asked as she poked at her salad. She'd eaten a few bites of pizza but not much else.

"She told me—and the police—that she had no reason to believe someone was after her, but she never stopped shaking the whole time the police were there. Whoever broke in, for whatever reason, has left her terrified."

Harper said, "Maybe she knows something she hasn't realized yet. And the person who killed Abby is now after her. Way to go, Darcy, leaving her with Aunt Ve when there's a possible serial killer stalking her."

She was definitely feeling better. "I'll pluck you, too," I threatened her.

Archie chimed in. "'Tis not such a menacing suggestion as it seems on the surface, Harper, as your eyebrows are, shall we say, rebellious? You should take Darcy up on the plucking offer. Soon."

Harper's fingertips went to her brows. "Hey! I've been sick. Dying, even. For the love. Sheesh." She leaned in close to Mimi's face. "Are they that bad?"

I was heartened by her reaction. This morning Harper wouldn't have cared if she had ferrets for eyebrows. It was good to see she was starting to care about her appearance again. But I had to wonder, once more, if this change in her had to do with feeling better . . . or Marcus.

"Depends on your definition of bad," Mimi said diplomatically as she assessed Harper's unruly, bristly brows.

"On a scale of one to Higgins?" Harper asked.

Mimi looked at Higgins, then Harper. Harper, then Higgins. "They're up there with Higgins."

"Great," Harper said, slapping a hand over her forehead. "You all can stop staring at my eyebrows now. How did we get started on this anyway? Weren't we talking about Quinn?"

"Plucking," Archie reminded.

Mimi added, "After you said Darcy was leading a serial killer straight to Aunt Ve."

"Oh, that's right. How good is that protection spell on Ve's house?" Harper asked with a hint of a smile, turning her full attention on me.

How she could joke about this, I'd never know.

"The best. Ve will be fine. Quinn, too, if someone tries to come after her there."

Nick said, "I have patrol watching the house as well, just in case."

Just in case. I didn't want to think of that kind of scenario.

"But someone, like *who*?" Harper asked. "Duncan Cole?"

"Revenge," Archie said. "A classic motive. Perhaps he's after everyone who worked at Balefire."

"'With great vengeance and furious anger . . .'" I said, glancing his way.

He folded his wings and looked away.

"Oh, come on," I said, then started humming the final *Jeopardy!* music.

"Not the *Jeopardy!* music," he cried out. "Curse you! It's *Pulp Fiction*."

"Don't make me separate you two," Harper said, pointing at Archie and me.

"There's no evidence Duncan was involved," Nick said. "Yet."

I added, "It'd be nice if he would come forward for questioning."

Nick's trip to interview Duncan had proven futile. He hadn't been home, nor had the apartment manager seen him in a couple of days. The trip to Wakefield hadn't been a complete waste of time for Nick, however, as the apartment manager not only had on file Duncan's vehicle information but an updated phone number, too. Nick had called it and left a message. If Duncan didn't return the call soon, Nick would have no choice other than to label Duncan a person of interest in the case and splash his picture all over the media.

So far Duncan hadn't called back.

The only phone that had rung tonight had been mine—a return call from Stef at the Sorcerer's Stove.

Sometime between the crashing vase and the interrogation by the police, Quinn had a change of mind about my helping with Abby's memorial.

Stef and I had managed to work out a lot of the catering details over the phone, but I was meeting with her tomorrow morning to go over some last-minute planning. I'd also phoned Lydia Wentworth from the Black Thorn at home and called in some favors for help with the flowers.

And I'd texted Glinda that I could meet her on Tuesday at the Gingerbread Shack. It gave me a day to plan how to handle that situation.

Higgins' head suddenly came up, and he raced to the back door, barking. Missy quickly followed suit, though she raced past him and went straight out the dog door.

"Is Mom here?" Harper asked loudly over the barking.

"I don't think so," I said. The back patio was brightly lit, and I didn't see her out there.

Higgins scratched fervently at the door, and Nick went over to let him out. Higgins flew out the door.

I walked over. "What is it?"

"Not sure," he said, flipping on the flood lights that illuminated the whole backyard.

Both dogs raced back and forth along the fence line at the back of the yard. There was a good twenty feet of woods behind the fence, separating our yard from the Enchanted Trail.

Harper and Mimi joined us at the door. "I don't see anything," Harper said.

Mimi squinted. "It's probably a raccoon."

"Probably," I said. But I'd seen Missy and Higgins harass raccoons before. This was a different kind of behavior. Frantic, almost. "Archie?"

"Aye, aye," he said, saluting with a colorful wing.

I held open the door and he flew out and soon disappeared into the woods.

"Look," Mimi said. "Missy and Higgins are calming down."

It was true. Both had stopped barking but hadn't left the fence. I opened the door and called for them.

Nick's phone rang as he said, "It's work. I'll be right back." He strode toward my office to take the call.

I kept a close eye on the dogs. They were taking their sweet time. I called to them with a little more urgency in my voice.

"Do you want me to go get them?" Mimi asked.

"No," Harper and I said in unison.

I glanced at my sister and guessed the look of apprehension in her eyes mirrored my own. I called the dogs again, and this time, they listened. I let out a breath of relief as they turned toward the house.

Archie circled above the back yard, then flew back inside and landed on his perch. "It's too dark to see much of anything back there, but I noted some footprints near the fence. Whoever they belonged to is gone."

Footprints. Whose? And why was someone back there?

As soon as the dogs were inside, I locked the door, and also Missy's dog door. I didn't want her going in and out tonight.

We were still at the door when Nick came back. Before I could tell him about the footprints, he said, "I have to go. Duncan Cole's car has been located."

"Where?" I asked, feeling dread spiraling through me.

"In the playhouse parking lot. Duncan's somewhere in the village."

I didn't like that news one little bit.

"What does Higgins have in his mouth?" Harper asked as Mimi tried to corral him to wipe his paws. "Is that a leash?"

"I don't think so," I said, crouching down. Higgins thought we were playing keep away as I reached toward his mouth. He tossed his head this way and that, preventing me from getting a good grip on his new toy.

In his sternest voice, Nick said, "Drop it, drop it, Higgins."

Higgins glanced up at him, then reluctantly let go of what he'd dragged inside.

My breath caught when I realized exactly what it was.

A noose.

"Is that blood?" Harper asked, horrified as she pointed at red specks on the thin, blue, braided rope.

Mimi grabbed hold of my hand, squeezed it tight. "That's sick."

Nick took a closer look at the frayed rope. "I don't think so. It's . . ." He squinted. "Lint. I need to get this into an evidence bag. I'll be right back."

I stood in silence, trying to take in what had just happened.

And trying to ignore the fact that the noose had my name written on it in dark, permanent ink.

Chapter Nineteen

I was on my way out for my Monday morning run with Starla, wondering if I should have canceled, when I spotted Ve coming down the sidewalk toward my house.

It had been a long night.

Police officers had been at the house until the wee hours, searching the yard for any footprints they could use to take an impression—and unfortunately, there hadn't been any usable ones. The noose was now evidence. It had been made of a short piece of rope and wasn't long enough to hang so much as an eggplant, but the threat came through loud and clear.

I'd upset someone with my questioning. But who?

And I couldn't shake the feeling that the rope looked familiar. However, I couldn't place where I might have seen it. In the Mad Dash event tent, maybe? I simply wasn't sure. If it had been there, any number of people had access to it. All the Mad Dashers. The Bryants. Quinn. Possibly even Duncan Cole. The list was endless.

One thing was abundantly clear to me: Time wasn't on my side with this investigation. I could only guess that whoever had killed Abby was now after me—to stop my investigation. If my questions had agitated someone enough to make a threat on my life, what would push them over the edge to *act* on that threat?

The sooner I found Abby's killer, the better. Not only to bring justice for Abby, but because now *my* life depended on it.

But I couldn't just hide out here in the house, as much as I wanted to. I had a job to do. My mother—and the Craft—were counting on me. Until I figured out who'd hurt Abby and threatened me, I'd just have to be extra careful. Carry protection charms with me at all times and avoid potentially dangerous situations.

While we as a family were all on edge, last night we'd decided as a group to try to carry on as usual. A little more careful than usual, but still. After a long night of little sleep, Nick had left to drop Mimi at school then head to the station. Harper was still sleeping, and Archie had been summoned by my mother. I'd already been on the phone this morning, raiding my contact list for a crew to work as servers for the memorial reception tonight. I had a list ready to take with me when I met with Stef later on.

"Good morning!" Ve called out when she spotted me. "Cute hat. One of Harper's?"

My usual running hat was my pink Balefire beanie, but I couldn't bring myself to put it on this morning. Instead, I'd grabbed a woolen hat Harper had made in her crochet group. A fluffy pom-pom bounced against my head every step I took. Even though it was another rare warm day, well over freezing, I liked to keep my head toasty when I ran. "She made it for my birthday."

Ve inspected it. "She's getting good. I was just coming over to check on her before getting some coffee and muffins from the Witch's Brew. How are you all doing this morning? You had quite a night."

Half the village had strolled by our house last night, wondering what was going on with all the police cars. When Ve heard the sirens, she came straight over to check on us but hadn't stayed long because of her houseguest. "We're okay," I said. "I'm extra grateful this morning for the protection spells on the house."

The spells that undoubtedly kept the intruder from coming inside the yard.

In what might have been related news, there was no news on Duncan Cole's whereabouts—he'd never returned to his car. And while the police wanted to question Duncan, at this point he was simply a possible witness. So no manhunt.

Had he been the one to give Higgins the noose?

Was it one of the Bryants? If one of them was guilty, they wouldn't want me to keep nosing around.

We had no way of knowing who it was who'd been behind the house quite yet. Hopefully some DNA could be extracted from the fibers of the rope, but those tests could take weeks. Months, even.

But one thing was clear. I'd hit a nerve somewhere. It was just a matter of figuring out where.

I could, however, rule out Quinn. She'd been at Ve's during that time.

Ve's coppery hair was twisted back and pinned in place, but a few strands fluttered in the chilly breeze as she said, "I have to admit I'm surprised to see you going out for a run. After everything . . ."

She wore a knitted shawl, pinned at her shoulder with beautiful agate broach that I knew was a protection amulet. I was glad to see her . . . alive. I hadn't wanted to let on, but Harper had freaked me out last night with her "leading a serial killer to Ve's house" talk.

"I'm a little surprised myself," I said. "But I don't want to live in fear. I'm not completely crazy, however. I'm meeting Starla, and we'll be sure to stick to well-traveled paths."

"I'm glad to hear you say so. How's Harper feeling this morning?"

The sky had clouded over, and forecasters were predicting a sharp drop in temperatures and another storm tonight into tomorrow. Mimi was already giddy at the thought of a potential snow day. "She's still sleeping, which is a good thing, I think."

"It most definitely is." Ve threw a glance toward the house. "I won't disturb her then."

"How was your night with Quinn? I'm guessing no piña coladas since you're upright."

"Unfortunately, no. No Tom Selleck, either, alas. Quinn went straight to the guest room and has been in there since. I did hear her speaking to someone on the phone during the night. She was crying, but I couldn't make out what was said, even with my ear pressed to the wall. She did ask if she could stay with me again tonight. I, of course, agreed. I'm happy to have her."

I was glad to hear Quinn had asked to stay. As long as she was at Ve's, she was safe. "It might be in our best interest to enlist some tiny ears for a stakeout tonight."

"Ooh, yes. Good thinking."

"I'll pay a visit to Pepe and Mrs. P after my run." I wished I'd thought of the idea last night, then we might have known who Quinn was talking to. "What's your take on Quinn?"

"She's a skittish thing. Which I'd say was justified since someone broke into her home."

"True enough."

"Has Derrie been by this morning?"

Derrie—Ve's nickname for my mother. "Not today. She summoned Archie before dawn, and I haven't heard from either since."

"I wonder if they're meeting about the Harper situation."

The Harper situation. It hurt just thinking about it. I wished there was some way Harper could know what she was facing.

But there wasn't.

Ve shook her fists. "That Dorothy . . . I loathe that woman."

"You're not alone in feeling that way." I put an arm around her. "But she seriously miscalculated the lengths mothers will go to in order to protect their children."

"Probably because she doesn't have a loving bone in her body. I feel sorry for Glinda. And Vince should be grateful he escaped Dorothy's narcissism."

I wasn't sure he'd agree about that, though Ve was probably right. Vince was searching for love. True love. Unconditional love. The kind of feeling most mothers had for their children.

The kind of love my mother had for Harper and me.

The kind of love Harper already had for her child.

Dorothy only loved herself.

And I hoped beyond hope that would lead to her downfall.

* * *

"Did Harper call Marcus to thank him for the gift?" Starla asked as we jogged across the village green toward the Enchanted Trail.

I'd been updating her on the whole Harper-Marcus saga. "Not that I know of. If anything, she'd probably text him. And I'm not sure she'd tell me she did."

We were squeezed together tightly on a wet path, boxed in by melting snowbanks, and needed to drop into single file whenever we passed by someone.

"*Hmm,*" she said.

The pom-pom on my hat bounced against my head in rhythm to my steps. "*Hmm,* what?"

A thermal headband kept her ears warm while her braided ponytail slashed the air. "While I was in the Witch's Brew this morning, I was standing a couple people behind Noelle Quinlan. She was on the phone, and even though she was trying to keep her voice down, it was easy enough to eavesdrop on her side of the conversation."

"I'm not sure Noelle knows how to whisper."

"Exactly. Anyway, she was saying something about how it was too late to get out of the contract and that there was nothing they could do, but that she could try to find him a new place in the village. I'm pretty sure she was talking to Marcus."

I nearly tripped over my feet. I caught my balance and said, "What makes you think it was him?"

She laughed and said, "Because she called him Marcus."

Did I know another man named Marcus in this village? I couldn't think of a single one. "When was this?"

"Maybe an hour ago?"

"And it took you this long to tell me?"

She shrugged. "Good things come to those who wait?"

I gave her a little shove.

"Hey! Assault!" she said, smiling wide.

I smiled too. "It has to mean Marcus changed his mind about moving, right? I'm not just jumping to conclusions because I'm hopeful, am I?"

"If you're jumping, then I am too. With both feet. Are you going to say anything to Harper?"

"I don't know. I don't want to get her hopes up until I know something for certain." I was trying to figure out when I could squeeze in a visit to see Marcus today. After this run, I needed to stop to see Pepe and Mrs. P. Then I had to stop at home and change before my meeting with Stef at the Stove. I also needed to see Vince about those surveillance tapes, too, before meeting with Lydia at the Black Thorn. Then this afternoon, I had plans to question Joe and Madison Bryant before Abby's memorial.

"You have more restraint than I do," Starla said. "I want to rent a plane to fly a banner."

"I just don't want to get Harper's hopes up if we're wrong. She's been through so much."

As we passed the playhouse, I couldn't help throwing a glance toward the adjoining parking lot. I didn't know which car belonged to Duncan Cole, but I did notice there was a village police car parked nearby.

"Then I suppose I'll put a hold on the plane. For now."

Taking a side path behind the playhouse, we emerged onto the Enchanted Trail. The path widened, allowing us some elbow room. We turned right, and soon were behind the Sorcerer's Stove, the site where Abby and Ben had reportedly argued Friday night. It was possible someone who worked at the restaurant had heard them—I'd ask around when I saw Stef later.

Starla and I fell into a rhythm as we jogged, splashing our way down the path. I was feeling guilty for not sharing the information about the Eldership, but I hadn't thought to ask my mother yesterday if I could spread the word to those we trusted. Like Starla and Evan. The more people on our side to protect Harper and the baby in the next few months, the better.

Then, of course, there was Glinda. I was meeting her tomorrow at the Gingerbread Shack, but I was thinking of canceling. I still questioned her role in her mother's plans and wasn't sure I could hide my emotions from her so easily. Did she really need my help with her wedding? Or was she using me—and our friendship—to get information for Dorothy?

Starla and I chatted as we ran, discussing Abby's death and throwing around theories. Nothing made much sense where that case was concerned, so we always ended up right back where we started.

After three miles, we neared the turnoff that led to her house, where we parted ways most mornings.

"Let me know if you learn anything about Marcus. Or Abby."

"I will," I promised.

She shifted foot to foot, hesitating to run off.

"What?" I asked.

"How about I take the long way home? Past the Bewitching Boutique?"

The news of the noose had freaked her out.

"Don't be silly. It's way out of your way."

"I don't mind."

"Starla, go home. I have a protection charm in my pocket. I'll only be on this trail a minute more, and look, there are a lot of people out today. I'll be just fine."

She turned and looked for herself at all the people on the path. Drawing in a deep breath, she said, "Okay, but run really fast. Don't take any chances."

"I won't."

"Promise?"

"Promise."

With another deep breath, she loped into a jog. She threw her arm up in a wave as she veered off, out of sight. I continued on the trail toward the main square and the Bewitching Boutique.

As I neared the turnoff, I looked ahead and saw Madison Bryant crouched next to a jogging stroller, pointing at something in the woods. I slowed as I neared and saw what they were looking at: a male cardinal, his feathers bright red against the snowy backdrop.

"Look, Aine, birdie," I heard Madison say before she looked up when she heard my footsteps. She was decked out in fancy running clothes.

I hesitated for only a moment before I approached. It was my job to question her, and where better than out here in the open? With lots of witnesses.

"Beautiful morning for a run," I said.

She side-eyed my hat before saying, "It is. We just stopped for a moment to bird-watch."

Aine looked cozy in the stroller. A well-loved red fleece blanket decorated with white hearts was tucked tight around her body and her casts, but her arms were free and her mittened hands were waving all around. Her face was pink from the wind and chill in the air, and her eyes bright beneath the hood of her coat. She smiled at me when she saw me peeking in and my heart melted.

"She looks like she's enjoying herself."

"These morning jogs are her favorite part of the day. She loves the wind in her face. When she's finally able to walk, I have the feeling I'm going to be chasing her all over the village."

"How long until she gets her casts off?"

"Hopefully by summertime."

"She'll be running alongside you before you know it."

A shadow crossed her eyes, and she was suddenly busy with a loose thread on her sleeve. "Actually, the doctors have warned us that she might not be able to run at our kind of level. High-impact sports aren't usually recommended for someone whose dysplasia was so severe."

This was, I realized, the longest Madison had ever talked with me, and I wondered why she was being so chatty. "Does Lucinda know that? I only ask because when I was talking to her yesterday she mentioned being eager to get Aine started training in a few years."

Madison rolled her eyes. "She knows. She's simply refusing to accept it. Joe, too. They think the Vincicrafter in Aine will overcome, but Aine is already showing signs that Terracrafting is her dominant Craft. She happiest outside, and she's enamored with trees and flowers and nature. It calms her when nothing else will."

It sounded to me like that might be case. No one would know for certain, however, until Aine was a good bit older. "In the end, all that really matters is that she's happy and healthy, right?"

The baby gurgled and smiled a drooly grin that reminded me of Higgins.

Madison nodded and picked at the loose thread again. "I'm glad I bumped into you out here. I was going to call later . . ."

"About?"

"The meeting this afternoon. I need to cancel it. With Abby's memorial today and everything, it's just not a good time. Maybe later this week? Thursday? Friday?"

Ah. This was why she was being so chatty. Easing me into the news that she was canceling our appointment. I should have been more shocked, but I wasn't. Not after Joe's and Ben's reactions toward me yesterday. Too bad for Madison that I wasn't in the mood to play her games. "That's not going to work. Time is crucial right now, and I know Joe is leaving town on Wednesday."

She had the grace to blush. "Even still, this afternoon isn't going to work. I'll call you." She swiveled the stroller and kicked into a jog.

More likely, she wouldn't call at all.

What was with these people? They all knew they'd have to face the Elder if they continued to evade my questions.

I couldn't let her get away without answering at least some of my questions, so I followed her. "How about now?"

Aine babbled as the stroller glided along the path. Madison didn't miss a step as she said, "Now what?"

I appealed to her competitive nature by saying, "We run one mile together. You answer as many questions as I can throw out. My pace," I clarified. Because she could easily sprint off, leaving me in the dust before I could even get one question out.

"Okay," she said. "One mile. Shoot."

"Where were you when Abby was killed?"

She slowed to a stop. "You're kidding. You think I hurt Abby? Why would I do that? I loved Abby. She was like family."

Like family. But she hadn't been. And besides, I knew firsthand from my investigations that family status didn't exclude murder.

"I'm actually trying to rule you out. But if I was looking for a motive, I'd say something along the lines of Abby discovering that you and Joe have been stealing from the company. She told Ben she noticed something was off with the race accounting. Maybe he said something about it to Joe, since the race was your pet project. The next day, Abby was dead. From what I've heard, Abby played by the rules. She would have turned you and Joe in. Did you or Joe kill her to keep her quiet?"

"You're out of your mind. No, we didn't kill her." Color rose up her neck and she started running again. "You make it sound like the bookkeeping thing was a big deal. It wasn't. It was just a few dollars here and there. Certainly nothing to kill someone over."

"I'm pretty sure embezzling is a big deal."

"It's not embezzlement when you own the company. It's *our* money."

I hadn't thought about that. It was true.

"We use it to pay January property taxes on our house," she said. "Money's tight around that time of year."

Obviously, this had been going on for a while. Except for this year . . . because they hadn't needed the extra money since the Mad Dash's proceeds were going to the family. It was probably why I had been allowed to help with the race as well. No one ever expected Abby would look at *last year's* accounting. Or share those books with me.

"Why not just give yourself a raise?" I asked. "Or draw cash as the owner?"

She shrugged.

"You're using it to pay property taxes, but do you pay taxes on the money itself?" I asked, suddenly realizing why they'd hide the extra income. So they wouldn't have to report it.

She shrugged. "Joe handles the taxes."

Joe, who was avoiding me. "If you're not paying taxes on the money, Madison, that's tax fraud. And it's a felony."

She wrinkled her nose. "I'm sure it's not. It's not worth the trouble of you looking into it."

I didn't want to argue, so I pressed on. "You never did say where you were the morning Abby died."

"I was in the Witch's Brew with Aine most of the morning, then we went over to the event tent, then to the starting line."

"Did you see Abby that morning?"

"No. The last time I saw Abby was the night before at the Stove."

Which reminded me of another question. "Do you know what Abby and Ben fought about behind the restaurant Friday night?"

"They fought?"

I took that as a no. "So I've heard. Where was Joe when Abby went missing?" I wanted to see if she'd verify his bathroom alibi.

"He didn't kill her. He loved her."

It seemed everybody loved her. Which didn't quite explain why she was very dead.

"That's not what I asked." We were coming up on the half-mile mark. "Where was Joe?"

"He was out and about. Doing his warm-up. Meeting with people. Catching up."

"Do you know if he saw Abby?"

"You shouldn't be wasting your time on us. We didn't kill Abby. This is ridiculous."

"Joe wasn't at the starting line. Where was he when the race went off?"

"Using the woods as a bathroom, since the portable bathrooms were locked. It took longer than he thought, and he couldn't make it back on time. He caught up with the pack not long after they passed by him. He disqualified himself from the race, so that's not a big deal either."

"Can anyone verify where he was?"

She shrugged. "I don't know. I'm sure someone can. There were a lot of people around that morning."

My chest was starting to hurt from exertion—and I was running out of mileage. "Do you know why Duncan Cole was in the village on the morning of the race?"

"Duncan was in the village?"

I was getting nowhere fast. "He was. *Is*. His car is parked in the playhouse lot. No one knows where he is, though."

"Do you think he was involved with what happened to Abby?" she asked, her eyes brightening.

As though she was *hoping*. "Do you?"

"He and Abby did have a bad breakup."

"I heard they broke up because someone at Balefire set him up with a fake positive on his doping test."

"How do you know that?"

"Doesn't matter. All that matters is I *do* know."

"Duncan was an issue," she finally said. "He'd been impossible since Abby told him about the Craft. Making snide remarks, being reckless around mortals. He had to go."

"With a nice, tidy memory cleanse on his way out so he couldn't remember that you guys have magic on your side."

"Exactly."

"You could have ruined his career."

"What career?" she asked. "He's a mortal. He's good, but not great."

"Great like Joe and Ben and Lucinda."

"It sounds harsh, but it's just reality."

I didn't like it. Not one bit. And suddenly felt extra sorry for Quinn.

"How was Ben and Abby's relationship?"

"Good," she said. "Solid. I played matchmaker between them, so I should know. They were much better suited."

"Because they're both Crafters."

"Right," she said, missing my sarcasm. "Now you understand."

I understood that I wished I'd never known this side of the Bryants. It was disconcerting to know Aine was going to grow up around this kind of insular thinking. Absently, I wondered if my mother could step in somehow, someway.

I gave up all pretenses and said, "Had either Ben or Abby mentioned that they were eloping this week?"

She laughed. "No! You're kidding, right?"

"I'm not kidding. They had plans to elope tomorrow. Abby had a dress made at the Bewitching Boutique and had ordered a cake from the Gingerbread Shack."

She slowed to a stop again. "You're sure?"

"Positive."

She looked like she had the wind knocked out of her. "I . . . I don't know what to say. Are you really sure?"

"I saw the dress myself. Quinn has it now."

"Quinn knew about the elopement?"

"It was probably too hard a secret to keep from her, seeing as how she and Abby were best friends and lived together."

"I just can't believe Ben would do that. Not tell anyone, I mean." She looked off in the distance, then bent down to adjust Aine's blanket.

My lungs were on fire, and I tried to catch a full breath. "What do you know about the break-in at Abby's house yesterday? I saw you in the crowd outside afterward."

"I don't know anything about it." She picked fluff off the pilled blanket, let it float away. "I need to go."

"Wait, one more question."

"What?" she said impatiently.

"Where was Joe last night?"

Her brow furrowed. "Last night? What happened last night?"

Aine waved and cooed at a woman passing by. Her sweet innocence both filled my heart—and hurt it. Because I knew it wouldn't last forever. "Someone left a noose at my house with my name on it."

Redness slowly infused Madison's face, and she wouldn't meet my eye as she said, "And you think Joe did it? That's absolutely . . . preposterous! We're done here. Bye, Darcy."

Before I could squeak out a protest, she sprinted off. I didn't bother to chase her. I didn't have that kind of foot speed, and she'd answered most of my questions. Whether they were honest answers remained to be seen.

Her over-the-top reaction about the noose made me think I had hit a little close to home with my questioning. But what I really needed was verification of Joe's alibi for the time Abby had died. Madison might be naïve enough to believe that doctoring the books wasn't a big deal, but Joe was a savvy businessman. If he was hiding money, it had to be because of taxes. And tax fraud was a felony. A felony that carried jail time.

It was definitely a motive for murder.

And it was quite a coincidence that he couldn't be accounted for during the same time Abby had been killed.

A very big coincidence, indeed.

Chapter Twenty

Godfrey was busy with a customer when I strolled into the Bewitching Boutique, which was a good thing as he despised my workout attire. He held a deep loathing for sweatpants and would probably keel flat over if he saw the state of my stained and torn long-sleeved tee beneath my running jacket. I tugged off my hat and gave him a quick wave before making a beeline for the workroom at the back of the shop.

I'd already called Nick and left a voicemail for him to call me when he had a chance, and stopped at the Ginger-bread Shack to chat with Evan about a cake tasting tomorrow morning, letting him in on the secret about Glinda's upcoming nuptials. While I was there, I picked up a treat for Pepe and Mrs. P. It never hurt to soften them up with cheesecake before asking a big favor.

I swished aside the heavy curtain separating the boutique's large work space from the showroom and stepped inside. I took a blissful moment to look around, soaking in the magic of the room. It was one of my favorite places in the village.

Shelving filled with bolts of fabric lined two walls. Bold colors, muted pastels, bright patterns, subtle prints. Sparkly, matte. Lace, tulle, silk. It was all I could do to not walk around the room to touch and admire.

"Ma chère!" Pepe said from his spot at a work station in front of the notion wall, which was an organizational masterpiece. His pointy nose sniffed the air, and he took off his glasses to give me a speculative glance. He lowered his voice and asked, "Is that cheesecake I smell?" He dropped the needle and thread he'd been using to fasten sequins to a blouse and bounded over to the edge of the table. "Whatever it is you want, it is done."

With his Cloakcrafting abilities, he'd have the blouse finished in minutes, rather than hours. His eye for detail was impeccable, his stitches precise.

I held up the snack box. "It is. Why are you whispering?"

"Doll!" Mrs. P poked her head out of the tiny door in the baseboard. "I thought I heard your voice."

Pepe groaned. "That was why I was whispering."

He held out his hands for the bakery box. "Quickly, *ma chère!*"

I laughed. "Is Mrs. P on one of her health kicks again?"

He shuddered. "Indeed, and it is abysmal. I had a wheat bran muffin for breakfast. Wheat bran. *Quelle horror!*"

"What is that smell?" she asked as she scurried up the table leg.

She wore her usual pink velour dress, and I thought it was high time she added a few more outfits to her wardrobe. I said, "Wheat bran does sound pretty dismal."

Mrs. P scampered across the tabletop and sat next to Pepe. The hair between her ears was standing straight up, in its regular style. She'd been a familiar for more than a year now and sometimes it was hard to remember what she had looked like in her human form.

"My tongue," Pepe continued, motioning toward his lips. "Hours later, and it is still sticking to the roof of my mouth."

To him, she said, "If you'd stop popping the buttons on your vest, you wouldn't need to lose a few ounces." She jabbed little fingers into his rotund belly, then looked at me. "He's had to sew the buttons back on three times last week." She sniffed loudly. "Is that . . . cheesecake?" Whiskers twitched, and her dark eyes rounded with interest.

I held up the cheesecake. "Should I just take this home with me, then? I don't want to cause a rift between the two of you."

"No!" they both said at the same time. Then laughed together.

"I suppose there's no harm in a little cheesecake," Mrs. P said. "Pepe can always sew more buttons." She smacked her lips. "My tongue is stuck to the roof of my mouth too. Wheat bran. *Blagh.*"

"Or maybe it's time to sew a slightly bigger vest?" I suggested as I set the cheesecake between them and sat on a rolling stool. Familiars did not have to worry about things like cholesterol or diabetes. They were immortal until they chose to cross over.

Pepe bowed. "My heartfelt gratitude for your kindness in using the word 'slightly.'"

I laughed and kissed his head. A blush swept across his cheeks.

"Now, don't go making me jealous, doll face," Mrs. P said.

I kissed her head too. "How's that?"

"Better. Much better." She patted my cheek.

Pepe broke off a chunk of the cheesecake and handed it to Mrs. P. She nibbled and sighed happily before saying, "What brings you by, doll?"

"A top-secret mission, if you're interested," I said.

Her ear wiggled. "Do tell."

I told them all about Quinn staying with Ve and her late-night phone call. "If we have eyes and ears in her room, we might be able to learn a little more about what she's hiding if there's a similar call tonight. Are you up for it?"

"Of course!" Mrs. P wiped her lips.

"And perhaps after you're done with Quinn, you can eavesdrop on Joe and Madison Bryant as well?" I filled them in about the noose situation and my concerns that Joe might be behind the threat and also Abby's death.

Pepe twirled his whisker mustache. "*Absolument!*"

Absolutely. "Thank you both. Your reconnaissance is invaluable."

"I just love a stakeout!" Mrs. P said enthusiastically. "But hopefully we won't have the same disastrous results we had at Dorothy Hansel Dewitt's house last night."

This was news to me. "You were spying on Dorothy?"

Pepe went for seconds on the cheesecake. "*Oui.* At the request of the Elder."

It seemed the war was well underway.

"My poor tail." Mrs. P held it up to show me.

It looked as though the fur had been burned off the tip. "What happened?"

"We were creeping up to Dorothy's home, nearing the foundation, and next thing we knew, we were thrown backward!" Mrs. P explained, using expansive hand gestures to demonstrate. "My tail took the worst of the blow. I must have turned my back at the last second."

"There must be a protection spell on the home," Pepe said.

"But that looks like a burn." I gestured to Mrs. P's tail. "Protection spells don't harm. Oh. Oh, no."

"What, doll?" Mrs. P asked.

To Catch a Witch

 231

"Protections spells don't harm, but hexes do."

Pepe twirled his whiskers. "Indeed, they do. Dorothy must have commissioned a hex from Vince."

"A hex to protect her house?" Mrs. P asked. "That doesn't make sense. Protection is helpful."

"It was probably a hex on intruders or something similar," I said. "Not a hex for the house itself."

"Curse her!" Mrs. P cried. "Is that not against Craft law?"

Pepe said, "*Non.* Dorothy did not use *her* magic to harm."

"But," she argued, "Dorothy must have asked Vince to use his dark magic to help her."

"There is no law against that," I said. "Unfortunately."

Mrs. P threw her little fists into the air. "Curse them both!"

"I'll talk to Vince," I said. "See what I can find out. Maybe there's a way around the hex."

I really wished Andreus Woodshall was in town. If anyone knew how to counteract a hex, it would be him. If worse came to worse, I supposed I could call him.

Or, better yet, ask Ve to call him.

I glanced at the wall clock and stood up. "I need to get going. You two be careful tonight, okay?"

"Will do, doll. You let us know if you need any more help."

I was about to ask if they could sneak into Glinda's house to see what they could see, hear what they could hear. But ultimately decided not to.

I needed to deal with Glinda myself.

* * *

I hustled back home to shower and change before going to the Sorcerer's Stove to meet with Stef.

Harper was still asleep when I checked on her. Whatever Dr. Dreadful had done to cure her insomnia had worked like a charm. Sleep, he had explained, was great medicine for her body to heal and strengthen, so the more she slept the better. She'd been surrounded by furry friends when I looked in, including Missy who seemed to be spending a lot more time at home now that Harper was there. It was as though the animals sensed Harper needed their protection.

When I left, I made sure to double-check all the windows and doors, turn on the alarm, and lock the mudroom door behind me. I had only taken a few steps down the driveway when my phone rang. It was Nick.

"Do you know that everyone loved Abby?" he asked with a sardonic tinge.

"I've heard that a time or two in the past couple of days."

"I shocked Joe with the news of Ben's elopement plans."

"And I shocked Madison with the same information."

"You saw Madison?"

"It's why I called you earlier." As I walked along the square, I told him about my literal run-in with her. And how she admitted that she and Joe had used creative accounting.

"Hold on a sec," he said. I heard muffled talking in the background before he came back on the line. "Sorry. Just having Joe brought back in. He neglected to tell me anything about that when I asked him about those bookkeeping ledgers. I'll contact the IRS as well."

I wanted to feel bad they'd be facing an investigation, but I didn't like them very much right now. "Did Joe give you an alibi for the time Abby was killed? Or where he was last night?"

"As for where he was on Saturday morning, he told me pretty much the same thing he told you. He was using the bushes as his personal bathroom."

The same thing Madison had said as well. But it didn't mean it was true. "And last night?"

"Said he was home all night and Madison could verify that."

I'm sure she would—even if it wasn't true.

I kept checking over my shoulder as I walked along. The square was crowded, but I wasn't taking any chances. That noose had freaked me out, too. I told him about enlisting Pepe and Mrs. P's help with Quinn. "I can't help thinking that Quinn knows more than she's letting on. Who was she talking to in the middle of the night? Why did she react to Duncan Cole's name like she did?"

"I should to talk to her again," Nick said.

"Get in line," I teased. I waved to Vivienne Lucas inside The Furry Toadstool as I passed. "I need to talk to her too."

"I have more manpower than you do."

"I have the Elder on my side."

"Quinn's mortal."

"Is she? Or is she a Halfcrafter?" I was still suspicious after her mention of magic.

"You'd know better than I would."

"My mother will know best of all."

"You haven't talked to her yet today?"

"Not yet. Hopefully soon. Any news on Duncan?"

"Nothing. He's vanished. I'm trying to get a warrant to search his apartment and car."

It made me wonder if Harper could do the lost and found spell to find him. It seemed unlikely, since we couldn't get one of his hairs.

Not to mention that Harper was off the Craft right now.

"Oh, I got a call from Noelle this morning," Nick said.

"About the closing?" It was supposed to be tomorrow afternoon. "Or something to do with Abby's house?"

"The closing. Looks like it's been pushed back to Friday morning. Another problem with the buyer's loan."

"I don't like the sound of that."

"Me, either, but Noelle didn't seem worried."

"Noelle never seems worried about anything."

He laughed. "That's true. Okay, I've got to run."

We said our goodbyes and hung up just as I was walking up the pathway to the Stove's front door. Inside the vestibule, I paused to look at the community board. I noticed a flyer for the Crafty Hookers and wondered if this was where Harper had found that particular club.

The dining room was busy with the late breakfast crowd. The air was heavily scented with bacon and something sweet. Blueberry muffins or pancakes perhaps. I told the hostess I was there to see Stef, and she walked me to the back of the restaurant to one of the offices off the kitchen.

I had a weird sense of déjà vu as I followed behind her. It wasn't all that long ago I'd been investigating a crime centering around this restaurant.

A crime that had involved Glinda's adopted sister.

Suddenly Glinda's words from yesterday rang in my ears.

And I don't want to be a mother like mine.

"Darcy, hi!" Stef said, shaking me from my thoughts. "Sit, sit."

I sat and pulled a folio from my tote bag. "Quinn hasn't told me much about what she's already set up."

"I'm just happy she didn't have any hard feelings about the chocolate cake."

"That's because she doesn't know."

"Oh. Well, thank you, then."

"Accidents happen. It didn't seem like it had any lasting effects on anyone."

I noticed a picture on the desk of her and a man cuddled together on the beach.

She saw me looking. "My husband."

"Your husband? I thought you and Vince?"

"I'm a widow. And Vince . . ." She shrugged. "He helps pass the time. We're not serious. Or exclusive. He didn't tell you otherwise did he? I don't want to lead him on."

"No, no, he didn't. I didn't mean to infer that." I was happy to hear her say it, after what Vince had said about their relationship . . . and the fact that he'd been out with Noelle. "I jumped to conclusions, is all. I'm sorry about your husband. I can't imagine."

"Thank you." She waved a hand. "Anyway, let's get to work and take a look at this menu."

We went over the offerings, came up with a timeline on when to set up at Balefire, and I signed a contract.

I stood up and shook her hand. "Thanks for being so accommodating. I know this was last minute."

"I'm glad you were able to step in with the extra crew so we could make it work. I really wanted to help after what happened to Abby."

"I know the feeling."

"Any developments with the investigation?"

"Not really. Nick is interviewing lots of people, but the consensus is the same. Everyone loved Abby. But . . . there is one thing you might be able to help with."

"Anything."

"There's a rumor going around that Ben and Abby had a loud fight behind here on Friday night. Ben denies it. Did you hear anything?"

"I not only heard Abby have an argument but saw it, too."

Finally a witness!

"I was on a break and happened to be outside."

"What were she and Ben fighting about?"

"Oh, no. The fight wasn't with Ben."

"Wait. It wasn't?"

"Shoot. I should have let the police know about it, but I didn't put it together that there might be a connection until just now. I'm sorry."

My mind reeled. "If not Ben, then who was she arguing with?"

"I don't know who he was. I'd never seen him before. Tall guy, dark hair, big fluffy beard. Thin."

Duncan Cole. The description fit him to a T.

I wanted to shake Stef for not sharing this information before now. Instead, I said, "Did you hear what they were fighting about?"

"Something about a wedding happening soon. Abby was angry with him and kept saying he shouldn't be there. He kept saying he was tired of waiting. She just kept telling him to go. I stepped in at that point to ask if she needed any help. She said no, and the man walked away. Abby went back inside with me."

Tired of waiting? For what? "Did she seem scared?"

"Honestly? No. Just upset."

"I'll let Nick know about this. He's probably going to want to talk to you."

"Sure, sure. Anytime."

I gathered up my tote bag and practically ran for the door.

Duncan knew about Abby's upcoming elopement. Had he killed her to stop it from happening?

Chapter Twenty-One

It was close to noon by the time I made it to Lotions and Potions. I'd called Nick and left yet another message. Knowing that it was *Duncan* and Abby who had fought the night before her death would help him get the search warrants he needed for Duncan's apartment and car.

As I pulled open the shop door, I was amazed at how an hour ago I was thinking that Joe might have killed Abby, and now Duncan was at the top of my list.

Aloe and eucalyptus scented the air inside the shop, undercut with a hint of sage. Vince was dusting bottles and looked up as I came in. His hand, I noticed, was freshly bandaged.

There were a few people shopping, and a young woman was working the register.

Vince's face was somehow pale and flushed at the same time as he said, "Can I interest you in a cranberry-thyme moisturizer, miss?"

"I'm good thanks. Are *you* good?"

"I have moisturizer enough to last me a lifetime." He gestured to all his merchandise, then set the duster down. "I'm guessing you're here about the surveillance video?"

"No, I mean, yes, I'm here about the video. But I didn't mean moisturizer. Are you feeling okay?"

He fluffed his hair. "Am I not looking my usual handsome self?"

"You look feverish."

"Are you calling me hot?"

I followed him back to his office. "Vince."

"Darcy."

"Let me feel your forehead."

"Don't make me ask you to leave. I might have a little cold. I'm fine."

I narrowed my eyes.

"I'm *fine*."

"Fine."

We went into his office, a small room crammed full with a desk, filing cabinet, a couple of chairs, and drabness. He went behind the desk, and I pulled a folding chair up to the edge of it.

"Good. Now that we've settled that, I can show you the video." He booted up a laptop. "I already sent copies to Nick this morning for him to look over, but from what I've seen, Ben's alibi checks out." He pointed at the screen. "Here he is stomping back toward the tent. Note the time stamp."

I set my elbows on the desktop and leaned in to study the laptop screen. Through the blowing snow, I could pick out Ben and Quinn walking into the frame from the direction of the trailhead. They split after a few steps. Ben went straight to the tent and Quinn went toward Spellbound. So far it was just like Quinn had told me.

And Vince was right—Ben was stomping. Anger emanated from him, even from this viewpoint. The time had been 7:48. Twelve minutes before the race began.

Something else caught my eye. Or, rather, someone. Joe. He was milling about, doing stretching exercises. Jumping. Lunging. High knee lifts. Low squats.

He didn't appear to be a man about to commit murder, but I knew looks could be deceiving.

I scanned the crowd. I didn't see Duncan, but I did spot Lucinda warming up near Madison and Aine, who stood at the curb in front of the Witch's Brew. Lucinda was making Aine laugh with over-exaggerated jumping jacks. Quinn stopped to talk with them for a second before continuing on to the bookshop.

I was happy to see neither had made faces at her behind her back.

"Ben's inside the tent for almost five minutes," Vince said, glancing at a notepad.

He'd taken notes. I bit back a smile and the urge to tease him.

"Then," he continued, "Ben comes out and starts bouncing around like a deranged acrobat."

"You mean, warming up?"

"You can call it what you want, I'll call it what I want."

"How about Quinn? Do you have footage of her coming and going from Spellbound?"

He tapped a few keys. "Here. She's going into Spellbound."

We waited while the video played on.

A few minutes later, Quinn came out of the alleyway between Spellbound and Lotions and Potions, and walked toward the event tent.

So that was that.

"Can you go back to the starting line? Did Ben warm up and then go straight to the starting line?"

"It looks like he does," Vince said, using a fingertip to trace Ben's movements. "Yep. There he is."

So Ben couldn't have killed Abby.

Quinn couldn't have killed Abby.

"What about Joe?" I asked.

Vince found the footage of Joe warming up. We kept an eye on him. He finished his warm-ups and went to use the portable toilet. When he saw the line, he walked off. Out of camera range.

We kept watching for him to come back, but he never did.

"Intriguing," Vince said. "Where'd Joe go?"

"According to him, to go to the bathroom in the bushes since the portable toilets were not usable."

He grinned. "They weren't usable? I wonder what happened to them?"

I let out a heavy sigh. "I don't suppose you have a camera near the trailhead that would have caught him going into the woods?"

"No. Sadly, I've been trying to cut back on my spying."

"Glad to hear it. One last thing," I said. "Footage of the Witch's Brew about five minutes before the race starts?"

He pecked away with his good hand to zoom in on that area of the video. Madison and Aine were there, at the curb. Madison was glancing around as though looking for someone. Joe, most likely, since he hadn't come back from his bathroom break. Unbeknownst to her, Duncan Cole had slid in behind her, coming in from the direction of the trailhead.

"See that guy?" I said, pointing to Duncan.

"Yeah?"

"Can you follow his movements backward?"

"Who is he?"

"Duncan Cole."

"It is?" He squinted. "I didn't recognize him."

"I hadn't either. That beard changes his whole face."

"Kind of makes you wonder if he grew it that way on purpose, doesn't it?"

It did.

We tracked Duncan as far as we could, but ran into the same problem as we had with Joe: Duncan went out of range of the cameras.

I leaned back in my chair. "I know you gave a copy of this to Nick, but could I have one too?"

He opened a drawer and pulled out a disk. He slid it across the desk.

"You knew I'd ask."

"You're always asking for stuff." He wiped a sheen of sweat off his forehead. "You're kind of a pain in the butt."

I smiled. "Thanks for your help with this."

"Yeah, yeah. Did you see anything that helps the case?"

"I can rule out Ben and Quinn. That helps."

He nodded and looked at his watch. "I'm going to have to cut this short. I'm meeting Noelle to look at a house."

"Is that what you two were doing at the play*house* yesterday, too? Looking at houses?"

"Har har." He rolled his eyes but I noticed he wouldn't look at me. "What can I say? I'm hoping to get a better deal on a place."

"Is that so?"

He glanced my way. His whole face had flushed—chasing away all the paleness. "It's so."

"You like her!"

He shrugged with a mischievous grin. "It was only one date."

I said, "Noelle's not too . . . enthusiastic for you?"

"I like her energy. It's . . ." He searched for a word.

"Energizing?" I suggested.

"Yeah, that works. She's nice. I'm not looking to get married or anything, so don't go planning our wedding too." He stood up and came around his desk.

Ah, so he knew I'd agreed to help Glinda. "Speaking of . . ."

"Of what?"

I stayed put in my seat. "Planning weddings."

"Do not ask me to be ring bearer," he said. "I'm much too old."

"Noted. Glinda's adamant that Dorothy does not find out about the wedding until it's happening."

"A smart move on her part."

"And you won't tell Dorothy? She's suspicious. She might ask."

"I try not to tell anyone anything."

"Oh, I know." I stood up. "But would you help Dorothy with a hex if she asked?"

He did a double take as he walked toward the door. "Why would you ask that? Seems kind of out of the blue to me."

"Let's just say that it's suspected there's a hex around Dorothy's house, one that hurts trespassers."

The corner of his mouth lifted. "How would one know that unless one trespassed?"

"Lucky guess?" I said.

"What if there was? What if Dorothy is afraid someone wanted to spy on her and asked for a little help? Given this conversation, I'd say her fears were warranted."

"Is there a way around the hex?"

"There might be."

"Would you tell me?"

"Doubtful."

But, he'd already had by telling me there might be.

I tucked the disk into my tote bag and passed by him. I stopped in the hallway outside his office and faced him. "There's going to come a time when you'll have to choose a side, Vince. Good or evil. You need to think long and hard which side you're going to pick."

"You're right. That time is coming. But what makes you think I haven't already chosen?"

I eyed him. "Have you?"

"You're just going to have to wait and see, aren't you?" He strode to the back door and pulled it open. "I'll see you at the wedding."

As I left the shop, I found I was more confused about him than ever.

* * *

I stopped by the Black Thorn, which was a few shops away from Lotions and Potions, and worked with Lydia on picking out appropriate flowers for the memorial service.

Once that was settled, I texted Quinn to let her know everything on my end was set for the night. She texted back a simple thank you and added that she'd see me later.

On a whim, I decided to try talking with Ben one more time. If I let him know that video surveillance gave him an alibi, maybe he'd be willing to open up about Abby. And why they had been so secretive about the elopement and about her selling her house, too.

The temperature had dropped during the day, and I was already missing the warmth. It was a quick five-minute walk to Ben's place, but I made it in three because walking alone was giving me the heebie-jeebies. I took the stairs up to his apartment door two at a time, and then quickly knocked on his door before I had the chance to change my mind.

Not even a second later, he yanked open the door and sighed. "Not now."

I fought the urge to bust my way inside. It was only the ravaged look on Ben's face that stopped me. Dark circles rimmed bloodshot eyes. He appeared to have aged a decade overnight.

Behind him, blankets were tossed on the couch as though he'd slept there and not his bed. The scent of burned toast filled the air.

He saw me looking inside and closed the door a bit, using his body to fill the gap.

But not before I saw something very interesting on the floor next to the door.

Green shoes with orange horizontal lacings.

I recognized them right away.

"Look," I said, my heart beating a little bit faster. "I just wanted to tell you video surveillance shows you couldn't have been the one to kill Abby."

He rubbed his eyes. "Thanks, but I already knew I didn't kill her."

With that, he closed the door in my face.

I was starting to take the rejection personally.

I pulled my phone from my tote and was dialing Nick before I was even halfway down the steps.

I needed to tell him about those shoes.

Because they meant Duncan Cole was at Ben's apartment.

Chapter
Twenty-Two

"So Duncan was gone by the time the police arrived?" Harper asked.

I'd waited across the street on the village green for the police to show up at Ben's apartment. But by the time they arrived, Duncan was gone. He must have slipped down the back alley, because I hadn't seen him go by.

Ben claimed he'd never been there at all, but the shoes I'd seen on the floor near the door were missing.

Nick had hauled Ben in for questioning once again, and I went home. Last I'd heard, Ben had asked for his lawyer, stonewalling Nick's questions.

"Ben must have noticed me looking at the shoes. It's the only giveaway I can think of that would have tipped him off."

"You need to learn to be cagier, Darcy," she said, smiling behind the rim of a teacup I'd just handed her.

I'd only been home a few minutes. Just long enough to let Higgins out and make some tea. Missy wasn't around, so I checked her GPS to make sure she wasn't roaming loose in the village and saw she was back at Ve's.

Harper had showered, done her hair, plucked her eyebrows, and looked much better than she had in months. If she'd been battling morning sickness along with her other illness without knowing what it was, there was no evidence of it now, and I had the feeling she could thank Dr. Dreadful for that as well.

She sat in the middle of the bed, propped up on what seemed like half a dozen pillows. One of which had Annie lounging on top of it. The cat's eyes were closed, but her tail swished every now and again, so I knew she was awake. Archie had yet to return, and I was starting to wonder what he and my mother had been up to all day.

"I'll work on that." I told her about the rest of my day, finishing with my visit with Vince. "Did you have a chance to look at your surveillance footage?"

"I did. I sent a copy to your email. It's the same as Vince's. Quinn came in, used the restroom, and left again out the back door. Do you believe Joe's story?"

"Not really. I mean, it does have a ring of truth to it, because many people ended up using the woods as a bathroom that morning, but it just seems too coincidental."

"Nick should make him take a lie detector test."

"I'll tell him you said so. It would be nice if we could hook Duncan up too."

"He is a wildcard. What was he doing with Ben? Seems like they should be enemies, doesn't it?"

It did. "Ben denies Duncan was there. I know they were friends before the doping incident, but I can't imagine they still would be."

"Well, Duncan might not remember he was mad, because of the memory cleanse."

"Good point. I just feel like there are too many secrets with this case. And that usually means someone is hiding something big. I just haven't figured out what that is quite yet."

"You will," Harper said. "I have complete confidence in you."

"Thanks." I glanced at her hand. "Any reason why you have a death grip on your phone?"

She hadn't let it go, even to hold the teacup. She blinked at it as though not realizing she had hold of it. "Marcus called."

"Did he? What did he want?" My insides were doing a happy dance while I tried to keep my face serene.

"I don't know. I didn't answer."

My happy dance turned into a funeral march.

She went on. "He left a message saying he needed to talk to me and asked me to call him back. I haven't yet."

"Are you going to?"

"I want to, but . . ."

"What?"

Her face flushed, her jaw jutted, and her body tensed. "I'm just so . . . *angry*."

Tea sloshed as her hand shook, and I took the cup and set it on a side table. "It's understandable to be angry with him, but if you—"

"I'm not angry with him, Darcy. I understand why he did what he did. I know he was in a lousy position, having to choose. I forgave him a long time ago."

"Then who are you angry at? His mom? Dad?"

"Not that they aren't deserving, but no." She shook her head. "I'm angry at *myself*."

"I—" She'd shocked me. "I don't understand."

Her lower lip trembled. "All my life I thought I was *not* that girl. The one who falls apart when a boy dumps her. I don't need a man to be happy. I'm strong. Independent. Self-sufficient." She gulped in air. "And yet, what did I do the minute Marcus left? I fell apart. Not just apart. I was in tatters. It turned out I *am* that girl!"

"Oh, Harper." I wrapped my arms around her. I grabbed a tissue from the nightstand and let her cry it out. It had been a long time coming. As I rocked her, I had to wipe my eyes several times because I couldn't listen to her cry without crying myself. My emotions were tied to hers and always had been since the moment I held her in my arms shortly after she was born.

Annie took one look at us and ran out of the room.

"The more I struggled with him leaving, the madder at myself I became," she said, her words drawn out between sniffles. "I didn't know who I was anymore. Which made me struggle even more. Which made me even madder. Before I knew it, I was so lost. I feel so dumb."

"Listen," I said as Harper finally quieted, her sniffles turning into hiccups. "Listen to me. Dumb is not a word that has ever been associated with you and never will be."

She swiped her eyes with the tissue but wouldn't look my way. Her chest heaved as she tried to control her breathing.

"We are *all* that girl, Harper. And none of us realize it until we lose someone who holds a piece of our heart." I held her tighter. "You've never been in love before Marcus, so you didn't know about the pain. You need to forgive *yourself*, because you cannot be mad for something you didn't know."

Her lip quivered. "I should have known."

"How? You have to experience it. Live through it. Regroup and rebuild. It's some of the worst pain you will ever feel. It's not called heartbreak for nothing. But being brokenhearted doesn't mean you're not strong and independent and all those other things. And it doesn't mean you're dumb. It means you had the courage to let another person into your heart, and you lived through letting them go."

She gave me a side glance. "Barely."

"But you did. And you're going to be stronger than ever, with or without Marcus by your side."

We sat in silence for a few minutes. Me rocking her, her sniffling and shuddering.

Finally, she said, "I need to tell him about the baby."

"Yes, you do."

"I don't want him to leave, Darcy."

"I know. But you need to tell *him* that. And you need to brace yourself that he might still go."

She gave a mirthless laugh. "If I can live through these past few months . . ."

"You can get through anything. But heaven help me if you join another club."

"Hey. I like the clubs."

"Call Marcus back," I said. "Talk to him."

She stared at the phone. "I'm scared."

My eyes welled. I kissed her forehead and stood up. "Being in love is terrifying."

"A massive understatement." She took a deep breath. "Okay. I can do this. I can do this. Can I do this?"

"You can do it."

She nodded, then dialed.

I backed out of the room, and resisting the urge to eavesdrop, went downstairs. I let Higgins inside and was standing at the door watching snow flurries when two birds came swooping downward out of seemingly nowhere, one bright red and the other a soft gray.

I quickly opened the door and both flew inside.

"Good timing, Darcy!" Archie said as he landed on his perch.

The gray bird folded its wings over its chest and my mother appeared before me. "Very good timing." She kissed my cheek.

"Tea?" I asked. "The kettle's still hot."

"Please," Mom said.

"I do not suppose you have stocked any rum today?" Archie asked.

I set out a couple of teacups. "Have you considered that you might have a problem?"

"Oh, most certainly. Many problems. One of which is the lack of rum in this house. How long until Quinn takes her leave of Ve's home?"

"Tomorrow, I believe. Until then, you're going to have to suffer with tea or coffee, milk or juice, water or tonic."

"Gin and tonic?" he asked hopefully.

I stared at him. "I'm going to have to talk with Terry."

"Do I hear voices?" my mother asked, tipping her head.

"Harper's on the phone." I set tea bags in the mugs. "With Marcus."

Mom's mouth formed a little "O" as she floated closer to the stairway.

Archie crossed his wings over his chest, cleared his throat, and said, "'Whatever happens, I must not cry.'"

"*Shrek 2*. And you and me both. Where have you two been all day?"

"Here and there and Delaware," Archie said.

"Delaware, really?"

"We paid a visit to the Roving Stones," Mom said, floating back to the island. She pulled a necklace from her pocket and held it up. A small stone pendant wrapped in golden threads glinted in the light. "It's the most powerful protection amulet in the Craft world. It should keep Harper safe from harm as long as she's wearing it."

"And the baby, too?" I asked.

"The baby, too," Mom said.

Thank goodness. "How do we explain the necklace to Harper? Without worrying her, I mean."

My mother said, "*We* don't. Dennis Goodwin will give it to Harper and explain its protection value for the baby. There is no way she will deny the gift if it's meant to protect her child."

I touched the charm. Warmth seeped into my fingertips. When I heard footsteps above, I abruptly said, "So Nick had to bring Joe back in for questioning when—"

Harper stuck her head over the railing of the overlook, the interior balcony that looked down into the kitchen and family room. "He's coming over. It's okay that he's coming over, isn't it? Hi, Mom. Hi, Archie."

"Who's coming over?" Mom asked as if she hadn't heard a word about Marcus in her whole life.

"Marcus. He said he has a meeting but will be by around five. Is that okay?"

"Of course," I said, wishing I could be home for the visit. But I'd be at Abby's memorial service. "I won't be home, but that doesn't matter."

"I'll be here. Rum-less, but here," Archie said. "I can chaperone."

"Just tell Marcus to bring a six pack and Archie will leave you two alone."

"I do not drink such swill," Archie said. "Make it a bottle of wine, and I'll be practically invisible."

"Archie, have you ever considered that you might have a drinking problem?" Harper asked him.

He cursed under his breath, then grumbled, "You and your sister are spending entirely too much time together."

"How did Marcus sound on the phone?" I asked, ignoring Archie.

"He sounded . . . good." She smiled, then turned and went back to her room.

"Good is good, I guess?" I said.

" 'Tis a sight better than bad," Archie added.

"I'm feeling the winds of change," my mother said.

"Are you sure that's not just Higgins' tail?" Archie eyed the dog.

We heard footsteps again, and Harper appeared once more at the railing. "Hey, Archie, how about a *Pirates of the Caribbean* marathon until Marcus gets here?"

"Ahoy, matey!" he cried excitedly, flapping his wings. He soared upward.

The *Pirates* movies were at the top of his favorites list. "He's going to want rum even more now."

My mother waved her hand and a bottle appeared on the counter top. "I have the feeling you'll all need cocktails at the end of this day."

I carried the bottle to the pantry. "Not that I don't trust Archie to find this and drink the whole bottle in one sitting, but I'm just going to hide this for now."

My mother sat on a stool. "Wise woman. Now, when Harper was coming down, you were saying something about Joe? What was that about?"

I filled her in on all she'd missed today. "No one knows where Duncan is now," I said. "Or why Ben would have been hiding him."

"Is it possible Ben didn't know the police were looking for Duncan?" Mom asked.

"I suppose," I said. "Ben's been keeping to himself these past couple of days, so he could have been insulated from the gossip going around."

"Grief is a terrible and often lonely companion. Will the police release Ben in time for him to attend Abby's memorial?"

"Unless he's under arrest, I can't imagine Nick keeping him too long. He just wants some answers about Duncan. Oh, and I have a question for you about Abby," I said.

"What's that?"

"Did Abby get her powers back after Duncan Cole was memory cleansed?" Oftentimes in those kind of situations, Crafters could petition the Elder for the return of their powers. I knew of several witches who'd been granted the request.

"No, she didn't. She didn't ask."

I drummed my fingertips on the counter. "Isn't it strange she didn't ask?"

"Not everyone does. Vitacrafters in particular often feel burdened by their powers. Unless you're particularly nurturing—or emotionally manipulative—it's difficult to deal with the energy of others on a constant basis."

I could understand that, thinking of Lew Renault, an Emoticrafter, whose powers were the next level up from those of Vitas. He could physically *feel* the emotions and pain of others and had chosen to become a hermit to keep himself sane.

"How much does Duncan remember about the incident at Balefire?"

"Most of it except the parts about the Craft. He does not recall accusing the Bryants of cheating via magic, for instance, but he does recall accusing them of altering his lab results."

"I still don't know why they did that. They could have just let him go, without framing him for doping.

Abby knew the consequences if he spoke of the Craft to anyone other than witches. She wouldn't have let him run his mouth. The only reason he did was because he felt attacked by those lab results."

Mom sipped her tea and said, "But if they simply let him go, then Abby might have left too."

And everybody loved Abby. "Ah. That way, they kept Abby and got rid of Duncan."

She tipped her head in acknowledgement. "By accusing him of cheating and providing so-called proof, they knew Abby would break up with him, as she lived by a strict moral code."

"It's reprehensible."

"Agreed. But not against Craft law. They didn't use the Craft to change those results."

"Is it possible Abby told Quinn of the Craft as well? Can she do that after already losing her powers?" I explained about my conversation with Quinn, and how it'd seemed she was hinting that she knew of the magical world around her.

"It *is* possible, and she did. It's a loophole within our law that the Coven is trying to close. A witch, after losing his or her powers, can tell as many mortals as they please with no consequences whatsoever."

"That's a big loophole."

"Enormous."

"But why would Abby tell Quinn about the Craft?" I asked.

"I believe Abby shared the knowledge to enlighten Quinn on the world around her. And to explain the Bryants and their abilities and behaviors."

"So, Quinn *is* a Halfcrafter."

"Yes, but her knowledge is limited to what she's been told by Abby, which isn't much."

"Is she going to be memory cleansed now that Abby has died?"

Even if she was, she'd remain a Halfcrafter forever, just like Duncan. Despite not remembering being one.

"It will be brought up at the next Coven meeting."

"Which is when?"

She wagged a finger at me. "*Uh-uhn.*"

"It couldn't hurt to try." I was forever trying to get her to slip up and reveal information about the Coven of Seven.

She pushed her teacup away and rose off the stool. "I need to get back to the meadow. Dennis Goodwin is stopping by before his visit with Harper."

I walked her to the back door. "Do you know if Dorothy has learned about the baby yet?"

"She has not. Trust me, Darcy. When she finds out, we will all feel the full strength of her fury."

"Something to look forward to," I said drolly.

She laughed and floated out the door. In a blink, she turned into a mourning dove and flew off.

I heard my phone buzz and ran for it. It was a text from Glinda wondering about the cake tasting, if we were still on.

I wrote back that I'd see her at the Gingerbread Shack tomorrow at eleven.

As I hit send, I couldn't help wondering whose side Glinda was on.

Good. Or evil.

Chapter Twenty-Three

"I can't thank you enough, Darcy, for stepping in to help Quinn," Lucinda Bryant whispered to me as we stood at the back of Balefire, fifteen minutes after the memorial service had ended. She had Aine strapped to her in a wrap that crisscrossed her back, and the same red blanket with hearts that had been in Aine's stroller earlier was now draped across Lucinda's shoulder. The baby was sound asleep, her lips pursed as she nestled her cheek against the soft, worn fabric.

"You're welcome." Shelves had been pushed aside to make room for folding chairs. A large picture of a smiling Abby sat on a tripod at the front of the room, and my throat tightened every time I looked at it. The Black Thorn had done an amazing job with the flowers. Tall arrangements of ivory roses, calla lilies, and peonies laced with pale greenery flanked the photo and a smaller spray covered a makeshift lectern where at least a dozen people had shared stories of Abby and her vitality with all the mourners gathered.

Lucinda had given a brief welcome to all who'd come, but neither Ben nor Joe had spoken. Quinn and Madison had. Quinn had tearfully shared personal stories while Madison had talked of her beloved running partner.

And it was as everyone had said: Abby was well-loved.

I glanced around the room and found Quinn in a far corner, her arms wrapped around herself, her eyes glazed. Every once in a while, someone would stop to speak to her, but she was in her own world and the person usually moved on quickly.

None of them had been Bryants.

Ben, Joe, and Madison stood amid a group of Mad Dashers, and Ben looked much like Quinn, staring blankly at nothing at all. Joe and Madison kept sending me angry stares, and I tried not to let them bother me. Too much.

The longer I stayed, the more I wanted to leave. I wasn't comfortable here, and it was clear I wasn't welcome, despite Lucinda being the one to hire me.

Lucinda shifted foot to foot, rocking Aine. Absently, she picked one of the fuzz balls off the blanket. Then another. "You'll send me an invoice for your services?"

"There will be no invoice. Abby was my friend, and this was the least I can do for her."

"Well, thank you then. Again."

She wandered over to Ben and whispered something to him. His eyes came up to meet mine, then he quickly looked away.

My gaze skipped among the Bryants, wondering if it was one of them who'd knotted the noose with my name on it. My nerves ratcheted up a notch just thinking about it.

I checked my watch, trying to figure out a way to get out of here as soon as possible. Unfortunately, I needed to stay to clean up, so I'd be here another hour at least.

Stef Millet was directing a server who carried a tray of cheese tart hors d'oeuvres through the room. A small bar was set up near the door, which made me think of Archie.

Which then made me think of Harper.

I'd been checking my phone as often as I could manage. There had been no updates on the meeting with Marcus, and it was making me anxious. I couldn't even rely on Mimi to eavesdrop, as she had gone straight to Spellbound after school to work a short shift.

I glanced at my phone yet again.

Nothing.

As I was looking down, a bit of red caught my eye. I stooped low to scoop it up. Fluff. From Aine's blanket. I stared at the piece of lint in my hand, and my heart started pounding. It was identical to the lint that had been found on the noose.

My head snapped up, and I looked around. As I did so, my gaze caught on something I hadn't noticed earlier.

The display of jump ropes on a far wall. Among them, a blue one identical to the rope used to make the noose.

"Excuse me," Quinn said. "Darcy?"

I'd been so focused on the jump ropes that I hadn't heard her approach. I pressed my hand to my heart.

"Sorry," she said. "I didn't mean to startle you." She swayed a little and I caught her by the arm. "I don't feel well," she said unnecessarily.

That made two of us. I needed to talk to Nick as soon as possible to tell him about the lint and the jump rope. And how they definitively connected the Bryants to the noose. I didn't know which one of them had threatened me, but I had no doubt one of them had. My money was on Joe.

But first, I had to help Quinn.

"Come on, let's get out of here. I'll take you back to Ve's."

"I can't leave . . . Clean up."

"I'll take care of everything." I found her coat and mine, then tracked down Stef. "Quinn's not feeling well, so I'm going to walk her home."

"You don't have to do that, I can take her," Madison offered, coming up beside us.

I could hear my heartbeat in my ears and feel a cold sweat rise along my hairline. "No, no," I insisted. "You have guests. Stay."

I strode away before Madison could argue. I helped Quinn into her coat, then texted Ve that we were on our way. Wrapping an arm around Quinn, I glanced back at the store as we walked away. Ben stood at the window, watching us with anguish splashed across his face.

I walked faster, ushering Quinn along. When we reached the corner, Quinn automatically turned in the direction of Abby's house, before I steered her toward Ve's. She didn't say a single word, just kept her head down while tears streamed from her eyes and dripped off her chin.

Night had fallen, and the village twinkled under the glow of fairy lights. It looked so peaceful it was hard to imagine anything untoward such as murder happened here.

And thinking of murder suddenly had me thinking about nooses, and just like that, my heart was racing again. Which was probably why when we crossed the street I noticed something out of place as we neared a tall oak tree. A man leaned against its trunk, blending in with its shadows. As we hurriedly passed by, the man lifted his head. Our gazes met.

He'd shaved his beard, making him even more recognizable.

Duncan Cole.

The twinkle lights in the branches above his head glinted off the tears in his eyes and on his face. I glanced around to see if anyone was nearby, and when I looked back at the tree, Duncan was gone.

Quinn, with her head down, hadn't noticed the interaction. Nor did she say anything when I picked up our pace. I rushed her across the village green.

As we passed my house, I saw that Dr. Dreadful's car was parked at the curb, and I wondered if Marcus was still there as well. I hoped so. Some good news on this crazy day would be nice.

Ve was waiting for us on the side porch and immediately took hold of Quinn, ushering her inside with promises of soup and tea.

Quinn crumpled against her and sobbed.

"Now, now," Ve said, patting her head. "It's okay. You just go on and cry. Let it out."

Over Quinn's head, Ve said to me, "You go on. We'll be just fine. I have a wee sleeping potion I can whip up if need be, but most times, crying is the best medicine of all."

I thought of Harper crying this afternoon, and my voice cracked with emotion as I said, "Thank you, Aunt Ve."

"Anytime, darling. Anytime."

As soon as they were inside, I pulled my phone out of my pocket and dialed Nick to let him know what I'd seen at Balefire with the red lint and the jump rope and who I'd spotted on the green. I swore I could hear sirens before I even hung up with him.

Within minutes, the village was going to be crawling with police, and I had the oddest feeling of wishing Duncan wouldn't be found.

It had been that look in his eyes.

He didn't look like a guilty man. He looked like a man who'd just lost the love of his life.

It was out of my hands now. But still, I wished . . .

Since there was no way I was going back to Balefire, I headed straight home. As I walked, I knew I needed to let Stef Millet know I wasn't coming back, but I needed a reasonable excuse.

I was hurrying past Terry Goodwin's house when my phone rang. I nearly dropped it trying to get it out of my pocket, and was surprised to see the call was from Noelle Quinlan.

Puzzled, I answered.

"Darcy, oh thank goodness," she said in a rush, sounding out of breath. "I'm so glad you picked up."

"Is everything okay?" She sounded frenetic— something I'd never heard from her in all the time I'd known her. "Is this about Nick's closing?"

"Nick's closing? Oh! No, no. This is about Vince. Vince Paxton?"

Oh, God. "What did he do?"

"Do? Nothing. He's in the emergency room, Darcy. He collapsed when we were walking into the movie theater. He's really sick, some sort of blood infection, but he keeps saying your name over and over. Can you come here?"

* * *

"Just wait until you get my bill," Dennis Goodwin said as we walked into the hospital twenty minutes later. "I'm charging extra for all the house calls and these extraneous visits."

Snow had started falling, thick and heavy. It dusted his coat, his hair.

"Yeah, yeah," I said, not worried. He didn't bill Crafters unless they visited his office as a regular patient.

I would, however, come up with some way to thank him for everything he's done. Maybe tickets to a Celtics game or to the theater. I'd check with his wife, Amanda, to see what she recommended.

As soon as I hung up with Noelle, I texted Stef to tell her I was on my way the hospital due to a family emergency and sent my apologies that I wouldn't be able to make it back to Balefire tonight. I'd then run the rest of the way home and grabbed Dennis to help with Vince's infection, which must have been from when he cut his hand on Harper's window frame.

Dennis grumbled something beneath his breath. "Of all the weeks for my mother to leave town . . ."

"She'll be back soon enough, and you can go back to your normally scheduled grumpiness. But you know you'll miss me. And Harper too."

He glanced my way, and I caught his half smile. "You two do kind of grow on a witch. Like mold. Fuzzy mold."

"You always say the sweetest things. We don't call you Dr. Dreadful for nothing."

He made a strange noise, and I realized he was laughing.

"That's a good one," he said. "I might put that on my license plate."

We stomped our feet on the mat by the doors and went straight to the registration desk, where he fed the clerk some line about being Vince's family doctor. It wasn't long before we were whisked back to Vince's room.

Noelle paced the hallway outside Vince's door. Worry creased her forehead and darkened her eyes. "Thank goodness you're here."

I had never seen her upset, never mind frantic, and it made me all the more worried. "How's he doing?" I asked.

"Not good. They're saying he's septic? I don't even know what that means, but they're getting ready to transfer him to the operating room to remove the infection from his hand. The nurse is in there with him now. Who are you?" she asked Dennis.

"They call me Dr. Dreadful." He walked past her and went into Vince's room.

Noelle probably got whiplash when she snapped her head to look at me.

"He's Vince's doctor," I said. "Has a wacky sense of humor."

Her eyes were wide. "I'll say."

"I'm going to go in for a second. Maybe if Vince sees me, he'll stop saying my name."

She practically pushed me to the door. "Yes, go."

The door opened soundlessly into a bright room that smelled of bleach. There were at least three machines hooked up to Vince.

My gaze quickly went to the nurse who was slumped in a chair, her head tilted downward on her chest. I glanced at Dennis. "What did you do to her?"

"She was a bit tired. A power nap will do wonders."

"Darcy?" Vince murmured.

"I'm here," I said, rushing to his side. He looked worse than Harper had on Saturday morning, which was saying something.

"Hand," he said.

"Yeah, Mr. It's Fine. Look at you now. Next time, maybe take my advice when I tell you to go to a doctor?"

"Bossy," he mumbled.

"Tell me about it," Dennis said. Then he looked at me. "Block the door."

I stood in front of it, planted my feet, and shot my arms out to the sides.

No one was getting in.

Dennis rubbed his hands together, then placed them on Vince's chest right above his heart. One of the monitors started chirping like crazy. Then he moved his hands to cover Vince's injured hand.

Dennis closed his eyes. A moment later, he murmured a spell and blinked his left eye twice. The spell had been cast.

Vince's eyes fluttered closed, but his chest rose and fell steadily. His coloring was immediately better.

Dennis opened his eyes and said, "His hand will still need surgery to remove the damage caused by the infection, but I've stopped the infection in his blood. He'll be asleep for a little while as my spell works its way through his circulatory system. Speaking of sleeping . . ." He walked over and gently touched the nurse's temple.

The nurse woke up, blinked, and looked around. "What's happening?"

"The monitor is going off," I said, trying to distract her from the fact that she'd been out cold for a couple of minutes. "Is he okay?"

She stood up, opened her mouth, then closed it again. She silenced the beeping monitor, then quickly checked Vince's blood pressure, then his temperature. "Normal," she said, staring at the thermometer like it was defective.

"I'm going to make a call," Dennis said. "I'll be out in the vestibule should you need me."

The nurse eyed us suspiciously.

I smiled wide and pointed to the hallway. "I'll just be out there."

Nothing to see here. No magic happening at all. Nope. No, sirree.

As soon as I stepped into the hallway, I heard her using the intercom on Vince's bed to ask someone to page a doctor.

It wasn't long before a doctor came running, his hand holding his stethoscope close to his chest as he rushed into Vince's room. Two nurses followed.

"What's going on?" Noelle asked.

"I don't know," I lied. "The nurse in Vince's room said his fever had broken and his blood pressure had stabilized."

"Really?" Noelle took a deep breath and leaned against the wall. "Thank goodness."

We stood there pressed to the wall for a few minutes before the doctor came back out.

"I've never seen such a turnaround," he said. "I need to run more tests, but it appears his body is fighting off the infection on its own. He'll still need surgery, however, the sooner, the better."

It wasn't long before Vince was taken off to the operating room, and Noelle and I went to find some coffee while we waited for news. I hadn't seen Dennis since he went to make his call and hoped he hadn't left me behind, since he was the one who'd driven here.

Noelle talked as we walked. "We were going to a movie, then dinner. He told me he just had a cold. Men. He collapsed and an ambulance came, then the doctor kept asking me how Vince hurt his hand, and I had no idea. That's when Vince started saying your name over and over."

"I was there when he cut his hand. It was in Harper's apartment. He'd been trying to get the window open. It was stuck."

She winced. "I'm glad he's going to be okay."

We found a snack bar near the OR waiting room and ordered two coffees. "I'm glad you were with him. So, dinner and a movie? And the playhouse yesterday . . ."

Giving a little shrug, she said, "He's an interesting guy."

The mama hen in me started pecking. "Is he still going to be interesting after he buys a house?"

She smiled. "I think so. I don't know. Maybe?" Color rose up her neck. "Has he said anything about me?"

"He likes you." I took a sip of my coffee. "How do you feel about fixer-uppers?"

Her smile turned into a wide grin. "I adore them."

"That's good. Really good. Remember that," I said as my phone rang. "Sorry, I should take this. It's Nick."

"Go, go." She shooed me with her hands.

Since no cell phone calls were allowed inside the building, I answered and hurried toward a nearby exit. Snow continued to fall steadily.

"Everything okay?" Nick asked. "I got home and Harper said you'd rushed in here, grabbed Dennis, and dragged him out. Something about Vince?"

I quickly explained, then said, "Now tell me what happened with Duncan?"

"Officers found some footprints in the snow but eventually he hit pavement and they lost track of him."

"Did you check Ben's place?"

He chuckled. "Ben's place is being watched. Duncan can't hide forever. His face is all over news reports and papers."

I questioned why Duncan—if he hadn't killed Abby—was hiding at all. His actions weren't those of an innocent man.

"And Balefire?" I asked. "The blanket fuzz? The jump rope?"

"I'm working on drafting a search warrant for Joe and Madison's house right now. I'll get it before a judge first thing tomorrow."

"Do you have a team watching Joe and Madison?" If Joe killed Abby because she found out about his tax fraud, then he threatened me with the noose because I was asking questions about the bookkeeping . . .

"Unfortunately, no. I'm out of manpower. Between the search for Duncan, watching Ben and Quinn . . ."

The hazard of a small-town police force.

I tried to console myself with the knowledge that Joe couldn't possibly think silencing me at this point would help him in any way. The information I'd discovered was already out there.

Unless he simply wanted to seek revenge because of what I'd uncovered.

Giving my head a good shake, I tried not to think too hard about it.

Nick said, "Be extra careful, Darcy. Don't take any chances, okay?"

I was beyond grateful that Dennis was here at the hospital with me. "I promise. Now, enough of the Bryants. Tell me what you know about Harper and Marcus. He'd already left when I ran in and stole Dennis. What happened?"

"I don't exactly know," he said, dropping his voice. "But he came back. He and Harper are upstairs talking. And laughing. There's been a lot of laughing."

I did a little jig. A person walking by widened the distance between us.

"You should see Mimi dancing around the kitchen."

"Oh, I can imagine," I said. "Easily."

"Are you going to be home soon?"

"I'll probably wait until Vince is out of surgery. I should call Glinda, too." I hadn't thought about it, that he had family who could be here to support him.

Somewhere along the line I'd come to think of myself as part of his family, which I suddenly realized was why I had such a soft spot for him. Family was everything to me.

Vince was the pesky little brother I'd never had.

I fought a sudden wave of tears, said my goodbyes, and went back into the hospital.

"Everything okay?" Noelle asked as I sat back down.

"It's been a rough few days," I said, not really knowing how to answer that question. There was still so much unresolved.

"I still can't believe what happened," Noelle said. "It feels like yesterday that Abby was sitting in my office, talking about selling her house. You, ah, haven't found out who inherits the house, have you?"

She and Vince might just be a match made in heaven. "No. As far as anyone knows, there's no heirs and no will."

"Rats."

"Hey, you mentioned the other day that Abby asked you to hold off on listing the house until Wednesday."

She bobbed her head. "That's right."

"Did she happen to say where she planned to move to?" It was one of those little details bothering me. Ben lived in such a tiny apartment. It didn't make sense she'd move in with him, when he could easily live with her.

"Oh, sure. She had me looking for a new house. I found a charming little Gambrel not too far from a training facility she planned to rent. Sadly, she was supposed to be looking at it today."

"Really? Where is the house? Here in the village?"

"No, no. In Wakefield."

I found myself repeating what I'd said the other day. "Wakefield? As in twenty minutes away Wakefield?"

"Yeah. Why? Is that important?"

I wasn't sure.

But I highly doubted it was a coincidence that it was the town where Duncan Cole lived.

* * *

It was after midnight by the time I left the hospital, and I was beyond grateful Dennis hadn't seemed to mind staying so late. As I exited the emergency room doors, I tried to remember where Dennis had parked—he'd left a few minutes before me to clear the snow from the car and get it warmed up.

I blinked against the heavy snow and spotted him in the distance, the glow of the taillights a dead give-away to his location.

I was lost in my thoughts as I hurried along, thinking about the bombshell Noelle had dropped about Abby moving to Wakefield and how it had to be connected to Duncan.

But how?

I cursed him for not coming forward. By now, he had to know the police wanted to talk to him. So why was he still hiding? Or better yet, *what* was he hiding?

"Darcy! Look out!"

I barely registered Dennis's words and the fact that he was sprinting toward me before I heard the footsteps crunching in the snow behind me. I spun around in time to see someone dressed all in black—their face covered in a three-hole black ski mask—raise a tire iron above their head. I threw my arms up to block the blow and cried out in pain as the tire iron hit my arm.

The attacker quickly ran off, dodging parked cars. A moment later, Dennis was at my side. He threw a look in the direction the attacker had gone, but didn't give chase. It would have been pointless, since the person was already halfway across the lot.

Even in the deep snow.

Obviously, it was someone who had great speed and athletic ability.

Pain washed over me, making me nauseous. I cradled my arm as tears filled my eyes. If I hadn't turned around, that tire iron would have landed on the back of my head.

My knees went weak and Dennis grabbed me. Carefully, he lowered me to the ground and knelt next to me. "Let me see your arm."

I gritted my teeth, and with his help, I wiggled out of my coat.

My forearm was already swollen to nearly twice its normal size, and just seeing it made me dizzy.

"Close your eyes," he said.

I didn't need to be asked twice.

"It's a good thing you had on a thick coat," he said.

I felt his warm hands on my skin, and immediately the pain ebbed. My arm was healed.

I opened my eyes. "Thank goodness you were here."

"I'm not sure who you've been hanging out with lately, but I think you need some new friends."

I blinked, then burst into tears.

Awkwardly, he patted my back, then ran a thumb across my forehead. "Take a deep breath."

I did as he said and felt warmth flood through me. I heard sirens in the distance and noticed a hospital security guard running toward us.

"You're okay," Dennis said.

And I was. Thanks to him. "You're angling to have Harper's baby named after you, aren't you?"

He smiled. "Yes, yes, I am."

Chapter Twenty-Four

"It was Ben," Mrs. P said late the next morning as she sat on the kitchen island, her tail dangling. The tip of it was wrapped in a strip of white gauze. "Quinn didn't talk to him long, but she clearly said his name."

Pepe and Mrs. P had stopped by to give me a full report on their nighttime adventures, which apparently had proved quite rewarding.

Fighting a yawn, I propped my elbows on the countertop. "What did she say?"

I'd been up most of the night dealing with the aftermath of the attack. Nick had met Dennis and me at the hospital, and I was pretty sure Nick had promised to name one of *our* future children after the man. There was no doubt we owed him a lot.

The police had a copy of the surveillance video, but it didn't give much insight into who the attacker had been.

Between the snow and darkness, there was nothing much to be seen. The attacker was taller than I was, thin, and fast. It could have been any of the Bryants, except Madison, since she was my height. Or Duncan.

"Very little," Pepe said. He was eating a bite of cheese Danish. "There were many tears shed."

"And she was a little loopy," Mrs. P added, "thanks to a sleeping potion Ve had given her."

"Who called who?" I asked.

I looked out the window and smiled as I watched Higgins and Missy play in the snow with Mimi, who was out of school for a snow day. She was trying to make a snow angel, but every time she lied down, Higgins would jump on her. I'd been out there with them until my little mouse friends had shown up.

I was trying not to worry about someone possibly being out there, watching them. They were safe as long as they stayed in the yard. And Missy and Higgins had proved to be good guard dogs. They'd be the first to raise an alarm if someone approached.

We hadn't told anyone what had happened last night. Not yet. There was no need to scare them when I was fine. Thanks to Dennis.

My nerves were shot, however. Two threats on my life were two too many. I could not—and would not—take any risks where the Bryants were concerned. I wouldn't be interviewing any of them alone—I'd make sure Nick came with me. One of them was guilty. I just didn't know which one quite yet.

Harper and Archie were both still asleep. Harper because she was still healing, and Archie because he had found the bottle of rum last night. I hadn't had a chance to get Harper alone yet for a full rundown on her meeting with Marcus, but I knew the basics. He was staying in the village (though soon to be homeless), he was thrilled about the baby (yet worried about a miscarriage), and they were back together.

Nick had left for work already. He was on the warpath and planned to question all the Bryants again as soon as he could while he waited on the search warrant for Joe and Madison's house. But first he had to deal with the warrants that had finally come through for Duncan's car and apartment. We both hoped Nick would find something to explain why Abby had planned to move to Wakefield.

After they eloped, were she and Ben planning to partner with Duncan to open a training facility? Had they been keeping the big picture secret, fearing a backlash from Joe and Lucinda?

I could see them fearing such a thing. I could see it quite clearly.

But did it factor into why Abby was dead?

Ben hadn't given any insight into the matter, either, when Nick questioned him yesterday. He'd lawyered up, and Nick hadn't had enough evidence to arrest him. His hands were tied.

Mine weren't, however. Ben had been summoned to see the Elder. He was going to have to answer her questions or face dire consequences.

"Yoo-hoo! Doll!" Mrs. P clapped her little hands.

I blinked. "What? Sorry. I was lost in thought there for a moment."

"I'll say," she said.

I rubbed my tired eyes. "Where were we? Quinn's phone call, right?"

"*Oui*. It was Ben who phoned her," Pepe answered. "He claimed he was worried about her. When she continued to cry, he asked her if she wanted him to come over."

"What did Quinn say?"

"She didn't answer him," Mrs. P said. "She just kept saying 'they're going to find out' until she fell asleep."

I was having trouble wrapping my head around all this. "How bizarre. Find out what?"

Mrs. P shrugged tiny shoulders.

"Ben showed up at Ve's not long after," Pepe reported.

"What time was this?" I asked.

Pepe said, "Around about midnight, give or take a few minutes."

So it hadn't been Ben who'd attacked me. It was good to cross one suspect off that particular list.

Mrs. P added, "Ve assured him Quinn was just fine and sent him on his way."

Part of me hoped she slammed the door in his face.

"I tried to break into Quinn's phone," Mrs. P said, "while she slept, but the cursed thing was locked. New-fangled technology." She blew a raspberry.

"And Joe and Madison's house? Did you learn anything there?" I asked.

"Alas," Pepe said, "by the time we arrived, Madison and Aine were asleep. Joe was awake and watching race footage of himself."

"Yawn," Mrs. P added.

"What time was that?" I asked.

"Around one o'clock," she said.

"Could you tell if he'd been home all night?" I asked as casually as I could manage.

Pepe's ear twitched as he studied me. "*Non.*"

Mrs. P held out her tiny hands, palms up. "Sorry, doll."

"No, no! Don't be sorry. You were a big help. You've given me some new leads."

Not that I had much time to explore them. Ben and Joe were leaving the village tomorrow to go to the race in New Zealand. Before they left, I needed to figure out what was going on with Quinn and Ben, and find out if Joe had an alibi for last night's attack on me.

I had a lot of work to get done.

And time was running out.

* * *

My first stop of the day was to question Quinn again. Try to find out what she'd been hiding, especially where Ben was concerned.

Finding out, much to my dismay, wasn't as easy as I'd hoped. Mostly because she was nowhere to be found.

When I went to Ve's, she'd told me Quinn had just left to run a few errands, but hadn't specified where she was off to. Her bags were packed and in the mudroom. When Ve had taken the liberty to snoop through them, she found a plane ticket to New Zealand with Quinn's name on it.

Was she supposed to have gone on the trip with the Balefire team? For work?

It was possible. Probable, even.

But why had she kept the ticket if she had quit? Was it possible she was still planning to be on that plane?

I called her cell phone but it went to voicemail.

I checked Abby's house, thinking perhaps Quinn had returned there to finish packing. While there were fresh footprints in the snow, no one had answered the door and Quinn's car was gone. When I cupped my eyes and pressed my face to the living room glass, the living room looked much the same as it had the last time I'd been there.

Boxes on the floor. The wig on the table.

But no. Something seemed different. I scanned the room but couldn't place what was bothering me.

Eventually I gave up and pressed on. I stopped by Balefire, but it was closed and dark. By the time I made it around the village, it was time to meet with Glinda for the cake testing.

I texted Ve and asked her to call me when Quinn returned.

I had a pit in my stomach where Quinn was concerned, and I didn't like it one bit.

Not even the sweet aromas of the Gingerbread Shack calmed the feeling.

Evan lit up when he saw me come in and said, "I heard about Harper and Marcus!"

I had told Starla what I knew this morning, so I wasn't the least bit surprised that Evan had already heard the news. I had no doubt it would be known throughout the village by dinner time.

"Wedding bells for Harper, too?" he asked.

"I don't know yet. I haven't had a chance to talk to her. She's sleeping about twenty hours a day lately."

"Must be nice," he said dryly.

"While I don't want to be as sick as she was, I could do with a full night's sleep. Is Glinda here yet?"

"In the back, looking through wedding cake books. Uh-oh," he added. "Wicked witch at two o'clock."

I glanced over my shoulder. Dorothy was walking by with her husband, Sylar, and had spotted me. She glared. I glared back.

Evan shuddered. "What's wrong with her? She's been more evil than usual lately."

"Everything?" I said, glad Glinda couldn't be seen from her spot in the kitchen.

"Well, it's a good thing Glinda's keeping this wedding quiet then. Come on back."

Glinda lit up when she saw me. "I just came from the hospital. Looks like Vince might be released today."

"So soon?" Evan asked.

"It's like magic. Imagine that," Glinda said. "Thanks for getting Dennis Goodwin involved, Darcy. I don't like thinking what could have happened otherwise."

I owed Dennis for many things and didn't know how I would ever repay him. "I don't like thinking about it, either. If Vince hadn't been so stubborn . . ."

"He's already joking about the lectures he's going to get from you."

"Your specialty, Darcy," Evan said, pulling up two stools. "I've been on the receiving end a time or two myself."

"You bake, I nag. We all have our strengths. It works."

The bell on the door jangled and Evan said, "I'm going to leave you two to look through these books to get a feel for design style for a couple of minutes while I cover the front. I have someone coming in to work the front at eleven-thirty, so I'm shorthanded until then."

My phone buzzed with a text message from Harper. I glanced at Glinda. "Do you mind if I read this? It's from Harper."

"Go ahead." She tapped the book. "I have plenty to keep me occupied. Who knew there were so many cake designs?"

"Not me. Give me a layer of devil's food cake and I'm good to go." I leaned in close to her and whispered, "Don't tell Evan I said so."

I unlocked my phone and opened the message screen.

HARPER: *Can you please bring me a couple of devil's food cupcakes when you leave the bakery?*

Finally, her appetite was returning. Thank goodness.

ME: *Sure.*
HARPER: *I'd also like one or two macarons.*
    Three. Three macarons.
ME: *Okay.*
HARPER: *And one of those little tiramisu bars.*

I sent her an angry emoji.

HARPER: *I love you.*
HARPER: *But really. The tiramisu.*
ME: *See you soon.*

I was shaking my head yet smiling as I tucked my phone back into my pocket. "Sorry about that."

"No problem. How's Harper doing?"

"Much better." I pulled a cake book over and cracked it open. I listened to hear if Evan was still with his customer, and he was still taking the order. "I wanted to say thanks for not telling Dorothy about Harper's pregnancy."

Glinda flipped a page. "She won't ever hear it from me."

I swiveled to look at her. "I heard about her plans for the Eldership."

She faced me. "I figured you would as soon as you talked to the Elder, what with Harper's pregnancy."

We sat looking at each other for a long moment. The silence stretched. I coughed. "I mentioned to Vince yesterday that he was going to have to choose a side eventually. Good or evil."

"I imagine that went over well. You might have noticed he doesn't like being told what to do."

"He pretty much kicked me out of Lotions and Potions."

She laughed. "And yet you still saved his life last night."

"Because I know what side I'm on."

She waited a beat, then said, "Well?"

"Well what?"

"Are you going to ask me what side I'm on? After all, I'm Dorothy's daughter. The person she wants to take the place of your mother as Elder."

I searched her gaze. In it, I saw all the changes she made in the past year. The acts of kindness. Turning the other cheek. The apologies. The amends she tried to make. I saw the hardness in her eyes shift to softness. The selfishness to openness. I recalled her horror at learning of Harper's baby and understood it was because she knew how her mother would react. And how she had told me that she didn't want kids of her own, so she wouldn't be a mom like hers. And I recalled the gift she had given me when I moved into my house. That beautiful besom to make sure my home was protected from evil. "No."

"No?"

"No, I'm not going to ask you. I know the answer."

Glinda blinked rapidly and tapped a page in the book. Smiling, she said, "What do you think? Two tiers or three?"

"How many people?"

"About twenty."

"Two is more than enough, then."

"You're forgetting that you and Mimi will be there."

"You're right. Definitely three."

She glanced at me. "My mother believes I'm pretending to be your friend and am using you to help her. I want her to keep believing that, do you understand?"

"I understand." She was trying to protect me, and it made my heart swell.

"Okay. I just wanted to make sure."

I smiled. "You're very thorough. It's one of your strengths."

"Better than nagging," she said, poking me with an elbow.

I heard a bell jingle, then a moment later Evan was back with us. He started setting out dessert plates. A dozen plates easily, each topped with two thin slices of cake. Then he grabbed a small platter that held a selection of cream puffs and set them before us as well. "Glinda, if you're thinking traditional, two tiers is more than enough—"

Glinda and I started laughing.

He set his hands on his hips. "What did I miss?"

"Nothing, nothing," I said. "Go on."

With a pout, he handed us forks and gave us a spiel about tiers, complementing flavors, fondant versus buttercream, and added, "If you rather nontraditional, you can do individual wedding cakes, pies, cupcake tiers, cake pops, a macaron tower, a croquembouche. The sky's the limit."

"A *croakemwhat*?" Glinda asked.

"Do not," he warned, "let Pepe hear you pronounce it that way. A *croquembouche*," he said with a flourish. He slid the plate of cream puffs towards us and then flipped through the cake book. "Here, look. It's a beautiful tower of cream puffs held together by a web of thin caramel strands."

The sugar work alone was whimsical and ethereal. It was a stunning cake, but not what I wanted for my wedding.

But this wasn't my wedding.

Glinda tipped her head side to side. "Maybe. I do like chocolate cream puffs."

"Do you? I can give you a deal. I have about a hundred of them in my freezer. Abby Stillwell had ordered a croquembouche, chocolate cream puffs with hazelnut cream as her wedding cake, and I have a ton of them frozen. They'll go to waste before I ever use them."

"You practice?" Glinda asked.

"There's magic," he said, "then there's foolishness. Of course I practice."

"Wait, wait." I held up a hand as his words sank in. "Back up. You said Abby ordered a cream puff tower? Chocolate cream puffs with hazelnut cream? Did she also want dark chocolate icing?"

"How'd you know?"

"Isn't it strange that chocolate cream puffs with hazelnut cream and dark chocolate drizzle are *Quinn's* favorite dessert?" She'd told me so herself a few days ago.

His shoulder lifted in a halfshrug. "I just thought Quinn had turned her on to them. They were room-mates. It makes sense."

My mind whirled with this new information, and I tapped the picture of the cream puff tower.

"What is it?" Glinda asked.

It was all starting to make sense in a strange sort of way. I'd been so blind to what was going on, when it had been in front of my face the whole time. "I don't think the cake was for Abby's wedding."

Evan said, "What do you mean, not for Abby's wedding? She's the one who ordered it."

"Yes, but not for her. I think it was Quinn's cake. And oh my gosh. The wedding dress!"

I suddenly realized it's what had been missing from Abby's living room when I peeked in earlier. Quinn must have stopped by to pick it up this morning.

"What about the wedding dress?" Glinda asked. "Godfrey made it for Abby."

"I bet if we ask Godfrey, he'll tell us Quinn was there when Abby picked out the dress. Don't you see? Quinn and Abby were the same size. They shared clothes all the time."

"Okay, even if all that is true, who is Quinn supposedly marrying?" Glinda asked.

"Ben Bryant." The way he'd watched from the window of Balefire last night made perfect sense now. He'd been concerned for Quinn. The phone call, too. Asking to come over. And how Quinn said he was the only nice Bryant . . .

"But wasn't he Abby's boyfriend?" Evan asked. "I'm so confused."

"Me, too," Glinda added.

"I don't think he was ever her boyfriend." I looked at Glinda. "Don't you see? It's just like you and me and what we're doing here, but taken to the next level. I think Ben has been Quinn's boyfriend all along. Ben was using Abby to cover-up his relationship with Quinn."

"But why?" Glinda asked. "Why wouldn't Ben just openly date Quinn? Why go through all the trouble of pretending to date Abby? And why would Abby go along with it?"

"Ben's family doesn't like Quinn. She's *mortal*. Or at least they thought so. It's like how your mom doesn't like Liam . . . that's how Ben's family is with Quinn."

"Wow," she said. "Then yeah, I can see why they'd hide it. But again, why would Abby go along with it?"

"I'm not sure. I know Quinn called her selfless. Maybe she felt bad for them, having to sneak around behind everyone's backs?"

Sneak. Around.

"The wig!" I said. "That makes sense now, too."

Quinn, with her blonde hair would be easily recognizable going in and out of Ben's apartment. But with a dark wig that resembled Abby's hair, and being the same size, she could pass as Abby from a distance. Just enough to fool anybody who might see her. Like Joe or Madison or Lucinda. She'd probably borrowed Abby's backpack, too, which was why the wig hair was on it in the first place.

"What wig?" Glinda asked.

Evan rapped on the tabletop. "Wait a sec, Quinn's *not* mortal?"

I explained as quickly and best as I could. Then said, "I need to call Nick. He can confirm all this easily by looking at the wedding license. If they were supposed to be married today, then the license is already public record."

"But Darcy," Evan said, "does any of this explain why Abby was killed?"

They're going to find out.

I bet Quinn had been talking about the wedding. Her wedding. And was scared to death one of the Bryants was going to stop it from happening.

"I don't know. I need to find Quinn and Ben. It's time for them to tell me *everything* they know."

Chapter
Twenty-Five

"The wedding license was applied for on Thursday and picked up yesterday morning," Nick said over the phone.

In Massachusetts there was a mandatory three-day waiting period when applying for a wedding license, and I knew from past clients that it had to be picked up in person by both parties. "Who was on the license?"

I was jogging across the green, toward home. "Just like you thought. Ben and Quinn."

I hadn't heard from Ve, which meant Quinn hadn't returned from her errands. Had one of her tasks this morning been to elope? "Are they married yet?"

"Not yet. They had an appointment scheduled with the justice of the peace at the courthouse at eleven. They didn't show."

"But Quinn picked up the dress at her house."

"Maybe they decided to go out of state."

Maybe. Massachusetts bordered a few states that didn't require a waiting period, like Rhode Island, Connecticut, and Vermont. They could apply for a new license and be married right away.

"But Quinn has suitcases sitting in Ve's mudroom. Why would she leave them there?"

"I don't know what to tell you, Darcy. But I can tell you this. Ben and Quinn weren't the only ones secretly dating. So were Duncan and Abby. From what we found in his apartment, they'd been back together for quite a while now. They just cosigned a lease on warehouse space in Wakefield."

I'm tired of waiting.

It's what Duncan had said to Abby the night before the race when Stef heard them arguing. He must have known he only had to wait a few more days, but I could understand why his patience had run thin. His life with the woman he loved had been put on hold until Quinn married Ben.

"And I just had a call from Joe Bryant's lawyer," Nick said.

"Did he confess about the noose?"

"No, but an interesting preliminary report came in from the lab about the rope. The red lint we found on the rope *is* consistent with fleece, and also, there were several long blonde hairs found in the rope fibers as well."

Long blonde hairs . . . "Madison?"

"Most likely. I'll deal with her as soon as I can."

I was trying to wrap my head around the fact that it was likely Madison who'd left the noose for me to find. No wonder she thought it preposterous I'd practically accused Joe of the crime—she'd *known* he hadn't been involved with the incident.

I thought back to everything I knew about Madison in regard to Abby. Was it possible Madison was the one who killed her? No. Impossible. Vince's video footage had given Madison an alibi. And she couldn't have been the one who'd attacked me last night at the hospital—she wasn't tall enough.

So . . . why had she left a noose for me? To stop me from finding out her *husband* had killed Abby? Or was it possible they were partners in the crime?

"Joe's lawyer," Nick said, "was calling about Joe's alibi. They have evidence of Joe's movements the morning of the race. His GPS watch tracked his every step, including into the woods after the bathrooms were locked. His route on the race morning was loaded on the family's group account, and Joe didn't realize he had the evidence until he logged his run from today and saw the route from the morning of the race. The watch syncs to the app automatically when it's near a cell phone. The information exonerates Joe since the map didn't show him going anywhere near the Aural Gorge bridge Saturday morning. The lawyer is sending me Joe's watch—the information is still on it—and also the group's log-in information to the app's website, so I can see it for myself."

"Can the data be manipulated?"

"I don't think so. It all goes through the watch. You'd need to be a high-tech wizard to change it."

Stunned, I nearly stumbled. "Then the watch clears Joe." With that, I was back to thinking Abby had been killed because of the wedding plans. "We need to figure out who thought it was Ben and Abby eloping today."

"No one I've asked had known about it. How about you?"

I was still stumped as to Madison's involvement, but I didn't think she was that good an actress to feign her disbelief about the elopement. "No one. All were shocked by the idea."

Which made sense now. They hadn't seen love and passion between Abby and Ben, because it hadn't been there.

And he and Quinn must have been exceptionally good at hiding it.

"Look, I'll be home in ten, fifteen minutes. We'll go over every bit of evidence. We're missing something. Okay?"

As I came to the edge of the green, I looked at the house and slowed to a walk.

"Darcy?" Nick asked. "You there?"

"I'm here. I just got home. I might not have found Quinn, but I found Ben. He's sitting on our front step." He had his head down, resting it on top of arms folded across his knees.

"You'll only be safe in the house with him, so do not go anywhere with him, do you hear me?"

Safe, because of the protection spells. "I hear."

"I'll be right there."

I hung up and slowly walked toward Ben. His head came up when he heard my footsteps. Big fat tears filled his eyes but didn't spill over.

"Ben?"

"I need your help. Please help me. Quinn's missing."

Despite the doors being closed in my face the past couple of days, I hesitated only a second. "Come on," I said, motioning him upward. "Come inside. Nick's on his way home."

Higgins was trying to bark his head clean off as we went inside. Harper was sitting on the stairs again and had Higgins by the collar. I was happy to see she had the strength to hold him back, since he weighed more than she did. A lot more.

She said, "Ben's been waiting out there for you for nearly half an hour. I wouldn't let him in without you here. What with the noose and all."

I was glad to hear it. Being overly cautious was going to serve her well in the coming months.

"Noose?" he asked.

"Someone left a noose for Darcy," Harper said. "We assume because of her investigating Abby's death."

"That's . . . horrible," he said.

So was attacking me in the parking lot.

I didn't mention to him that I thought Madison was behind the noose. I wanted to hear what he had to say, and if he had any idea who had killed Abby. "Tell me about Quinn."

"Quinn and I were supposed to meet up," Ben said, "at ten, to go up to Marblehead."

"To get married, I know."

"To do *what*?" Harper asked, following us down the hallway. She led Higgins to the back door, let him out, where he promptly started chasing a sparrow.

I led Ben to a stool at the island and motioned for him to sit.

"Long story," I said to her. "Where's Mimi?"

"She went to a friend's house to make zombie snowmen. Ve drove her over. You know, because of the noose thing."

Good, good. I was glad they'd taken the extra step—and that she wasn't here.

Ben went on explaining, saying, "Quinn didn't show up. She's not answering her phone. I've looked everywhere. Help me find her. *Please*."

"First," I said, "do you think she'd stand you up? Is it possible she just up and left all this madness behind?"

"She wouldn't," he said. "We've been planning this forever. She texted me this morning that she had picked up her dress from the house and was on her way to get the rings. I called the jeweler. She never made it there. Something's wrong."

"Before we go any further, do you know who killed Abby?" I asked.

"What? No! I don't know what happened to Abby. I get sick just thinking about it."

He did look a little green. "Could it have been Duncan?" I asked. "I know they've been dating for a while and that he was upset with her the night before the race. Was he still angry with her Saturday morning?"

"*Duncan and Abby*?" Harper asked.

"Nick just told me on the phone," I said to her.

Ben raked a hand through his short hair. "Duncan wouldn't have hurt Abby. He was frustrated, that's all. And they weren't just dating. They were *married*. For about two months now."

My hand froze as I unzipped my coat. "*Married*? Had they ever really broken up?"

Harper sank onto a stool.

Ben said, "Yeah. After the fallout with the doping scandal, they split. They were both devastated. Abby, because he had been using performance enhancers, and Duncan because Abby didn't believe him that he hadn't."

"Did he, or didn't he?" Harper asked.

"He didn't," Ben said. "But Abby, Quinn, and I didn't know it at that point. All we knew was what we had seen on those lab reports. It was horrible."

It sounded like it.

"Duncan was barely out of the picture, when Madison ramped up her matchmaking between Abby and me, not knowing that Quinn and I had been dating secretly for more than a year at that point and had plans to get married. We were waiting for the New Zealand trip. Get married the day before here in the States, get on a plane, and not come back. We were going to relocate there, get away from the toxic environment at Balefire."

I said, "I don't suppose it's a coincidence you chose a location halfway around the world?"

"Hardly." He looked me in the eye. "The farther away, the better. My family . . . is complicated."

That was stating things mildly.

"We were just going to grit our teeth and deal with Madison's pressuring, but two things happened. One, the matchmaking was getting under Quinn's skin and she was having a hard time biting her tongue about it."

"And the second?" Harper asked.

"A few months ago, Quinn was cleaning the office and came across Duncan's lab report. The original one, the one that hadn't been altered. She showed it to me, I took it to Abby, and we all realized what had happened."

"Did you confront your family? Who changed it? Your mom? Joe?"

"Joe," he said, "but Madison knew about it."

"Did your mom?"

He shook his head. "As much as she wanted Duncan gone, she wouldn't have tolerated such a devious plan."

"Why didn't Joe and Madison tell you?" I asked. Higgins barked, and I went to let him back inside. I didn't bother to wipe his paws—he had his sights set on Ben, and I didn't particularly want to dislocate a shoulder trying to hold Higgins still. He galloped over to Ben to sniff him up-and-down.

"They knew I was good friends with Duncan. They didn't know if I'd go along with their plan to get him out of Abby's life. I wouldn't have."

"Did you confront them?" Harper asked.

"We were going to, but Abby wanted us to wait until after she talked to Duncan. She always played by the rules. Always. My family's deceit cut her to her core. She was crushed they'd do that to her and Duncan, knowing how much she loved him. She went to see him."

"In New Hampshire?" I asked.

He nodded. "He was on a new team there. She told him about the lab report. Begged forgiveness for not believing him. He forgave her, but told her he was never moving back to the village and didn't think he could do a long-distance relationship. He was really worried my family would just try to break them up again when they found out they'd gotten back together."

He had good reason to worry, I thought. I glanced at the clock, hoping Nick would get here soon.

Ben went on. "Abby had been wanting to leave Balefire to open a training facility, and Duncan had been planning to retire from racing anyway, so they moved up those plans. And Abby had the idea that if they were married, none of those things would go wrong. So they drove to Vermont and eloped that day."

All this eloping was really making me rethink my wedding plans. "Then how did Abby end up back at Balefire? And why pretend to date you?"

Harper added, "Did she and Duncan have another falling out?"

"No, they didn't. At some point in all their excitement, Abby realized that without her as a buffer at Balefire, Quinn wouldn't last long."

"Even though she was a Halfcrafter?" I asked.

"My family doesn't know that," Ben said.

"Why not?" Harper asked. "The knowledge could have eased some of the tension between them."

"Quinn didn't want us to tell them. She wanted them to like her for her, not because she was now part of the Craft. But it was never going to happen, whether or not they knew she was a Halfcrafter. To them, she'd always be a mortal. The Craft isn't in her blood. It took a year for my mother to forgive Joe for marrying Madison, and she *likes* Madison."

"But Madison is a Terracrafter," I said. "Why would she have a problem with Joe marrying her?"

"Because she's not a Vincicrafter. Mom wants grandchildren who are full Vincis to carry on her legacy."

My jaw dropped. "You're kidding."

"No. I mean, she adores Aine, but she knows there's no way Aine is going to end up an Olympian. Especially since we can all see she's starting to take after Madison."

"This is positively eugenic," Harper said, shaking her head.

"And after seeing what my family did to Duncan and Abby, I'm glad we didn't tell them. Quinn would have been memory cleansed and who knows how they would have framed her to get her out of my life? Maybe blame their little tax fraud scheme on her and get her sent to jail?"

I didn't doubt it. Joe and Madison, I was quickly realizing, were utterly ruthless.

Ben said, "Knowing Quinn would be under a constant barrage at Balefire without her there, Abby came up with the idea to pretend to date me until mine and Quinn's elopement date. That way, we could live under some semblance of normal."

"That's a lot to ask of Abby," Harper said.

"And Duncan," I added.

He said, "I know, but it was Abby's idea."

"Even with her strict moral code?" I asked.

"Even with. Maybe because of it. She wanted to right the wrongs that had been made. And she said she owed Quinn for finding the truth about Duncan, and beyond that, she loved Quinn. Wanted her to be happy. And she's happy with me. And we were grateful, because we needed her, especially as the elopement day got closer, so she could help Quinn pick out a dress and do all the wedding things."

Selfless, Quinn had called Abby. It was true.

"Why didn't you just go into the city for a dress and cake?" Harper asked. "Why risk being seen in the village?"

"We did for the rings, since they had to be sized to our fingers, but Quinn really wanted one of Godfrey's dresses. We figured if anyone saw Abby picking out a dress, if word got out, it wouldn't be a big deal for people to think *Abby* and I were getting married. Even if my family caught wind of it, they liked Abby. We actually didn't know Abby had picked out one of those cream puff cakes, until after she ordered it. She was going to call Evan on the morning of the wedding, to have the cake delivered to our hotel room that night."

"Aw," Harper said.

"It was the kind of person Abby was. I don't know who could have killed her. It had to have been some nutjob who caught her off guard. A wrong time, wrong place kind of thing." He glanced at me. "Right?"

"Maybe," I said. "We've ruled out you, Quinn, Joe, and now Duncan."

"Have we really ruled Duncan out?" Harper asked. "He and Abby fought Friday night. And why were you so mad at him Saturday morning, Ben?"

Harper, I thought, would make a great Craft investigator, should I ever want to quit the job.

"Duncan would not harm a hair on Abby's head," Ben said. "They argued because he was frustrated she was spending all weekend in the village, doing stuff for Balefire. He'd been there to pick her up, but she was running late dealing with last minute details for the race. He lost his temper. Abby calmed him down and that was that."

Harper asked, "And Saturday morning?"

"I was angry because I couldn't believe he showed up at the race. It was too risky. But he wanted to watch Abby compete—it was going to be her last race. When he didn't see her at the starting line, he went to look for her at her house. But . . . Abby wasn't there." He dragged a hand through his hair. "It drove him crazy, but he waited there until Quinn arrived to tell him what was going on. He's devastated."

"Where is Duncan now?" I looked again at the clock. Nick should be here any minute. "Why's he been hiding?

"He's with his lawyer. He was waiting until after Quinn and I got married this morning to go in for police questioning. He was honoring Abby's wishes by not wanting to ruin mine and Quinn's plans for today. He knew it was our way out. If he went to the police before today, everything would come out, because he wouldn't lie about his relationship with Abby. So he was waiting."

"So we're back to square one," Harper said.

"Let's go back to when this all started," I suggested. "Saturday morning. Is there any detail you can think of, Ben, that you haven't told us?"

He pushed the heels of his hands into his eyes. "No. You know everything. I'm just so upset with myself that the last time I saw Abby, I was angry." His eyes watered. "She'd even been trying to get me to laugh by saying how she was looking forward to the wedding on Tuesday because I'd most likely be less grumpy once I was a married man. And I held onto my anger. If only I could go back . . ."

"Wait," I said. "You talked about the elopement at the race?"

"Just what Abby said. Why?"

"Was there anyone nearby?" I asked.

"I mean, not really. A few people passing by, warming up. There was the line for the portable toilets not too far away. No one seemed to be paying us any attention."

Harper said, "What are you thinking, Darcy?"

I'd been thinking about what he'd said earlier. About how Lucinda wanted full-blooded Vincicrafter grandchildren. To be a full Vinci, the child would need to have two Vinci parents . . . it was the only way.

I added that to the way Lucinda was so sure Ben and Abby's relationship was casual in nature, rather than one headed for the altar. If she had known they were getting married, I had no doubt she would have put a stop to it somehow.

Even if it meant getting rid of Abby any way possible, since Lucinda believed she had only 'til Tuesday. There was no time to Craft an elaborate plot to get her out of the village.

I swallowed hard and said, "If your mother truly wanted you to marry a Vincicrafter and thought you and Abby were marrying on Tuesday . . ."

"You don't think . . . No." He shook his head. "She didn't know anything about the elopement. None of my family knew."

But I wondered if she'd somehow found out. I was thinking back to the video I'd watched with Vince. Lucinda had been with Madison and Aine, but I didn't recall seeing her again until the race went off.

I pictured the area, trying to imagine where some-one could overhear Ben and Abby's conversation. There was nothing around the trailhead but bushes and trees, which I realized, would provide plenty of cover. Lots of evergreen to hide behind. "Both Joe and Quinn had gone off to find other restrooms after seeing those lines. Joe ended up in the woods and missed the start of the race. Is that something your mom would do? Use the woods?"

He said, "All the time. You don't run dozens of miles on wooded trails without using the woods once in a while."

Why hadn't I suspected Lucinda before now? Because she was older? Because I'd seen the loving way she looked at her granddaughter? She was fast enough to get to the bridge and back before anyone knew it. And she ruled her family with an iron fist.

I was kicking myself mentally. "Is it possible your mom was in the woods nearby when you were talking with Abby?"

"I mean, it's possible." His face had scrunched up as though fighting the idea that his mom had done some-thing so terrible. Yet . . . he wasn't vociferously defend-ing her either. "But, Quinn. There's no way she knew about Quinn."

My heart was pounding. "I think she knows about Quinn because she was the one who broke into Abby's house. I questioned her right before the break-in," I con-tinued, trying to keep my breaking voice steady. "I must have unknowingly made her suspicious when I questioned her. I told her about Quinn picking up the wedding dress, and I asked her about the wig too."

Harper said, "You think Lucinda broke in to verify suspicions that it was Ben dating Quinn, not Abby?"

I nodded. "Photos or something," I said, thinking about the album Quinn had packed. Was it still there? Or had it been taken during the break-in and we hadn't noticed?

Ben swallowed hard. "There were pictures of Quinn and me on her nightstand."

I'd seen them. During the walk-through with the police officer. And if I'd seen them, so did the person who had broken in.

Lucinda.

Without a doubt, it had been my questions that had led us to this place and time. Guilt nearly swallowed me whole in one big gulp.

"If it's true that Lucinda killed Abby to stop *her* from marrying Ben," Harper said, her voice tapering off. "What would she do if she realized it was actually Quinn who was supposed to marry him?"

I almost choked on my fear. "We need to find Quinn."

Ben pulled out his phone. His hands shook as he dialed.

"Who're you calling?" Harper asked.

"My mother."

It couldn't hurt to try, but after several rings, he hung up. "She's not answering."

"Do you know where she is this morning?"

"She's supposed to be at the store," he said. "Doing inventory, but she wasn't there when I checked there earlier for Quinn."

The store had been dark when I'd gone by on my way to the Gingerbread Shack as well.

"This is crazy." He looked at his watch. "It's been more than an hour since Quinn and I were supposed to meet up. We need to do something."

I looked at his watch. His GPS watch. Quinn didn't wear one, but his mother did. "Is there any way to track Lucinda's current movements with her watch?"

He shook his head. "No, it only uploads when you've finished a route. You have to tell it you're done to upload. And only then when you manually connect it to your laptop, or if it's near your cell phone, will it sync automatically. People don't just disappear. How did you find Abby? Can we use that guy's drone to search the village? Maybe we can at least find Quinn's car."

"He's in the hospital," I said. "It could take hours before he's released. But we could use the lost and found spell to find *Quinn*." I should have thought of it sooner. "Harper? Will you help?"

She held up her hands. "I'll show you how, but I told you I'm done with the Craft."

Interesting, considering the amulet she was wearing. Apparently she was picking and choosing what kinds of Crafting she'd support. But now wasn't the time to argue. "Fine," I said. "We need Quinn's hair. Her suitcases are at Ve's. Harper, can you call over there and have Ve bring Quinn's brush or comb or whatever over here?"

"I'm on it." She pulled out her cell. As she dialed, she added, "You'll still need to know what Quinn's wearing or a piece of jewelry or something."

"She has to have a coat on in this weather. I know what it looks like—I helped her into it last night."

Ben looked shell-shocked as Harper talked to Ve. I gathered supplies and put the kettle on. I was grateful I also had a bowl from the Trimmed Wick, and with

Harper's guidance, I mixed spices together. Before we knew it, Ve and Missy had arrived.

The ruckus must have woken Archie from his stupor, because he was suddenly on his perch, rubbing his eyes with his wingtips, and saying, "What in Lucifer's name is going on down here?"

"No time to explain," I said as Nick came dashing in the door.

"What's going on?" Nick asked, studying the items on the island.

"We think Lucinda killed Abby, and now has Quinn," Harper said.

"Oh," Archie grumped. "That took forever to explain. Ages. Decades, even."

"*Shh*," I said to him.

He folded his wings in a huff but shut his beak.

"Now, pour the water slowly," Harper said to me, pointing to the ceramic bowl and looking like she wanted to take the kettle out of my hand.

The cloud plumed above the bowl and we all stared into its mist.

"I see Quinn!" Ve said. "Oh. Oh my. Oh dear."

Quinn was alive, but she wasn't alone. She and Lucinda were standing on the Aural Gorge bridge, and Quinn was clinging to one of the railings for dear life as Lucinda tried to push her over into the gorge.

Nick whipped out his phone and ran for the door.

How long until he could get there? It would take at least a couple of minutes to drive to the trail, even with his siren on. Another five minutes to get to the bridge on foot if he ran full-out.

I didn't know if Quinn had that kind of time.

"Oh god, oh god," Ben cried. He stood up to follow Nick, and it was Ve who snagged him.

"Let him go," she said. "He doesn't need your emotions complicating the situation."

"I can't just sit here!" he protested.

"What can we do, Darcy?" Ve asked.

I was at a loss, watching Quinn fight for her life. We needed someone there *now*. Someone who could buy Nick some time.

I turned a pleading gaze to Archie.

He saluted and said, "I'm on it."

Harper ran to the mudroom door to let him out.

Ben pulled out his phone again and dialed. In the cloud, Lucinda paused in the struggle as though she felt the buzz in her pocket, but she didn't stop fighting with Quinn, who now had her legs twisted around the railing as well.

Ben kept calling his mother's phone, alternating each call with a text message. But Lucinda was undeterred as she kept tugging at Quinn, who wasn't giving an inch.

Yoga had made Quinn strong and flexible. Lucinda had underestimated its power when she'd mocked Quinn for practicing the discipline. It was proving to be a fateful miscalculation.

"Look, look, Archie's already there," Harper said, her voice high-pitched with excitement.

In the cloud, Archie's vibrant scarlet color streaked back and forth, dive-bombing Lucinda. She swatted at him and we could see her yelling, too. As I manipulated the cloud, trying to see how far away Nick was, I wished we could also hear what was going on.

Or maybe I didn't want to know.

I caught sight of a flash of color and zoomed out. Nick had arrived—he must have taken his car onto the trail. It was the first time, perhaps, the little MINI Cooper had proved valuable.

We watched as Lucinda slowly backed away from Quinn and Archie landed on the railing, near Quinn's head.

Nick held his gun as he neared Quinn, and I could see him shouting at Lucinda.

"He's saying 'get down'," Harper said.

He was. It was easy to read his lips.

Ve clasped her hands together under her chin. "Have mercy."

Lucinda was shaking her head.

"Get down," Ben whispered.

We all watched in horror as Lucinda bolted forward toward the railing, only to stop short of flinging herself over as a bullet ripped into her leg. She crumpled on the bridge, writhing in obvious pain as Nick rushed over to her. As he slipped a pair of handcuffs on her, next to me in the kitchen, Ben put his head in his hands and wept.

Chapter
Twenty-Six

"I'm a glutton for punishment," I said. "Tell me why I'm here again."

"You're a good person," Nick said. "And have I mentioned how beautiful you look tonight?"

"Yes, thank you. And you don't look so bad yourself."

"Flatterer."

"I learned from the best."

We were dressed up, me in a high-necked aqua-colored lace dress and Nick in a navy suit, standing in Glinda's living room, watching as she and Liam gazed happily at each other. They'd been declared man and wife only a few minutes ago. Starla was bent low, snapping plenty of pictures. And I couldn't help thinking what a strange and wonderful life I led.

A year ago, Starla would have happily strangled Glinda with her camera strap.

Now, they were friends.

Not best friends. Not by a long shot. But there was peace between them.

There was not, however, any peace between Dorothy Hansel Dewitt and me.

If looks could kill, I'd be on the floor, outlined in chalk. She had been acrimonious since the moment she stepped into the house and realized, first, that there was a wedding happening and, second, that I'd been invited.

She'd asked to speak to Glinda privately but Glinda had refused, and I thought for a minute there she was going to pop a vein and bleed out on Glinda's Persian rug.

While Dorothy had somehow managed to keep quiet during the ceremony, she'd been doing nothing but sniping, snorting, and scowling since.

I was trying my best to avoid her all together. "Glinda looks happy."

Nick put his arm around me, holding me close. "She does."

"I'm happy for her."

He kissed my temple. "I'm happy you're happy. It's been in short supply this week."

It had been only a few days since Lucinda Bryant had been arrested. Days of sadness and remorse, of grief and guilt. I knew I wasn't the only one who had been questioning if what had happened could have been prevented.

Ben and Quinn were, too. They were living in chaos right now, trying to pick up some of the pieces of their lives while dealing with the police investigation, Lucinda's arrest, and Joe and Madison's sudden abandonment. They'd cut Ben off completely, blaming him for everything that had happened.

The bullet Nick had fired had hit Lucinda in the thigh. An infection much like Vince's had set in, and she was still in the hospital, under police watch. Doctors said it could take weeks, but she was expected to fully recover.

It was clear to me as she ran toward the railing on the bridge that day that she would have rather died than be arrested. Whether that had been because of shame for what she'd done, or because she didn't want to go to prison where she'd be surrounded by mortals, or for some other reason, wasn't yet known. She was heavily medicated and had been since arriving at the hospital. But doctors were optimistic about her recovery, and soon she'd be formally charged with the murder of Abigail Stillwell, the attempted murder of Quinn Donegal, and with criminal harassment charges from the tire iron incident. It had been Lucinda who'd attacked me in the hospital parking lot, after fearing that Quinn had told me of her and Ben's relationship and thinking I'd realize what had happened with Abby.

Quinn had confirmed my speculation about what *had* happened to Abby was correct: Lucinda had been in the bushes near the trailhead the morning of the race. She'd told Quinn everything after she waylaid her heading to the jewelry shop Tuesday morning, telling her someone had attacked Ben on the trail during his morning run, and that she needed Quinn to come with her.

Once they'd reached the bridge, the situation had taken a dark turn when Quinn realized Lucinda had lied to her about Ben being injured and that she was trapped—she couldn't possibly outrun Lucinda. She'd grabbed onto the railing and started screaming.

The ruse with Ben, we'd learned, was the same thing Lucinda had told Abby the morning of the Mad Dash. Lucinda had told Quinn so. And Abby, wanting to help, had willingly followed Lucinda to the Aural Gorge bridge . . . to help save her dear friend's life. Only to lose her own.

And if describing what had happened to Quinn hadn't been enough of a confession, data collection from Lucinda's GPS watch had proven the path she had taken the fateful morning that Abby had died.

Joe cutting off his brother stuck like a thorn in my side and only verified what Ben and Quinn had believed all along—that the Bryants never would have supported his and Quinn's relationship. Ever.

Joe and Madison had problems of their own, however, with an IRS investigation. Madison also faced charges for threatening to commit a crime—the result of leaving that noose for me to find. According to her, she'd simply been trying to warn me from looking too deeply into Balefire's bookkeeping, but I was hoping a judge would throw the book at her. It was too early to know the outcome of either investigation yet, but a part of me hoped they would both spend a lot of time behind bars, just for being horrible people. Time would tell.

In the end, it seemed like Ben and Quinn had lost just about everything. But they still had each other, and I had the feeling they would come out of this in the long run stronger than ever.

Noelle Quinlan sidled over, clutching a glass of champagne for dear life. She leaned in. "Does Dorothy hate me?"

I said, "Dorothy hates most everyone."

She winced and gulped her drink. "Oh dear."

"Fixer-upper, remember?"

She let out a shuddering breath. "Don't remind me."

I didn't think it had been an accident that Vince had chosen Noelle as his date tonight. I suspected he'd been trying to divert Dorothy's vitriol from Glinda. However, he'd been unprepared for the fact that Dorothy had plenty of animosity to go around.

He kept looking our way as Mimi talked his ear off. His hand was in a soft cast, but once his incision healed, he'd be practically good as new.

"Nick," Noelle said, "again, I'm so sorry about your contract falling through."

Despite postponing the closing for a few days, the buyers hadn't been able to secure their financing. Nick's house was already back on the market. But not for long.

"It's all right," he said. "Sometimes these things happen for a reason."

"I'm sure you'll be under contract again soon," Noelle assured. "It's a great house."

That contract was going to happen sooner than she could imagine. Once Harper had heard about Nick's deal falling through, she'd been on the phone to Marcus.

They were going to buy Nick's farmhouse and renovate the workshop garage into a guest house, so that when Marcus's mother came for extended visits to the village, she had a private place to stay.

"Oh! Did you hear the news about Abby's house?" Noelle asked. Then she looked at Nick and laughed. "Of course you have. I'm just thrilled it isn't going to be defaulted to the state."

I bet she was.

Since they had been married, Duncan had inherited Abby's house.

The last I'd heard, from Quinn this morning, was that Duncan planned to eventually sell the house and invest the money in the training facility he and Abby had dreamed of opening together. And he had new investors: Quinn and Ben would be joining him in the venture, deciding that the three of them sticking together was more important than moving halfway around the globe.

Noelle glanced at me. "How long do you think we need to stay?"

"At least until cake," I said, glancing over at the dessert table. The beautiful three-tiered ivory cake had one continuous Shakespeare quote decorating each level in golden lettering. "When I saw you, I fell in love, and you smiled because you knew." The wedding topper was a pair of golden birds, which was appropriate, I thought, given the whole theme of this so-called party.

"I do like cake," she said, smiling.

"We should go save Vince from Mimi's interrogation," Nick said. "She's not going to leave him alone until she has every detail of his infection, from first cut to final suture."

I shuddered at the thought. I'd already teased him about his hospital adventures earlier, and when I asked him if he still thought Craft magic was lame, he'd given me a shrug and a small smile.

Baby steps.

We crossed the room, taking the long way around to avoid Dorothy, and Noelle snagged another glass of champagne from a tray, replacing her empty one.

Vince eyed it wistfully. "If not for the medication I'm on . . . How soon can we leave?"

Noelle laughed and linked arms with him.

I swore I heard a growl from Dorothy behind me.

"After cake," Noelle said.

"Isn't it so pretty?" Mimi asked. She looked at Nick and me. "I can't wait to see what kind of cake you guys pick out. It'll be chocolate, right?"

"Of course," I said.

Nick smiled. "Every tier, I'm guessing."

"Of course," I said again.

"I can't wait for summer," Mimi said, beaming. "The wedding. And then Harper's baby is due in September. It's going to be—"

"Baby?" Vince asked.

"Baby?" I heard Dorothy screech.

Oh, no.

Glinda heard the shriek and came rushing over just as Dorothy elbowed her way into our group. "Did you say baby?" she asked Mimi.

Mimi didn't pick up on the caustic undertones and kept on talking. "You haven't heard? Harper and Marcus are having a baby. Can you imagine? A little Harper running around?"

"It's a girl?" Dorothy said, her tone deadly.

"Well, we don't know yet. It's too soon." Mimi glanced around and noted our stricken faces. "Is it okay I said something? I thought that since Harper and Marcus are back together now . . ."

"It's okay, Mimi," Nick said. "Don't worry about it. Maybe we should get going . . ."

"You don't have to leave," Glinda said. "The party's just starting."

"Oh, they should leave," Dorothy said. "Right now."

"What's going on?" Noelle stage-whispered to Vince.

He was watching me with worried eyes as he shrugged, clearly brushing off her question to avoid having to explain.

Dorothy's burning gaze swept from Glinda to me to Vince, but finally settled on Glinda. Rage infused her face, plumping her cheeks, making her eyes bulge. "Did you know?"

"No," Glinda said without hesitation, lying so effortlessly that I believed her even though I knew the truth.

"Know what?" Noelle asked.

Dorothy spun on her. "Shut. Up."

"Mother," Glinda said. "Don't be rude. This is a party. We're *celebrating*. Sorry, Noelle."

Noelle nodded, but had shrunk into Vince.

"*Don't*," Dorothy warned Glinda, "tell me what to do."

Liam rushed in and laughed nervously. "Everything okay here?"

"We were just leaving," Nick said, pulling Mimi in to stand between the two of us. Protecting her.

She looked my way with tears in eyes. I took hold of her hand, held it tight. "That's right, we were."

"No," Glinda said. "I want you to stay. Please. We can all get along for one night. For *me*. Please," she said again.

"No, we cannot," Dorothy said, stepping forward. She opened her mouth, then snapped it closed. Without another word, she stormed to the door and walked out, slamming it behind her.

* * *

Across the village, a restless Melina "Missy" Sawyer stood, stretched her paws, turned in a circle three times, then scratched just the perfect spot on a fleece blanket and tried to settle down. Not an easy task, considering her mood. Not even the distraction of a young, toned Tom Selleck was helping. But she had to admit the more she watched, the more she was starting to understand Archie's adoration for *Magnum, P.I.*

Archie let out a catcall as Magnum marched across a beach in those tiny short-shorts of his and Ve laughed, shaking the couch.

Although they'd been watching for nearly half an hour, Mel couldn't say what the plot of the show was about. She was too busy worrying.

Glinda's wedding was tonight.

Dorothy and Darcy in a small room was a recipe for disaster, but she hoped the happiness of the occasion would overshadow any hostility.

Ve had been trying her best to take Mel's mind off the event all night, offering every now and again to fix her a mai tai—they had tired of piña coladas—to help her relax. Mel kept turning the offers down. She didn't want to turn into a lush like Archie.

And she didn't think it was possible for her to relax until Mimi, Nick, and Darcy were safe at home.

She noted, too, that she wasn't the only one worried.

Derrie had been fidgeting in her chair all night, throwing anxious glances at the clock. The later the hour, the more agitated the Elder became.

"Maybe we should go over there," Mel finally said. "Put our minds at ease."

"We've been through this," Ve said, muting the TV. "Dorothy isn't likely to cause a scene tonight that will jeopardize her chances at overthrowing Dee's Eldership."

Derrie sent her a weary glance.

"What?" Ve said innocently. "I didn't say she was going to succeed."

Archie said, "'Tis true she would not want to jeopardize her chances, however, as calculated as Dorothy can be, it is important to remember she has trouble controlling her temper."

Derrie added, "And the wedding itself is provocation enough, since Glinda is marrying against Dorothy's wishes. Anything can happen tonight. We mustn't be complacent."

"We should have had Pepe and Mrs. P there spying on the wedding," Ve said after a moment. "It would have set your minds at ease."

Archie said, "Darcy is there."

"More provocation," Derrie pointed out.

"Maybe we should go over there," Mel said again. "Mimi's there . . . and I don't want her caught in crossfire."

It had been hard enough for Mel these past few months, separating herself from her daughter. It was for the best, she knew, to eventually live with Ve, but it was going to be so difficult to leave Mimi behind. The thought of Dorothy possibly doing anything to harm her . . .

Mel shook her head to banish the thought and her ears flopped around. One flipped inside out. Ve reached over and fixed it for her. "Thanks." Would she ever fully get used to being in this Schnoodle form? She was starting to think no and wondered if other familiars felt the same about their bodies.

"Dorothy's target isn't likely to be Mimi," Derrie said.

Mel knew that to be true, but . . . "If she's angry enough, anything is possible."

Aiming the remote at the TV, Ve turned it off. "Maybe we should all go over there."

Suddenly Ve's cell phone buzzed.

They all looked at it, vibrating on the coffee table.

Ve grabbed it. "It's a text from Darcy."

"What does it say?" Archie asked.

Ve's hand trembled. "All it says is 'she knows'. Have mercy. Dorothy must have found out about Harper's baby."

Just then a huge gust of wind shook the house, rattling it from rafters to foundation. Vases wobbled and a picture fell off the wall, the glass shattering.

"What in the world was that?" Mel asked. "An earthquake?"

Derrie said solemnly, "No. That was Dorothy unleashing her full fury. We knew this time would come. It's just come a little sooner than we thought. But we're ready."

"We are?" Archie asked, sounding quite uncertain.

"We are," Derrie said, nodding. "And we will win this war."

Mel's heart pounded. She was glad the Elder was so confident going into this battle with Dorothy.

Because she wasn't.

Not at all.

But she was ready to fight. To the death, if need be.

Of course, that was easy enough for her to say. She was already dead.

She glanced at Ve. "I think I'll have that drink now."

Acknowledgments

A heartfelt thank you goes to my agent, Jessica Faust, for her endless encouragement and guidance. I'm so grateful to have her by my side on this journey.

To Anne Brewer, Jenny Chen, and the whole team at Crooked Lane, thank you for all you do—and have done—for Darcy and me. We couldn't be in better hands.

Finally, to all the readers who follow my stories wherever they may take me—I appreciate your support and encouragement more than I can ever fully express. Thank you, thank you.

Read an excerpt from

A WITCH TO REMEMBER

the next

WISHCRAFT MYSTERY

by HEATHER BLAKE

available soon in hardcover from
Crooked Lane Books

CROOKED
LANE

NEW YORK

Chapter One

"This wedding might be the death of me, and I'm not even the one getting married. So much to get done, so little time."

Startled by the statement, I studied my sister Harper a little more closely. June sunshine highlighted the humor in her big golden-brown eyes. She was joking, which made sense since the wedding ceremony would be a small affair, fifteen to twenty people max. "We both know there's not much left to do at all, and please don't tease about the death thing."

I'd seen enough death in the past couple of years to last me a lifetime.

Maybe two lifetimes.

While some of the deaths had been natural, most of them had not.

As we wended our way along one of the paths that twisted through the vast village green on our way to Divinitea Cottage, a tearoom where my informal bridal luncheon was being held in fifteen short minutes, I didn't want to think about death. Any death . . . but especially Harper's. Not too long ago, she'd had a close call. It had been enough of a scare. I couldn't even bear the *thought* of life without her in it.

But as hard as I tried to dissuade morbid thoughts from encroaching on what was supposed to be a cheerful day, I couldn't keep from remembering all the murder cases I'd been involved in during the two years I've lived in this quaint village. The cases had scarred me. Some literally. All figuratively.

While the Enchanted Village, a touristy witch-themed neighborhood of Salem, Massachusetts, appeared at first glance to be postcard-perfect, it wasn't always. Every so often, evil visited these charming cobblestone streets. It walked past the boutiques with their colorful awnings, drank a glass of wine at the Cauldron, and watched kittens play in the window of the Furry Toadstool pet shop.

And sometimes . . . the evil came to stay, residing alongside the magic.

Both of which were well concealed.

Especially the magic. What most people didn't know was that witches inhabited this village, working and living alongside mortals who simply thought the Enchanted Village was a popular tourist area. Here, witches like my sister and me—Wishcrafters, who could grant wishes—could practice the Craft out in the open without fear of being caught.

Well, *I* could.

Harper was currently off witchcraft.

Abstaining. Again.

I was holding out hope that she'd change her mind about using her Craft abilities. Soon. Otherwise . . .

Drawing in a deep breath, I forced those particular worries from my thoughts and tried to think only of the afternoon ahead at Divinitea. Time that would be spent celebrating my upcoming wedding to Nick Sawyer, the village police chief. Waiting for Harper and me at the cottage were a few of my nearest and dearest, and I was looking forward to enjoying an afternoon of love and friendship.

With a smirk, Harper said, "I think your sense of humor is lost somewhere under that hat, Darcy."

"This hat *proves* I have a sense of humor." Before we left my house, Harper had presented me with an ivory fascinator decorated with tall, glittery feathers, rhinestones, and a birdcage veil that was nothing short of overwhelming.

Glancing up at the hat perched on my head, she laughed. "It's a work of art."

"Oh, it's *something*, all right." I smiled at someone who openly stared at the ostentatious creation.

I hadn't been receiving too many curious glances, only because it was the third day of the Firelight Psychic Festival. Here on the green, I was literally surrounded by curiosities in the form of mediums, animal communicators, tarot readers, chakra specialists, crystal healers, palm readers, astrologers, and many more mystics. Despite most of the vendors looking like your average everyday joes and janes, there were some who took their appearance to the next level with turbans, caftans, top hats, and long coats. With the fascinator, I blended in.

Amid all the booths, tents, and demonstrations, the village buzzed with upbeat energy. Music thumped, the scent of fried dough permeated the humid air, and the thrum of voices chatting and laughing surrounded us.

"And there *is* plenty to do still—for the reception, especially." Harper wore an emerald-green maxi dress that flowed behind her as she strode along, her tiny, rounded belly leading the way. She was six months pregnant. She held up a hand and started ticking off a list. "Final fittings, final check-in with vendors, pick up your rings, follow up with the people who haven't RSVP'd, finalize the music playlist . . ." She lifted her other hand. "Package wedding favors . . ."

In two weeks, Nick's and my wedding would be held in our backyard, attended by only our closest friends and family. The reception, however, was going to be a big party right here on the village green that practically the whole village was invited to. I wasn't the least bit stressed about any of it.

I was concerned with other big life events that I didn't even want to *think* about.

I suddenly felt queasy as we walked along. Worry and anxiety weren't good companions to the thick fried-oil smell hanging in the air.

But there was time enough to stress about everything else later. Today was supposed to be a happy, joyous day.

Thankfully, Harper had everything with the wedding under tight control. I could only imagine how she was going to behave when she was an actual bride, but I'd find out soon enough. She and village lawyer Marcus Debrowski planned to marry at Christmastime. He was currently out of town, helping his mother settle into her new house in Florida, and I thought some of Harper's hyperfocus on my wedding had to do with his absence. Harper didn't think he was coming back until Tuesday—the day of her twenty-fifth birthday—but that was because she didn't know we were having a little surprise party for her Monday night, where a bonus surprise would be Marcus's early return.

I reached over and forced her closest hand down. "Everything with the wedding will be fine," I said. "Take a deep breath before you deprive your poor baby of oxygen."

After a rocky start to the pregnancy, Harper and her baby were now as healthy as could be, thanks to a little magic and some modern-day medicine. I glanced at the amulet she wore on a long chain that bumped against the top of her belly as she walked—a protection amulet she hadn't taken off since the day she put it on back in February. It had done its job remarkably well, and I thanked my lucky stars for the magic in my—and her—life.

Tufts of her light-brown pixie-cut hair fluttered in the breeze as she said, "I know, it's just that I want everything to be perfect for you and Nick. You both deserve it."

I smiled at her. "It will be."

"But—"

"Hush. No more worrying today, okay? Today's about celebrating. There are people waiting for us at Divinitea, so let's get a move on."

I hadn't wanted a big, fussy bridal shower, much to Harper and my best friend Starla Sullivan's collective dismay. To appease them, I'd suggested a luncheon instead, and they'd jumped at the idea, even though I capped the guest list at seven. Including me.

Holding the festivities at Divinitea Cottage had been a favor to Dr. Dennis Goodwin. He wanted to ensure the tearoom, which was owned by his wife Amanda and her cousin Leyna Noble, was booked solid for its grand opening. I'd gladly agreed to Dennis's plan, since Harper and I literally owed him our lives— he was a Curecrafter, a healing witch—but he needn't have worried. Divinitea, which also specialized in tea-leaf reading, had been packed solid since its doors opened a few days ago.

"Look, it's Feifel Highbridge's tent," Harper said with an impish look in her eyes as she stepped off the path onto a thick carpet of freshly mowed grass. She patted her belly. "Should we see if he can guess what I'm having?"

Feifel "Feif" Highbridge was one of the top-billed psychics at the festival, and over the past couple of days I'd overheard people raving about his readings. But a psychic proclamation wasn't necessary when it came to the gender of Harper's baby. "We already know what you're having."

At Harper's last obstetrical appointment, a detailed ultrasound had revealed she was carrying a little boy.

A perfect little boy.

"I know, but let's ask Feif anyway." Harper grabbed hold of my arm to steer me toward a large ornate tent that looked like it belonged on the set of *Arabian Nights*. Domed, the tent was draped in yards of gossamer and satiny fabrics colored in deep reds, purples, and golds. "Let's see how good of a psychic he really is."

I dug in my heels. "Let's not. Don't you think it's rather rude of us to attempt to debunk *guests* of the village?"

"It's not personal, Darcy. It's *research*."

The arched entrance to Feif's tent had an OUT TO LUNCH sign clipped to it. "What a *shame*," I said with a shrug. "He's not here."

"Yes, I can feel your disappointment. But aren't you curious, Darcy? Can people really see the future, read people's minds, talk to the dead . . . ?" Harper gestured far and wide, sweeping all the tents and booths into her question.

"I'm not curious at all." I lifted the veil out of my eyes as a breeze kicked up.

"How can you *not* be curious?"

"It's simple," I said. "I believe in things I can't see. In things I don't quite understand. I believe in magic."

She put her hands on her hips. "That seems a little naïve to me."

"Does it? Do I need to remind you that we're"—I dropped my voice—"witches?"

Despite that particular—and undeniable—fact, Harper still didn't fully believe in the wonder of magic. The skeptic deep inside her longed for *scientific* proof that magic was real, and I had the uneasy feeling she'd never completely accept her abilities and her heritage until she found what she was looking for: one big *aha!* moment that would explain everything.

It simply was never going to happen.

Not with the Craft.

And not with these psychics, no matter how much she *researched* them.

Harper looked around and said, "What if some of these people are phonies?"

Whether Feif—or any of these mystics—had true psychic ability, I didn't know. As long as they weren't hurting anyone, I was of the thought to live and let live.

Do no harm. The tenet was the cornerstone of the Craft. Witches couldn't use the Craft to emotionally or physically hurt one another. Not without dire consequences, at least. It was my greatest wish that everyone would adopt the rule, whether they were a witch or not. But even though I could grant wishes for others, Wishcraft laws stated I could not grant my own. Otherwise the world would have been a much more peaceful place.

"What if they are phonies?" I asked. "Are you going to throw them out of the village?"

The corner of her mouth lifted in a half smile as she looked around. "I might."

I couldn't help laughing at the thought of her strong-arming anyone. At just five feet tall, she was more elf than henchwoman. Yet . . . "I don't doubt it, Harper. I don't doubt it. Now, come on. We're going to be late."

"All right, but don't you think there's enough time for a quick stop at one of these food stands?" She eyed the offerings—everything from fried Oreos to lobster rolls. "I do."

"You know Divinitea has food waiting for us—lots of it."

"But not corn dogs."

I could hardly argue. The menu offerings for today's tea included items such as salmon-and-herb sandwiches, shortbread, scones, custards, and quiches. No corn dogs.

"Do you want one?" she asked.

"No, definitely not."

"Your loss." Grinning, she veered off to stand in a long line.

Since I certainly wasn't going to deny a pregnant woman her craving, I found a shady spot next to a tree to wait.

From here, I could just see the top of Divinitea's quaint eyebrow dormers and thatched rooftop at the other end of the village square. That the tea cottage's opening had overlapped with the arrival of the Firelight festival wasn't a coincidence but had been planned carefully, as the festivalgoers were ideal long-term customers.

That Divinitea had managed to open this week at *all* was a bit of a miracle. There had been issues with obtaining the property, hoops to jump through regarding zoning, and construction troubles. The renovation issues hadn't had anything to do with the ability of the crew and everything to do with vandalism—thefts, graffiti, and property damage. It had stopped only when Amanda and Leyna commissioned a protection spell. Even though the culprit had never been caught, most every witch in the village had a suspicion of who had been behind the acts: Dorothy Hansel Dewitt.

Dorothy, newly separated from her husband, Sylar—and therefore newly jobless as well, since she'd worked for him—had fought bitterly to buy the property herself to open a gift shop to feature her handmade woodcrafts. As a Broomcrafter, a witch who could work magic with wood, she had an undeniable talent for creating masterpieces, ranging from wooden bowls to stunning besoms. She hadn't been pleased when the previous owner of the cottage rejected her offer to buy the place in favor of Amanda and Leyna's bid. Much to everyone's relief, Dorothy had not tried to set the place on fire. It was no secret that she was a firebug—especially when she was angry.

Dorothy was not a witch used to being denied something she wanted.

Something I knew quite well.

"*Psst!* You! Hey you! You there."

I glanced around and found an older woman eyeing me from a booth across the path. A large banner behind her had PSYCHIC written on it in silver curlicue letters.

I put my hands to my chest. "Me?"

The woman nodded and beckoned me closer.

"No thanks." I stayed put. "I'm not interested in a reading."

Not that I wasn't curious, but there were too many secrets tucked inside my head that I wanted to stay exactly where they were, thank you very much.

"Come here, child," she said in a stern voice.

Ordering someone around perhaps wasn't the best way to snag a customer, I reflected.

Yet . . . I oddly found myself crossing over to her, so maybe she knew precisely what she was doing. She still wasn't going to get a reading out of me, no matter what tone she used. I could, however, make idle conversation until Harper was ready to go. I didn't want to be rude.

The booth smelled of roses and was filled with displays of stones, glass balls, candles, and delicate crystal figurines of fairies, cats, and witches. Eyebrows raised, I approached with caution.

The woman thrust out a thin, arthritis-gnarled hand and said, "I'm Mathildie. You can call me Hildie. That's with an *ie*. Nice hat." There was a slight warble in her voice that came with age and a mischievous gleam in her eyes that I instantly suspected had been present her whole life long.

Hildie with an *ie* was a tiny woman with clear blue eyes flecked with gold that were sharp yet playful. Her ivory skin was deeply lined—almost cross-hatched in appearance. Black and white strands wove through glittery silver hair that was pulled back and clipped at the nape of her neck. She wore loose jeans rolled at the hem, a red tee, and black Converse sneakers. She had to be eighty if a day. I guessed closer to ninety.

I held out my hand to shake. "Thanks." I didn't bother explaining the hat. "I'm Darcy."

"I know who you are." Her warm, baby-soft palm met mine, and she quickly added her other hand to the mix, trapping my hand between both of hers.

"You do?" I tugged my hand, but she held firm.

"Darcy Ann Merriweather. Daughter of Deryn Devany Merriweather and Patrick Merriweather."

Shock rippled through me that this stranger knew of my family. After all, my mother had died when I was seven. My father had passed a couple of years ago. It wasn't as though she'd just met them as they wandered the village green. "How did you—"

"*Shhh*. I'm trying to concentrate."

"Hey, stop that!" Tingles spread from my hand up to my elbow. I tried to yank myself free, but for a petite woman, she was strong. "Let me go!"

Abruptly, she released my hand, and I stumbled backward.

"Just what I thought," she said with a firm nod and a sly smile.

"What do you think?" I watched those clear eyes carefully.

They gave away nothing.

Had she divined that I was a witch? Or picked up on any of the other secrets I was keeping? About the Renewal. About the . . . No. I wasn't going there. I'd promised myself I wouldn't even *think* about that particular secret for a few more days.

I wasn't sure what this woman knew. All *I* knew was that I didn't have any memory cleanse with me because I'd left my purse at home. I threw a glance at my house, on the other side of the green, and then at Harper, who was still in line at the corn dog stand. I was going to have to run home to get—

"Stay right there," Hildie said as she turned to rummage through a large apothecary chest that had to be a nightmare to haul from festival to festival.

I froze, wondering if Hildie could read minds as well.

What had I gotten myself into?

Setting a hand on my stomach to quell the queasiness, I took a deep breath. I could fix this. A little memory cleanse worked wonders.

Her wobbly voice carried as she said loudly, "A blind leap of faith brought you and Harper to this village. My question to you, Darcy, is this: do you have enough faith in yourself and your abilities to keep on leaping?"

Everything around me quieted while my head buzzed with the sound of the woman's voice and the knowledge that she knew *all* about my life. I had no doubt she was aware that I was a witch, and I instantly suspected she was too. It set me at ease. Somewhat. This was all so very strange.

Her question rang in my ears as I thought about everything I'd learned since arriving in this village, the people I'd met, the love I'd found for the enchanted world I lived in. The answer was easy. "Yes."

Hildie returned to me, a pensive look in her eyes. "In weakness, there is strength. Out of darkness, there comes light. From the ashes, there is rebirth."

Chill bumps raised on my arms. "I don't understand."

"Take this." She held out a closed fist, and the blue veins on the top of her hand fairly glowed through thin skin. "Keep it safe until you need it. You'll know when the time is right."

Warmth radiated into my hand as she dropped a shiny silvery-green seed, a little bigger than a watermelon seed, onto my palm. She then rested her hand on top of mine, and a sense of calm washed over me.

There was an air of benevolence about her as she steadied her gaze on mine and said solemnly, "You must trust your faith, because it will be tested. The first test is not telling *anyone* what I've given you until after you have used it. That includes your mother—or all will be undone. Understand?"

"But—" I had so many questions that I didn't know where to start. What was this seed? Who was this woman?

"Darcy?" Harper called out, interrupting my thoughts. "Are you ready?"

Keeping tight hold of the seed, I glanced over my shoulder. Harper had already eaten half the corn dog and was wiping her lips with a napkin.

"Just a second," I said, wanting to find out exactly how much Hildie knew. Did she know my mother *was* the Elder?

The Elder, the governess of the Craft, was a role that could be held only by a witch who had already passed away and become a familiar. My mother's reign had begun nearly twenty-five years ago, and her identity was top secret to all but a dozen or so witches. *I* hadn't even learned the truth until a year ago. The rest of the confidants were mostly family members, trusted friends, and the Coven of Seven, her council of advisers.

To my knowledge, Hildie was none of those. The truth of the Elder's identity was revealed only at her discretion. If other witches spoke of it without permission, there were steep consequences. If Hildie knew the Elder was my mother, Deryn, then she knew because my mother had told her.

I turned back to question Hildie further, but she was gone. The booth stood empty.

Of everything.

Only the banner remained, flapping gently in the salty sea breeze.

Absently I heard sirens in the distance as I looked all around, wondering if I was going crazy. But no . . .

my palm was warm. I opened my hand and saw the seed sitting there, plain as day.

"Did"—I coughed—"did you see the woman I was talking to?"

Harper's eyebrows dipped. "I didn't see you talking to anyone."

How was that possible? Hildie had been *right here*. The apothecary chest, the bits and baubles . . . My heart pounded. What was going on?

Harper sniffed loudly and looked around. "Do you smell that?"

As soon as she said the words, I caught the scent of something burning and scanned the horizon. Black smoke spiraled above a building in the distance.

A building with a thatched roof and eyebrow dormers.

"Is that . . . ?" Harper asked, horror in her eyes.

It *was*.

Dealing with whatever it was that had just happened between Hildie and me was going to have to wait. I grabbed Harper's hand and started running.

Divinitea was on fire.